THE SNOWBALL EFFECT
A FULL-LENGTH ROMANTIC COMEDY

AVERY KANE

KISSINGSHARK PUBLICATIONS

1
ONE

Summer in Bellaire was waning, but Ava Mason didn't mind. Sure, she loved warm weather as much as anybody—there was nothing better than kayaking on the Au Sable River or relaxing on a float in Torch Lake—but fall was her favorite season. She loved winter too. Ava was one of the few people who didn't participate in winter sports but still enjoyed what could be a brutal four months in northern Lower Michigan. Fall was definitely her favorite, though. That was why she was more than happy to sit with a latte in the local café and wax poetic about what was to come with her friend Lindsey Torkelson.

"I'm telling you it's going to be great," she enthused as she watched Lindsey flip through the local weekly newspaper.

Lindsey, her dark hair hanging over one side of her face as she leaned forward, didn't respond.

That only made Ava more determined. "Did you hear me? It's going to be great."

Slowly, Lindsey raised her chin. "What are you prattling on about?"

Lindsey was nothing if not blunt, which was one of the reasons Ava loved her so much. She didn't have to guess what Lindsey was feeling at any given moment. She would say it, whether anyone wanted to hear it or not.

"It's almost fall," Ava said. "You know how I feel about fall."

"Yes, it's your favorite season until winter."

"No, it's my favorite season of all of them."

"You're only saying that because it will be fall in three weeks." Lindsey licked her finger and flicked another page in the newspaper. "In three months, when we both have turkey hangovers, you're going to be raving about how winter is your favorite season. Then at the end of February, you'll do the same thing for spring."

"Spring is never my favorite season," Ava argued as she tucked a strand of her shoulder-length hair behind her ear. Some people said it was strawberry blonde. Others said it was auburn. But Ava had never been able to pin down the exact color. It was uniquely her, which suited her just fine. "Don't be ridiculous. The first half of spring is actually the last gasp of winter, and you know how I feel about dirty snow."

"It's the way we all feel about dirty snow," Lindsey agreed. "It's stupid."

"It's totally stupid. And the second half of spring isn't really spring anyway. Or ... well, it hasn't been in years. We seem to get two weeks of spring now then jump right into summer. Basically, it's like we have three seasons now. Spring is an illusion."

"Right." Lindsey narrowed her eyes as she studied the real estate listings.

"You're not listening to me. Why is it that you never listen to me?"

"Because you don't prioritize your words," Lindsey replied evenly, smiling at the café owner, Maya Markham, when she appeared with the coffee pot to top her off. "Isn't that right?"

Maya, who had grown up in Bellaire before moving away for a decade, grinned. "Isn't what right?"

"She talks too much."

Ava pouted. "I don't talk too much. I just happen to be an effusive individual."

"We all love effusive individuals," Maya replied. She smiled a lot, Ava noticed. Ever since she'd gotten engaged to her former best friend, Nick Griffith, she'd done nothing but smile. "What are you being effusive about today?"

"I love fall."

"What's not to love? The clothes are cute. The drinks are to die for. Also, you can eat as many pastries as you want without worrying whether you'll still fit in your bathing suit the following weekend."

Ava bobbed her head. "That's a very good point."

"Yeah, yeah, yeah." Lindsey waved her hand. "I bet I know something that will ruin your good mood."

Suspicious, Ava asked, "What?"

"Why would you want to ruin her good mood?"

"I don't *want* to do it," Lindsey replied. "It feels necessary, though. If I don't tell her, someone else will."

"What?" Ava demanded. All the joy she'd been feeling seconds before had disappeared. "Do I even want to know? I bet I don't."

"So do you want me to tell you or not?"

"I don't know." Ava chewed on her bottom lip. "Give me a hint."

"Okay." If Lindsey was thrown by the demand, she didn't show it. "What's the one thing you want more than anything else?"

Ava cocked her head, considering. "A three-Chris sandwich," she replied. "We're talking Evans, Pine, and Hemsworth. I don't want Pratt in there."

Lindsey blinked several times. "That's a wish well worth dreaming about. I don't even care about the logistics. But I'm being serious. It's something you've been talking about nonstop for the past six months."

Ava's forehead creased. "I don't... Wait." Realization dawned. "The Holden farm. I've been talking about when it goes on the market." She turned to Maya. "I'm going to buy it, renovate it, and turn it into a bed-and-breakfast."

"Oh yeah?" Maya didn't look nearly as excited at the prospect as Ava had anticipated. "Isn't that a lot of work?"

"So much work," Lindsey agreed. "That farm is falling down."

"No." Ava wrinkled her nose and extended a warning finger in her friend's direction. "While I agree that the barn needs a lot of work, the house is still pretty cool. All the plaster walls will need to be taken down and replaced with drywall, but I'm prepared for that. I know exactly what I'm getting myself into."

"You're going to turn a farm into a bed-and-breakfast?" Maya appeared to be having trouble wrapping her head around the concept. "How is that even going to work? What about the animals?"

"There are no animals," Ava replied. "There haven't been in years. Well, there were goats at the end, right before Chuck passed away." She frowned. It hadn't escaped her that she was angling to buy her favorite parcel of property in the area so soon after her close friend's death. Chuck had been nothing but kind to her over the years, and she loved him dearly. His death had hit her hard. But that didn't mean she would back away from her plans. No, she knew exactly what she wanted. And she was going to get it.

"She's been obsessed with that farm for as long as I can remember," Lindsey volunteered. "Like ... *obsessed*. When we were teens, when everybody else was getting jobs up at the resort during the summers, she worked out at the farm, even though she made half as much money as we did. It was ridiculous."

"Money isn't the only thing that matters," Ava countered.

"That's easy for you to say. Your grandmother left you a million bucks when she died. A million freaking dollars! You don't have to worry about money like the rest of us."

Lindsey was right. Ava's grandmother had been an eccentric soul, refusing to talk to her own daughter—Ava's mother—for the ten years prior to her death. Nobody knew that Ethel Kingsley had a million dollars tucked away in an account. She lived in a nondescript cottage out by the river. It was more of a shack, really. And when her will had been read, and the truth was revealed, Ava's mother had thrown a fit. Being bypassed in her own mother's will wasn't easy to swallow, but she eventually stopped pouting and instead started angling for Ava to do something beneficial to her with the money. But the only thing Ava wanted to do was buy the Holden farm.

Her mother had been sore about it for three years. The farm was a bone of contention, with both sides refusing to bring it up.

"That farm is pretty big, if I remember correctly," Maya mused. "I can see turning it into a bed-and-breakfast. It looks old from the outside, though. We're talking black-

and-white-movie old. Are you really going to funnel a bunch of money into that place?"

"Yes." Ava bobbed her head. "I totally am. It won't be as much money as you think, either. I've already had a construction crew out there, looking. At most, we're talking two hundred grand."

"That's a lot of money," Maya argued.

"It is, but it will bring in at least ten grand a month once it's renovated."

"Do you really think you can make that much?" Lindsey asked.

"I really do. I've had an accountant look over my estimates and everything."

"You mean your uncle Phil?" Lindsey drawled.

"He's an accountant, isn't he?" Ava knew she sounded shrill but couldn't stop herself.

"Yeah, but he invested money in Beanie Babies. We're talking a grown-ass man with Beanie Babies as his retirement plan. You can't take what he says seriously."

"He's not the only one I've been talking to," Ava snapped. "I have a business plan. Oh, why am I even discussing it with you?" She crossed her arms and dramatically jutted out her lower lip. "You're a dream killer, Lindsey. You've always been that way. And by the way ... I'm going to do this no matter what you say."

Lindsey blinked several times, and when she spoke again, it was in a softer tone. "Actually, Ava, I don't think you are."

"You don't think I'm going to turn that farm into the best bed-and-breakfast ever? You don't even know all the plans I have. I've been keeping them from you because I didn't want to be made fun of."

When Lindsey darted her eyes to Maya, she looked

resigned. "Ava, that's not what I meant. Honestly, no matter how much I tease you, I think you can do anything you put your mind to. I mean, you did build that ridiculous blog on your own and make it a success, didn't you?"

Even though she was annoyed, Ava couldn't help smiling. *Buzzing around Bellaire* had started as a project of her heart and turned into an actual moneymaker, thanks to various local businesses—including Maya's café—advertising. The blog was a mixture of small-town announcements, like when the senior center had decided to expand its outdoor patio, and gossipy tidbits that were nobody's business, like when Casey Brighton and Ed Carter had started dating, even though they were both still married and living with their spouses. Ava would never get rich off it, but she was making enough to pay her monthly bills.

"So what's the problem?" Ava asked. "If you acknowledge that I'm good at what I do, why don't you think I can manage this?"

"Because you're not going to get a chance to buy the farm," Lindsey replied. She paused. "Wait ... that came out wrong. Don't you die when you buy the farm?"

Maya shrugged. "That's my understanding. I knew what you meant, though."

"Of course I'm going to buy it," Ava argued. "It's going up for auction in September. Lynn at the bank told me. I'm going to be right there in the front row the day it goes on the block."

"That's what I'm trying to tell you." Lindsey looked frustrated, which wasn't like her. Even when life went wrong for Lindsey, she was stoic. She always managed to hold things together. "The house isn't going on the market."

"A bunch of back taxes are owed," Ava persisted. "The

bids are going to have to be high enough to cover them. I know exactly what it'll take. It's sixty grand. I've got it. Don't worry."

Lindsey stared at the table for an extended beat before speaking again. "Ava, that's what I was just reading in the newspaper." She turned the real estate sheet toward Ava so that she could read it. "The back taxes have been paid. The house isn't going on the market. It says so right there."

"But … no!" She found the notice Lindsey was referring to, and sure enough, the taxes had indeed been paid. "Who the hell is Griffin Holden?"

"Well, if I had to guess, I'd say he's a relative of Chuck Holden," Lindsey replied. "I mean, the last name is sort of a dead giveaway."

"I don't understand." Ava wasn't a crier. She was far too happy and upbeat, especially in front of others. But she found herself blinking back tears. "How can this be happening?"

"Hold on," Maya said, plopping down next to Ava and boxing her in before she could flee. "Let's see if we can find the name, huh? Maybe he paid the back taxes because he wants to fix up the property and sell it himself."

"Then it will be too expensive for me," Ava whined. "If he puts a bunch of money into it—and that's what he's going to have to do to get it up to code—then he's going to have to charge a lot to get his money back."

"Let's not panic," Maya insisted. Her expression was intense as she studied her phone screen. "Here we go. Griffin Holden. Says here he was an architect—that sounds like a fun job, huh?—and he worked for his father's company." She pressed her lips together and kept reading. "Most of this is press releases. 'Griffin Holden breaks ground on the old Taft Building renovation.' That sort of stuff."

"If he's an architect, doesn't that suggest he's going to have big plans for the Holden farm?" Lindsey asked. She, too, had her phone out. "Oh, wait. Here's Chuck's obituary. He had three grandsons, and one was named Griffin."

Ava's fury was about to sprout wings and fly off to lay waste to the village. "Why would a Detroit architect want to come up here?"

"I have no idea," Lindsey replied.

"I think I do," Maya offered. "I found something that's not a press release."

"And what's that?" Ava was beyond hope, bitterness her new best friend. But that didn't mean she was above hearing any sort of dirt Maya managed to dig up.

"Do you remember that building that fell in Detroit about five months ago? It was a high-rise that was under construction."

That sounded vaguely familiar. "I think so," Ava said. "They said something about faulty construction."

"Faulty design," Maya corrected. "Griffin Holden designed the building."

"Was anybody killed?" Lindsey asked.

"Two people, both on the ground. I guess they were homeless. That's terrible. The whole thing is just a tragedy."

"No, the tragedy is that guy is buying my farm," Ava snapped. "How is that even fair?"

"I hate to state the obvious, but life isn't fair," Lindsey replied. "He's family. I wonder if he's heading up here to lie low. People here would be less likely to know about that thing with the building."

Ava didn't want to be a spiteful person—really and truly—but an ember of hate flared to life in her heart.

"Oh no," Lindsey intoned when she caught Ava's

expression. "You're going to do something weird, aren't you?"

"Define weird."

"You're going to write about Griffin Holden's woes on your little blog in an effort to force him out of town, aren't you?"

"I didn't say that." Ava tried to portray the picture of innocence.

"It's what you're *not* saying that's starting to become apparent. You can't put him in your blog, Ava. You don't know anything about him or what happened. You could live to regret it."

Ava didn't believe in regrets. "I didn't say I was going to do anything," she insisted. The heaviness that had been weighing her down only moments before was gone. "I'm just sitting here, minding my own business. Don't worry about a thing. I've got it all under control."

"Oh, jeez." Lindsey slapped her hand to her forehead. "You're going to go off the rails, aren't you, and declare war on this poor guy."

"I'm going to do what needs to be done."

"And what's that?"

"I guess you'll have to wait to see." Ava gave Maya a benign smile. "Can I have another muffin? I think I might need the sugar buzz."

Maya didn't look thrilled, but she nodded all the same. "Sure. I mean, what could possibly go wrong?"

"Oh, you've jinxed us now," Lindsey said. "You're about to find out just how wrong things can go."

2
TWO

Griffin Holden arrived in Bellaire the last week of September and immediately wondered if he'd accidentally ventured into a hellish dimension. Though he knew that wasn't possible, he'd always had an overactive imagination, he couldn't shake the feeling of dread threatening to take him over.

He was a city boy who had been relegated to living in the country. *How did this even happen?*

Grim-faced, he eyed the farmhouse, which he hadn't visited since he was a child, and sighed. "Well, it's definitely haunted."

Nobody was around to reply. If they had, he would probably have assumed they were a ghost, jumped into his Jeep Compass, and fled back to the city—but he was bothered all the same.

He hadn't known his grandfather well. Chuck Holden had been something of an enigma when Griffin was growing up. His father and grandfather weren't close, so even though Griffin enjoyed spending time with Chuck, there were very few opportunities, other than when his father decided it was easier to dump Griffin on the farm for the entire summer. That stopped happening when Griffin was twelve, other than one unfortunate summer when he was sixteen and his father was between wives, but he still had fond memories of the farm.

Unfortunately for him, the memories weren't living up to the reality.

"What a dump."

Resigned, Griffin let himself into the farmhouse. The decision to pay the back taxes and claim the property after his grandfather's death had been a rash one. He could admit that, since he was almost six weeks removed from it happening. At the time, he'd been feeling the walls closing in and figured the best thing he could do was get out of Dodge.

When the Peck Building had fallen, all eyes were on him. He was the one who had designed the building. That meant he was at fault, and even though nobody had cared about the individuals who were killed when they were alive, suddenly, they were martyrs in death.

Griffin didn't like to think about the two individuals who had been found in the rubble. It didn't even occur until two weeks after the catastrophic fall. Nobody had been reported missing, so at first, the building's collapse had been considered a terrible accident. Then the bodies were discovered, and everything changed. He'd had to undergo a criminal investigation, and although he'd been cleared in the eyes of the law, the public still hated him. He might've been able to live with that, but he couldn't also deal with his father, given what he was feeling. That meant fleeing the city, and the farm was a perfect place to hide.

Griffin dropped his duffel bag and suitcase in the living room, his eyes automatically going to the hardwood floor.

He remembered it being shiny and slick, the sort of floor you could slide across when wearing socks. But it had become faded and scratched. It would need a good buff. That would be one of the final steps, however. Other things had to be done first.

"Plaster," he muttered as he touched the wall. The farmhouse was old, so there wouldn't have been drywall when it was constructed. Clearly, nobody had bothered to switch it out in the years since. "That will be an expensive trade."

Griffin did the math in his head. The taxes had been sixty grand. If he'd been dealing with corporate funds, he wouldn't have blinked an eye. But he'd used his own money, and while he was a saver, he didn't want to blow all of it on the farmhouse when he had no idea if he'd ever be able to get the money back out. At the moment, he was looking for a distraction, and his grandfather's beloved farm seemed a good place to start.

"Okay." Griffin exhaled heavily and clapped once. "What we need here is a list." He moved into the kitchen, frowning when he saw that nobody had bothered to clean the last of the dishes.

"Okay," he said again, steeling himself. "More than a list—we need cleaning supplies." Even considering construction would have to wait. Griffin couldn't sleep in a house so filthy. He wasn't a neat freak or anything, but he was fussy. That meant cleaning came first. The other stuff would have to wait. "I think it's time to head to town." He clutched his keys, gave the kitchen another cursory look, then headed for the door. "There's not enough Mr. Clean in the world to make this place habitable, but we're going to give it a try."

· · ·

BELLAIRE WASN'T BIG BY ANY STRETCH OF THE IMAGINATION. It boasted three stoplights, a two-screen theater, several golf courses, a resort, what was billed as a decent brewing pub, and exactly one grocery store, which was where Griffin headed.

Once in the aisle, he looked around dubiously. He was used to super centers, which boasted multiple aisles of cleaning supplies, all sorted for speedy selection. The small store had exactly one aisle for cleaning, and nothing was sorted.

"Well, this is just great," he muttered as he started collecting the things he needed. Toilet bowl cleaner was a must. Since he couldn't guarantee his grandfather had a toilet brush, he grabbed one of those too. He added three containers of multipurpose cleaner, two spray bottles for counters, three boxes of garbage bags, then topped it off with rags and a mop.

"That should do it," he said, surveying the contents of his cart again. "It'll at least get me through the day."

"Excuse me," came a female voice from Griffin's left, jolting him out of his reverie.

When he looked over, he found an older woman—she had to be pushing eighty—trying to get around him. "I'm so sorry." He shoved his cart to get it out of her way. "I didn't see you there."

With an easy smile, the woman replied, "That's okay. You were obviously busy talking to yourself."

Griffin's cheeks burned.

"Don't worry about that either," she said with a dismissive hand wave. "I talk to myself all the time. I think it's normal."

"Oh yeah?" Griffin was amused despite himself. "My father would say it was a sign of mental illness." Why he'd volunteered that, he couldn't say, but his anger with his father bubbled over at the oddest of times.

"He sounds like a schmuck."

"Oh, he is."

"Don't listen to him. Edie says it's okay to talk to yourself. That's all that matters."

"I take it you're Edie."

"That would be me. Edie Eggers."

"I'm Griffin Holden." Griffin automatically extended his hand. "It's nice to meet you."

Edie's eyes grew wide. "You... You..."

Confused, Griffin cocked his head. "Is something wrong?"

Edie seemed to be struggling with something. After a few seconds, she stood taller. All signs of welcome and mirth were gone from her face when she spoke again. "You're Chuck's grandson."

"I am," Griffin agreed, dropping his hand. Perhaps she wasn't a shaker. It was expected in the city, but he was in the country, so maybe it was different. He would have to be the one to adjust. "Is that a problem?"

"Of course not." The way Edie darted her eyes to the left made Griffin think otherwise. "We heard you were coming to town."

"Oh yeah?" For some reason, that struck Griffin as funny. "How did you hear that?"

"It made the paper."

Griffin jolted. "The fact that I was moving into my grandfather's house made the paper?"

"No, the fact that you paid off the tax lien on your grandfather's property made the real estate page," Edie replied. "That's public record. People pay attention to that stuff up here."

"Oh. I hadn't considered that. It makes sense, though."

"Yes, well, we're all glad that Chuck's farm isn't going to fall into disrepair. Well, more disrepair than it already is. He couldn't keep up with the workload for the last couple of years, and he refused to hire anybody to help him. I'm assuming you have quite a task on your hands." Her gaze flicked to the contents of the cart.

"It's a bit messy," Griffin confirmed. "I'll clean as much as I can today, then start dumping stuff tomorrow."

"Right." Edie studied his face. "Well, good luck." With that, she was gone, leaving Griffin to stare in her wake.

"Well, *that* was weird," he muttered.

Things got weirder. Since he was in the grocery store, he decided to grab some food to get him through the next few days. Nothing fancy, but he needed to survive, and Bellaire didn't have a lot of fast-food options.

In the bread aisle, two women watched him from the far end, their heads bent together as they whispered. They did not smile back when he offered a friendly wave to them.

While he was in front of the peanut butter display, a middle-aged woman glared at him so hard that he was surprised her eyes didn't pop out of her head. He had crunchy peanut butter in his hand, so he switched to creamy in an effort to earn her approval. It didn't work. She continued to burn holes in him as he moved on.

In the canned soup aisle was where he was almost thrown over the edge. He was positive the old man who rammed him with his cart had done it on purpose, and it wasn't because he snagged the last can of chicken and stars.

By the time he reached the checkout area—no self-checkout, unfortunately—he was at the end of his rope and ready to flee. He couldn't wait to get out of the store and back to the haunted farmhouse. *Who knew ghosts were preferable to people?*

"You cleaning something?" the young woman working the register asked. Her eyebrows were halfway up her forehead as she rang up all the supplies he'd gathered.

"My grandfather's farmhouse," Griffin replied darkly. "He died more than six months ago, and I'm certain nobody has been inside since."

"You mean Chuck Holden?" The girl focused on Griffin fully. "Are you the grandson everybody has been talking about?"

Leery, Griffin replied, "I am."

"I'm Jenny Compton." Her smile was so wide it threatened to devour her entire face. "We heard you were coming to town, although nobody knew when it would actually happen. Some of the locals were saying you wouldn't bother because the farm is so old and needs so much work, but I knew you would come."

Jenny's reaction to him was so different from the others he'd encountered in the store that Griffin couldn't help but bask in her warmth. He had questions, though.

"If you don't mind my asking, how is it that you knew I was coming to town?" he asked as she steadily scanned his groceries.

"It was in the paper."

"I thought there was just a notice about my paying the taxes on the property."

"I think there was." Jenny turned thoughtful. "I'm not sure how that all happened. I just know about the thing that happened after."

"And what thing would that be?"

"Oh, you know. *The thing.*"

Griffin waited. When Jenny didn't expand, he had to

force himself to keep from exploding. "I honestly don't know what 'the thing' is. I would love some insight, though. I'm pretty sure everybody in this town is under the assumption that I'm a pariah."

"Oh yeah?" Jenny angled her head and looked down the line of people who were waiting. "You mean Edie?"

"She would be one of them. There were others, though. The guy in the soup aisle ran into me with his cart three times. I don't think it was an accident."

"Him?" Jenny pointed to three checkout lanes to the left.

Griffin followed her finger and grimaced. "Yes. Him."

"That's Carl Jenkins. He's blind in one eye. It's possible at least one of those collisions was accidental."

"And the other two?"

"He probably just hates you."

Griffin growled deep in his throat. "I would love to know what I've done to make these people hate me when I've been in town for exactly two hours, and this is the first time I've ever interacted with them." He dug into his wallet for his credit card.

"It's not you," Jenny assured him. "Well, I mean, it is. But it's more the stuff Ava wrote about you."

If Griffin thought he was confused before, it was nothing compared to what he was currently feeling. "What now?" he asked after several seconds. "What are you talking about? Who is Ava?"

"Ava Mason. She runs the local blog. *Buzzing Around Bellaire.* Maybe you've heard of it."

"I believe I somehow missed that stellar showing of journalistic integrity," Griffin drawled.

"It's not a newspaper," Jenny replied quickly. "It's just a blog. They're different."

Griffin had to leash his sarcasm. "You don't say." Well, mostly.

"She keeps track of what's happening in town," Jenny explained. "Like, last week, she broke the story that the high school was getting new basketball uniforms for the boys but not the girls—even though the girls haven't had new uniforms in twenty years—and she outed Fred Kingman as coulrophobic. That means he's afraid of clowns."

Griffin blinked several times. "I know about coulrophobia," he said finally. "Who isn't scared of clowns, though?"

"Right?" Jenny bobbed her head, as if they were having the most normal conversation in the world. "I know that movie clown is supposed to be the scariest, but old Lionel Givens dresses like a clown for birthday parties, and he honks the mothers' breasts. I think that's way scarier."

"It sounds like it." Griffin was determined to get the conversation back on track. "What does this Ava person's blog have to do with me?" he asked.

"Oh, didn't I tell you?" Jenny wrinkled her nose. "About a month ago, Ava wrote a piece on you. She said you were coming to town to claim your grandfather's farm ... and that you'd killed a bunch of people in Detroit. Now everybody thinks you're a serial killer."

Griffin's jaw dropped. "What now?"

"I didn't believe the serial killer part," Jenny offered hurriedly. "But I did google you once she wrote the post. It's sad what happened with that building. I figure you can't control where homeless people hang out, so that wasn't really your fault."

Griffin couldn't decide whether he wanted to run or scream. "She wrote about the Peck Building?" he rasped.

Suddenly, his stomach felt as if it were being invaded by squirming snakes.

"Oh, most definitely. She says we can't afford a killer in our community. She's mentioned you a few times."

"I see." Griffin signed the receipt for his groceries with an angry flourish. "And where can I find Mrs. Mason?"

"Miss," Jenny corrected automatically. "It could be Ms., too, I guess. Ava strikes me as a feminist, although that's totally a dirty word in this area, so shh." She pressed a finger to her lips, something Griffin would've found comical under different circumstances.

"Where can I find her?" Griffin demanded.

"She's renting a cabin out by the resort. You need the code to get past the gates, though, and I don't know it any longer. I'm sorry."

"She must hang out somewhere," Griffin insisted.

"She's in the coffee shop a lot. Most of the time, she just wanders around town, though."

"Do you have a photo of her?"

"No. That would be weird. But there's a photo on her blog."

"*Buzzing Around Bellaire?*"

"Yeah."

"Great. Thanks for the information."

Fury fueled Griffin as he stormed out of the grocery store with his purchases. He had no idea who Ava Mason was, but there would be a reckoning between the two of them before it was all said and done.

3
THREE

When a moving truck arrived at the Holden farm, Ava's worst fears were realized. Somehow—although it seemed like wishful thinking—she'd believed it had all been a mistake. She'd managed to convince herself that everything was going to be okay, and she would somehow be able to buy the farm. The truck meant she'd been deluding herself. She really hated it when that happened.

Because she couldn't help herself, she snuck into the trees on the east side of the farm. There, she had a good view of the front door and the barn. Ava had to use her phone to zoom in on faces, and it took her three tries before she found Griffin. She recognized him from his photo in the newspaper stories, although he looked paler and was sporting more stubble. Dressed in jeans and a flannel shirt, he looked as if he belonged at the farm ... even though it was supposed to be hers.

There weren't a lot of items in the moving truck, only a handful of furniture pieces and several boxes, so it only took the movers an hour to finish unloading. Then they were gone, and Griffin was alone. He retreated into the house and didn't come out again. Ava knew because she spent an entire hour waiting. Frustrated when he didn't emerge again, she decided to get a little closer.

A normal person would've left the man to unpack and take a breath. Moving was one of the most stressful things imaginable. But Ava wasn't a normal person. She was naturally curious—not a busybody, like her friends constantly suggested—and simply couldn't help herself. Before she knew it, she was in the bushes on the side of the house and was trying to look through the kitchen window.

It took her eyes a moment to adjust because it was dim inside the farmhouse, and the first thing she noticed was that the kitchen was a mess. Chuck had been a tidy individual—well, up until the end—and it was obvious the space hadn't been cleaned since his passing. There were items spread out across the counter, including dishes, and Ava wrinkled her nose when she saw the mess.

"Chuck wouldn't like that," she muttered.

"Oh no?" someone behind her asked.

Ava almost jumped out of her skin. Before she even realized what was happening, she tried to move out of the bushes and toward an open space that would allow her to run. But the bush came to midthigh, and she tripped on her way out, causing her to fall forward and hit the ground hard.

"I'm armed!" she blurted as she held up her hand. "I have a gun." When she focused on the individual standing on the other side of the bushes, his arms crossed, she found Griffin watching her with baffled amusement.

"You're armed?" he asked after a beat. "That seems a bit extreme."

"It's northern Lower Michigan." Ava rolled to her butt

and began a methodical check of her arms and legs to make sure she hadn't broken anything. "Everybody here is armed."

"Ah." Griffin nodded. "That makes sense. Well, since it's my property, I would appreciate it if you didn't shoot me."

"I can't guarantee that." Ava was in a precarious position and hoped that if she was bold enough, that would keep the newcomer at a safe distance. "I know nothing about you. It might be your property, but I still have a right to protect myself from a pervert."

"Uh-huh." Griffin scratched his cheek. He hadn't moved from his spot. "What makes you think I'm a pervert?"

"I didn't say you were a pervert. You could be one, though." Ava made a face when she realized she'd twisted her knee. It wasn't bad, but it ached enough that she needed to stretch it. That meant buying herself more time. "You kind of have the look of a pervert."

"I see." Griffin's lips twitched, but he didn't smile. "What does a pervert look like?"

"You know."

"I don't think I do."

"*You know.* Don't pretend you don't know."

Griffin narrowed one eye, seemingly debating, then managed a smile. It was devastating in its beauty ... not that Ava allowed herself to notice those things when dealing with the man who had stolen her farm. "I hate to be the one to point out the obvious, but you're the one trespassing. How do I know *you're* not a pervert?"

"Oh please. Look at this face." She scrunched her nose, giving Griffin a good look at her freckles. "Is this the face of a pervert?"

"I have no idea. Maybe I should google 'What does a

pervert look like' and see what I find. For all I know, your picture could be the first one that pops up."

"Go ahead," Ava replied, unruffled. "Please google the word *pervert* and tell me what you come up with. I'll wait."

Griffin scowled. "What are you doing here?"

"What are *you* doing here?"

"I asked first."

"Well, I asked second. A gentleman would defer to a lady." That was total crap, but Ava recognized she was standing—or rather, sitting—on shaky ground. She had to do whatever she could to get herself out of the predicament.

"Are you a lady?" Griffin queried.

"That's the word on the street."

His smile came back. "This is my house. I live here." He inclined his head. "Now you go."

Ava had a choice. She could make up a ridiculous story and hope he would be gentleman enough to accept it to ease her embarrassment, or she could tell the truth. She'd built her reputation on bluntness, so that was the avenue she took.

"I was curious and decided to spy on you. When I saw the moving truck, I knew you were finally here, and I wanted to see what you looked like. There have been a lot of stories about you."

"Is that a fact?" Griffin's lips twitched again. "I like how you just came right out and admitted you were spying. I thought you were going to tell me you were looking for a nonexistent cat or something."

"That's not really my style." Ava flexed her knee. "Besides, there was no way you were going to believe the cat story."

"Definitely not." Griffin edged out from behind the

bushes and extended his hand. "Come on. The least I can do is offer you a pop and make sure you haven't injured yourself."

Ava's eyes widened, but she took his hand. "What makes you think I would take a pop from you?" She grunted as she regained her footing. "We still haven't ascertained whether you're a pervert or not."

"If I'm a pervert, that means you can't accept a pop?"

"Of course. You could've drugged it."

"Ah." He managed a weak laugh. "You are something, aren't you?"

"That's the rumor." Ava dusted off the seat of her jeans. "Can I ask you something?"

"I guess."

"It's invasive."

"I would expect nothing less from the woman who was spying on me."

"How come you moved from the city to a farm? That also seems like something a pervert would do because a farm makes a better hiding place. You can hide bodies and stuff more easily on a farm than you can in a city."

"Oh, so now I'm a murderer on top of being a pervert. Good to know. As for why I decided to move here, that's a long story."

Ava already knew the specifics—or most of them—but that didn't stop her from pressing. "You don't plan on burying bodies out here, do you?"

"No. Can't I just like the country?"

"I have it on good authority that city boys hate the country."

"That sounds like a stereotype to me."

"Maybe, but there are no strip clubs in Bellaire. There are no late-night movies, and the grocery store shuts down at ten o'clock every single night. It's a different world from what you're used to."

"Maybe I'm looking for a different world."

"Why?"

"Why not?"

"You're evading." Ava shook her head. "I don't like it when people evade questions. It makes me itchy, like crabs … not that I know what it's like to have crabs. I've read about them, though, and know they're itchy. Wait… I think I went off on a tangent."

That time, Griffin's smile was accompanied by a gregarious laugh. He was so amused, apparently, that he had to bend over at the waist and rest his palms on his knees. His entire body shook. "I'm guessing you were the kid who was constantly in trouble for talking," he said when he'd recovered. "How many notes got sent home, admonishing you for talking during tests when you were younger?"

"Only twenty-two," Ava replied. "I don't think that's so bad, considering I went to school for twelve years."

"That's more than two reprimands a year some years."

"Yeah, but two times out of one hundred eighty days? That's nothing." She waved away the comment. "You still haven't told me why you moved here." She couldn't let it go. The conversation might've been witty—and he was nowhere near the ogre she'd been painting him out to be in her head—but she wanted actionable information. If she was going to figure out a way to get Griffin to return to the city, she needed ammunition.

"You still haven't told me why you were spying," he fired back.

"I was spying because I was curious. There's no deep, dark secret to it. I wanted to see what you looked like."

"In case I was a pervert, right?"

"The jury is still out."

Griffin gave a long, drawn-out sigh. "I needed a break from the city. The hustle and bustle got to be too much for me. I enjoyed visiting my grandfather when I was younger. Upon his death, I couldn't bear the idea of his house being sold at auction, so I figured I would give it a try."

Ava blinked. She hadn't expected him to unleash so many words at once. "Huh," she said finally.

"Is that all you have to say? That sounded like a loaded 'huh.'"

"I guess I thought maybe you were going to say that you were fixing it up to sell it or something," she admitted. If Griffin wasn't going to put a lot of money into the farm, there was still a chance he would grow bored with his purchase and unload it for the same price he'd paid just to make his escape in a month or so.

"Actually, that's the plan," Griffin said, dashing her hopes. "I need a project. Between the house and the barn, I don't think projects get much bigger than this one. It will serve as a distraction, and when I'm finished, if I don't want to live here, I can sell it for a sizable profit over my investment."

Ava's face fell. "Oh."

"You don't look happy about that."

"I just... I don't know." Ava tossed her hair over her shoulder and did her best to pretend she didn't want to find a hole to crawl into and die—or better yet, a hole that was big enough to hide his body. "I guess I don't like the idea of a stranger owning the farm."

"Did you know my grandfather?"

The question shouldn't have been surprising, but it threw her. "Everybody knew Chuck. He was famous around these parts."

"Oh yeah?" Griffin arched an eyebrow. "What was he famous for?"

"Up until about five years ago, he used to deck the farm out for Halloween and invite all the area kids to hang out for free. He made a corn maze at the end of the season, had treats and fresh cider, and would even dress up and pretend to scare everyone. It turned into a big thing, with all the high school kids volunteering to help every year."

"I didn't realize that. Why did he stop?"

"He couldn't get around very well after a while." Ava's smile disappeared. "He struggled and couldn't plant a corn crop any longer. Then the decorating got to be too much. People volunteered to help, but he didn't like that."

"He was never one to accept help," Griffin agreed. "People say I inherited that trait from him." He looked lost in thought for a moment, then shook himself out of his reverie. "I'm sorry to hear that. I didn't realize he was struggling so much."

"Maybe you should've visited more." The words were out of Ava's mouth before she could stop them.

"I definitely should have," Griffin replied softly. "I guess I got caught up in my own stuff. It makes me sad." He glanced around. "I didn't realize how bad things must've gotten until I went into the house. I don't think it's been cleaned in years."

"I offered to clean once a week for him, but he refused." Ava scowled. "Eventually, he stopped inviting me inside. I tried not to take it personally—I knew why—but it was still frustrating."

"It sounds like you were close." Griffin shifted from one foot to the other. "I'm just now realizing I don't know your name. I'm Griffin." He extended his hand.

Ava automatically put hers in his and tried not to notice

the sudden spark that erupted between them. Her hand suddenly felt tingly, as if she'd accidentally sat on it for an hour. It was weird but not worth dwelling on. "Ava Mason."

Griffin froze, his grip on her hand going tighter. "Did you just say your name was Ava Mason?"

"Yeah. Why? Did Chuck mention me?" The idea tickled her. Chuck had always called her a spitfire. She wondered what sort of stories he'd told his family about her.

"I don't remember my grandfather ever mentioning you," Griffin replied as he dropped her hand. "You're the one who runs the blog. *Buzzing Around Bellaire.*"

Ava froze. *How does he know that? Could he have found the piece I wrote about him? No, that's not possible. Why would he be looking at Bellaire blogs? He's a city boy.* "I see my reputation precedes me." She attempted a smile but was sure it came across as more of a grimace.

"It certainly does," Griffin agreed. "It's weird, but I was just reading your blog a few minutes ago. I particularly enjoyed the piece where you called me a murderer."

Ava internally cringed but managed to keep her expression neutral through sheer force of will. She wanted to run, but she didn't. Instead, she held his gaze. "I just thought the locals would want to know who was moving into the neighborhood. You *are* the one who took responsibility for that building falling, correct?"

"I am." Griffin's demeanor was stiff, with no hint of the smile he'd bestowed upon her earlier. "I don't suppose you've ever heard of an accident."

"Some accidents aren't really accidents."

"Do you really think I wanted that building to fall? Do you think I somehow benefitted from that?"

"I think two people died," Ava replied, refusing to back

down even as her stomach began to churn. "I think that's the sort of thing that shouldn't be swept under the rug."

"Because you're, what? A journalist?"

"Oh, don't say it like that." Ava made a face. "Just because I blog for myself and not a newspaper doesn't mean I don't provide a service."

"Yes, I'm sure all the editors of the *National Enquirer* say the same thing."

Ava's eyebrows practically shot off her forehead. "Did you just equate me to the *National Enquirer*?"

"If the gossip rag fits."

They faced each other, seething, their chests heaving.

"You've seen me. I'm not a pervert. You can be going now."

"I was just thinking the same thing." Ava turned to leave but had to slow her pace when he called out one more time.

"There's no reason for you to come back."

Ava could think of a million reasons, but she didn't offer up any of them. That man didn't belong in Bellaire. She'd never been more certain of that. She had to find a way to get him off her farm and out of her town.

How, though?

4
FOUR

Griffin was still stewing about Ava's spy mission the following morning as he stomped out of the house and headed toward the barn. He hadn't even checked it yet, and that felt like something he should do with winter right around the corner. The odds of fixing something significant were small so close to snowfall, but if there was something minor that would hold off something major through winter, he wanted to get ahead of it.

First, though, he had to walk to the end of the driveway to check the mailbox. He'd restarted mail service for the house, and he was expecting a huge pile of stuff to show up. Most of it would go straight into the garbage, but he didn't want to inadvertently miss something important.

As he walked, he grumbled to himself.

Exactly who does Ava Mason think she is? It was bad enough that she wrote nasty stuff

about me on her blog. Her freaking blog! How much more small town can you get? And her attitude. Just because I spent the bulk of my life living in the city, that doesn't mean I'm not eager to embrace country living. I don't have an attitude about the country. That's not who I am.

But his inner voice countered, *You just made fun of her blog.*

Griffin's scowl deepened. *So what? She shouldn't be writing about stuff she doesn't understand.* The Peck Building falling had ruined more than one life, including his. Ava probably didn't even understand the intricacies of designing a building. She was too busy spying on random people and calling them perverts. Her brain was too small to grasp how many bad decisions had to pile up to result in that building falling.

I should've called the police. The thought kept going through his head. When she'd showed up on his property and called him a pervert, he should've called the police and had her arrested—or at the very least had them scold her. She didn't belong on his property, sticking her nose into his business.

And who is she to call me a pervert? She was the one peeping through windows.

And why does her hair have to be so pretty? It was neither curly nor straight. And the color... Well, in the city, he would've assumed it came from a bottle. He knew women who would pay for that color. It was both red and brown, and somehow, she managed to have glowing strands of blond in there too. That color should be illegal.

He didn't want to think too much about her attitude either. He happened to like a sassy woman. Unfortunately, that sassy woman was trying to ruin his new life. *What did I ever do to her?* He just wanted some peace and quiet. He didn't need spies running around his property, calling him a pervert.

"Hey, man," someone called out when he reached the end of the driveway.

Griffin jerked up his head, wondering if Ava had returned with backup, and instead found a man running down the road. Unlike in the city, he wasn't running from the cops or anything. He was exercising.

"Hey." Griffin smiled. He'd been a runner when he was younger but had fallen out of the habit. Maybe since he was in the country, he should reconsider it. His therapist had suggested he needed a way to relax and zone out. Running might provide just such an outlet.

The runner slowed his pace, his smile never diminishing. He stopped in front of Griffin, pressed his hands to his sides, and tried to catch his breath. "I'm Nick Griffith. I'm the gym teacher at the high school."

"Oh, hey." Griffin forced his insides to relax a little bit. "I'm Griffin Holden."

"Chuck's grandson, right?"

Griffin nodded. "Did you know him?"

"Everybody knew Chuck." Nick smiled softly. "He was a good guy. He used to throw these Halloween parties every year. My fiancée loved to get dressed up and come out here. She wasn't my fiancée at the time or anything—that would've been weird. She was just my friend. Sorry for rambling. Anyway, we're getting married in a few months, and it's getting real."

Griffin grinned. He liked the guy right away. "It's okay. I understood what you meant. Obviously, you've always lived here."

"Pretty much. I went to college and lived in Grand Rapids for a few years, but I'm back here now and pretty settled."

"With your fiancée who used to be your friend?"

"It's a long story." Nick let out a low chuckle. "We were best friends forever. Lost touch after college. Then ended up back here at the same time and realized we wanted to be more than friends. Hey, look at that. The story wasn't that long after all."

Griffin's smile widened. "I'm sure she's lovely."

"She is. Maya owns the café downtown when you get a chance to go exploring. She makes fancy coffees and sand-wiches. The best things in there are the cheese Danish, though. She bakes like a dream. If you like cheese Danish, she's a master."

"Not that you're biased or anything."

"There's a reason I have to run five miles a day," Nick replied. "She's worth it, though." He turned his head toward the farmhouse down the driveway. "How much work does that thing need?"

"A lot." Griffin checked the mailbox, found it empty, then motioned for Nick to follow him. "You can look around if you want."

"I just might." Nick fell into step with him. "In the last few years of his life, Chuck didn't let anybody out here. People tried—I want you to know that—but he wouldn't have it. He had a certain opinion about what he called charity."

"He was a hardheaded son of a bitch," Griffin readily agreed. "I wish I'd come up here to check on him, but I was dealing with my own stuff."

"Oh, I know how it goes."

"I'm sure you read about my stuff on Ava Mason's *Buzzing Around Bellaire* blog." Griffin's expression darkened again. "Even if she doesn't know what she's talking about."

"I'm surprised you found the blog." If Nick was bothered about Griffin's past, he didn't show it. "That's a local thing. I think it gets like a hundred fifty hits a post, and that's considered great for this area."

"Jenny in the grocery store pointed me toward it."

"Oh, that sounds on brand." Nick bobbed his head. "You would appeal to her."

Griffin blinked twice. "What is that supposed to mean?"

"Jenny wants out of this town something fierce," Nick explained. "That's a regular occurrence for the teenagers and young adults. Most of them don't have the same opportunities a kid who lives south might have. The closest community college is over in Traverse City, although remote learning has helped some. Jenny wants out so badly she can taste it."

"I still don't know how that involves me."

"Well, as my future wife and her best friend would say while munching on pastries and mainlining caffeine, 'You're oh so very hot, and there's going to be a swoon fest.'"

Griffin's expression didn't change, even when Nick modified his voice.

"Yeah, I spend too much time with teenagers and women," Nick said ruefully. "My vocabulary is all messed up. I'm just saying that Jenny would see you as an opportunity to flee, since the gossip says you're only here to fix up the farm and sell it."

"Is that what the gossip says? What if I want to stay?"

Nick shrugged. "I didn't say I had an opinion on the subject. This is a small town, though. You're going to have to adjust to the gossip. When Maya moved back, I had no fewer than fifty people stop me to explain why we should get together. That's simply how it works in small towns."

Griffin forced himself to calm down. He liked Nick and

couldn't blame the guy for being honest. "I'm sorry." He waved his hand. "I'm just feeling a lot of stress. The house is in worse shape than I thought. And I haven't even been in the barn yet." He gestured toward the building, which looked dilapidated and sad. "I was just about to check it out."

"Then let's do that," Nick suggested. "I can help you look around. I'm not an expert on construction or anything, but my best friend is. He used to work for another guy but is just now launching his own business with my fiancée's ex-boyfriend."

Griffin wanted to let it go, but he couldn't. "Your best friend is going into business with your fiancée's ex-boyfriend?"

"Yeah, that's a small-town thing too." Nick huffed out a laugh. "It's okay. Maya and Blaine were a couple in college. He's a good guy, and we're one big happy family now."

"Of course you are. What else would you be?" He had to untie a rope from around the barn doors—it was the only thing keeping them shut—and he held his breath as he let them fall open. *How bad will it be?*

The first thing he saw was four cats sitting in the middle of the barn's dirt floor. One of them was an adult, and three of them were kittens ... and not very big ones.

"Oh crap." Griffin took a step forward, and the cats scattered. From the noise in the loft, he could tell more were up there, and they didn't sound happy about having their utopia invaded.

"Yeah, I'm not surprised about that," Nick admitted as he scratched his cheek. "We've been seeing a lot of cats in the fields surrounding the farm for the past few months. I bet this place is crawling with them."

"What do I do?" Griffin had never felt more out of his element.

"You could hire a company."

"Would they kill them?"

"Some of them work for rescues," Nick hedged. "Feral cats are often euthanized, though."

"I don't want to kill them." Griffin was disgusted by the thought. "That hardly seems fair. They're just doing what cats do."

"The good news is if you get the little ones into rescues right away, they can often be socialized and adopted out."

"Okay." Griffin wasn't opposed to that. "What about the others?"

"There's a program. Maya has donated her time to it ... and money. They capture the older cats and fix them. You know, so they can't add more kittens to the mix. Then they tip their ears so other rescues know that they're fixed and release them back where they came from."

"Into the barn?" Griffin wasn't thrilled with that possibility.

"Honestly, it's not the worst thing," Nick replied. "It will keep down the mice. You probably have thirty or forty cats in here, though. We need to get the babies out and catch the adults and take them in. The rescue will help you for free, but it's going to take work."

"Right." Griffin raised his eyes to the barn ceiling, which had holes. "Is it even worth it, though?"

Nick followed his gaze. "Those are going to have to be fixed. The barn won't survive another winter if we don't get in here and do some triage."

"You seem to know a lot about construction." Hope welled in Griffin's chest.

"Actually, I don't, but Bear does. He's the one I told you

about. Blaine does as well. I've just been listening to them talk a lot over the last few months. They would say this barn needs some TLC."

Griffin huffed a laugh. "Of course it does." He glanced around. "Do you think it would be better to save this barn or leave it over the winter and build a new one in the spring?"

Nick thought for a moment. "I'm not sure. I happen to be a big fan of restoring places like this. I guess it depends on what you want."

"If I knew that, I wouldn't be standing here frozen with decision paralysis. I don't know what to do."

"I can call Bear and get him out here," Nick offered. "At the very least, he can look around and tell you what you're dealing with. There might not actually be a decision to make if Bear sees things that I don't, which is likely."

"You would do that?" Griffin let out a breath. "I'd actually appreciate that. I'm an architect, not a builder. Some of the construction stuff is above my pay grade."

"I can totally do that," Nick said as he dug into his pocket for his phone. "I bet I can get him out here today."

"You're much nicer than some of the other people I've met here. I really appreciate the help."

"Who have you met that isn't nice?"

"Edie Eggers in the grocery store."

"Well, she doesn't count." Nick chuckled. "She's just an old busybody. Each one of the small towns in the area has ten of her. Just ignore her."

"Then there's the lovely Ava Mason," Griffin added with a glower. "She's been an absolute delight."

"You're talking about the blog post?" Nick's nose wrinkled. "I wouldn't get too worked up about it. Ava can't help prying into everybody's business. She's actually a good person … when she can control herself."

"How often can she control herself?"

"She's actually pretty good about it."

"Oh yeah?" Griffin crossed his arms. "What if I were to tell you that I found her hiding in the bushes outside the kitchen, spying on me, yesterday?"

Nick hesitated then laughed. "Did she press her nose against the window and make whimpering sounds until you let her in? I happen to know she's been dying to see inside the farmhouse. People are naturally curious because Chuck cut everybody off from the goods."

"She said she was spying to make sure I wasn't a pervert."

Nick laughed again. "That sounds like Ava."

"Then when I found out who she was and called her out on the blog post, she said she was providing a service to the community. She suggested I wanted that building to fall and was some evil megalomaniac who was happy to get away with murder."

Aghast, Nick replied, "Oh, that doesn't sound like Ava."

"How well do you know her?"

"Fairly well, actually. She graduated a year behind Maya and me. She was always spunky and fun and into mischief. But not big mischief. As for the blog, well, just ignore it. People will move on just as soon as another longtime couple implodes, and they have something new to gossip about."

"You sound pretty certain."

"My mom left my dad for the town loser, and now I have to have dinner with him once a month or risk her wrath, so I know how it goes."

Griffin's eyes widened, then he shook his head. "Small-town life is going to be an adjustment."

"It is. When I was growing up, I thought I wanted to be in a city. I was determined I could only get what I wanted if I left this place. Do you know what I found out?"

Griffin shook his head.

"Small towns can be magical. I didn't get what I really wanted until I came home. Now, did I see myself being a high school gym teacher and coaching the basketball team? I did not. That was not the dream. Maya was the dream I never knew I wanted, though."

"So you're happy here, even though this isn't how you thought your life would turn out."

"That's exactly what I'm saying," Nick confirmed. "I don't fully understand what happened with that building, but it's obvious you didn't want it to fall. It wasn't on purpose. You need to let it go."

"That's what I was trying to do. But now everybody here knows about it too."

"Yeah, but they'll move on. Trust me. Ava's blog will be a blip. As for the spying, well, she's just a busybody. She hates it when you call her that, by the way, but it's true. And she'll move on eventually too. You're just the new element."

"So what do I do?" Griffin felt as if he was in over his head.

"Let's start by getting Bear out here to look at this barn. Once he tells us what we're dealing with, we'll go from there."

Griffin let out a sigh. There was no sense panicking before he knew whether it was even warranted. He had to take it one step at a time, something he used to be good at but had come to fill him with dread.

"Please call your friend," he replied. "A fresh set of eyes on someone who's knowledgeable can only help."

"You got it." Nick grinned. "You're going to fit in fine in this place. Trust me."

Griffin had no idea whether that was a good or a bad thing.

5
FIVE

Ava's job was to hear things. Okay, it wasn't her *job* job. Still, she liked to know what was going on in her community. Since Griffin Holden had moved in several days ago, he was the only thing anybody had been talking about. Unfortunately, none of her normal gossip hounds had anything good. The only thing she'd managed to uncover was that Bear Torkelson had been seen at the farm thanks to intervention from Nick Griffith. She had no idea whether Bear was going to work for Griffin or if Griffin had decided it was too much work to renovate the farm and was looking to sell it. The Holden farm was like a black hole of information, and that drove her crazy.

Ava's run-in with Griffin was still fresh in her mind. Until he'd found out who she was, he'd been friendly and gregarious. He'd even been flirty ... or maybe she was making that up. Once he'd learned her identity, however, he'd turned cold faster than a Michigan winter.

Deep down, Ava knew the man didn't owe her anything. Nobody did. It was her own fault she'd planned her entire life around getting her hands on that farm. Still, she was annoyed. Griffin was a city boy. *Why would he possibly think he would be happy in the country?* Every movie she'd ever seen and every book she'd ever read told her that he couldn't be happy out of his normal environment. Sure, Hallmark movies said otherwise. But they were Hallmark movies. Marvel movies were based more in reality than Hallmark ones.

For the four days following their meeting, Ava told herself to stay away from the farm. There was nothing she could do. She had to wait for Griffin to make his decision. On the fifth day, she lost her head and decided another spy mission was in order. Nobody knew the Holden farm better than her. She could get close, take a look around, then disappear into the trees surrounding the house. The new owner—and his bad attitude—would have no idea she was even there.

Ava dressed for her mission with the utmost care. She went with brown leggings and a green top and tugged a gray knit cap over her ears before shrugging into her camouflage coat. She snagged her binoculars from the drawer before heading out.

She parked on the road, making sure the vehicle wasn't visible from the farmhouse, then went into the woods. By the time she reached the area surrounding the barn, she was sweaty and annoyed. *Why is this guy making my life so freaking difficult? What does he hope to accomplish here?*

The barn door was open, so she moved to a location where she could see inside. The lighting wasn't great, but she caught a hint of movement almost right away. Griffin was hard to mistake for someone else, with that strong build and chiseled jaw, and he seemed to be intensely pacing the barn.

What the hell is he doing?

Ava watched for several minutes longer, her jaw dropping as Griffin performed a series of jerky movements she couldn't identify. Then finally, when he stood, she realized he had a kitten in his hand.

"You're not going to kill that kitten, are you?" she blurted as she straightened.

Griffin, who clearly thought he was alone, jerked at the sound of her voice. Rather than drop the kitten, he cradled the tiny creature against his chest and glared at her. "Seriously?"

Her spy mission an abject failure, Ava sheepishly emerged from the bushes and made her way to the barn opening. She didn't risk venturing inside. Instead, she glanced around—it had been too long since she'd been inside the barn—before allowing her gaze to fall on him. "You can't kill that kitten. I'll report you for animal cruelty."

"That's going to be pretty hard if you're locked up for trespassing," Griffin fired back.

He had an edge to his voice, but he didn't reach for his phone to report her. Ava took that as a good sign.

"I'm not trespassing." Ava took a step into the barn and inhaled deeply. The faint scent of cloves hit her like a Mack memory truck. "I'm ensuring the safety of God's littlest creatures."

"Oh, whatever." Griffin made a face as he peered down at the kitten, who seemed confused. It regularly let out little hisses but didn't appear to be trying to escape. "The barn is full of cats."

"I know." Ava took a tentative step forward, her eyes on the kitten. "Barn cats are a regular thing in these parts. They help keep the vermin down."

"I think there are at least thirty cats in this barn," Griffin countered. "That has to be more than what's allowed under the law."

For some reason, that struck Ava as funny. "I don't think anybody is going to ticket you." Since he hadn't yet ordered her out of the barn, Ava took the final step and closed the distance between them. "May I?" She held out her hands toward the kitten.

"I'm not going to kill it," Griffin groused. He handed over the kitten despite his surly attitude. "It doesn't like me."

The kitten hissed when Ava took it. "It's feral. It's still young, though. I think it's only about six weeks."

"Are you a vet now too?" Griffin must've realized how aggressive he sounded. "I'm sorry. It's just... I wasn't expecting to find a cat colony in here."

"You're not going to tear the barn down, are you?" The mere thought had Ava's heart racing.

"That wasn't the plan." Griffin dragged a hand through his hair. "I called a construction foreman out here to take a look. He said the frame is still good, but it needs a roof and some wall work. But that can't happen until I get all these cats out."

"Well, you could catch them."

Griffin shot her a withering look. "That was already the plan. Nick mentioned a rescue, and I'm going to call them."

"Oh, you must be calling my friend Sabrina. I work with her team whenever I get the chance. I can help you."

"You want to help me catch kittens? Why?"

Ava shrugged. "It will get cold soon. Once these kittens hit about the ten-week mark, they can't be socialized. Well, I should take that back. There are always miracle cases of feral cats being adopted, but they're the exception to the rule. The faster we can catch them, the better."

She stroked the feisty kitten's head even as the creature continuously spit at her. "This little one, for example, could be completely socialized in a week."

Griffin's forehead creased. "You know a lot about cats." He held up a hand to stop her before she could respond. "Let me guess—you live in a house with twenty of them because nobody else can stand you."

"Stereotypes aren't polite." Ava sniffed.

"This is the second time this week I've caught you spying on me, and you want to talk about being polite? That's on top of your stupid blog post."

"That blog post was factual."

"So you think," he muttered. When he turned away from her, he sucked in a breath as if calming himself, and his face was impassive when he turned back. "You said once they hit ten weeks, they can't be socialized. What does that mean for the adult cats? They won't be killed, will they?"

He looked so upset at the prospect that Ava's stone-cold heart thawed a bit. *What the hell? He's the enemy,* she reminded herself. *He took your future. You can't suddenly start liking him.* Despite her brutal inner voice, she took pity on him. "You need barn cats if you're going to keep this place. The barn will be overrun by mice and rats if you're not care-ful. You don't want to put a bunch of money into fixing it up only to let it be overrun by mice."

"Nick mentioned that when I talked to him. I would prefer that not happen. If the adult cats stay out here, though, they'll just keep producing litter after litter of kittens."

"They will." Ava nodded. "That's why we have to trap them too. It's stressful for them, but it's for the best. There's a local vet who will give you a break on getting the adults fixed. He'll also check the cats over to make sure they're not sick or anything. There's no sense putting a sick cat back in the wild. When the cats are fixed, the vet will tip their ears. That will allow you to notice if a new cat moves in. You'll probably still end up with a litter of kittens here or there. But it will be nothing like this."

"Yeah, Nick mentioned tipping the ears too. That's what they do with feral cat colonies in the city." Griffin's eyes had drifted up to the loft, to where an orange kitten was watching him from behind a toolbox. "This barn is a mess."

"Chuck couldn't keep up with it in the last few years." Ava's heart squeezed when she thought back to the way Griffin's grandfather had struggled to get around. "I tried to help, but he was too stubborn. He kept thinking that some-how, he'd miraculously get better." She glanced up at the loft, to where another kitten had appeared. "I had no idea the barn had been taken over this way."

"Well, we need to do something about it."

Ava arched an eyebrow. "We?"

"I think it's the least you can do, considering I keep finding you on my property."

"I hate to be a wet blanket on your self-righteousness, but I know this property better than you do. You need me."

Griffin rolled his eyes. "I want to save as many kittens as we can. I know that's not much in the grand scheme of things, but it's something tangible. If we can find homes for them..."

Ava was horrified to discover that her heart was melting yet again. "We can save the kittens." She handed the one she was holding back to him. "Do you mind if I take a peek up there?" She pointed toward the ladder that led to the loft.

"Actually, I do," Griffin replied. "You strike me as the

type to sue if you fall—even if it's your fault—so I think I should be the one to climb up there."

"I'm not going to sue," Ava replied, offended. "That's not who I am. Besides, I've been up in that loft a lot more recently than you. I know which parts of the floor are weak."

"You just told me that you haven't seen the inside of the barn for years."

Ava hesitated. "That's not entirely true. Chuck wouldn't let me help him with the cats, cleaning, or anything. But he let me sit in the barn."

"He let you *sit in the barn*? Why would you want to do that?"

Ava squirmed under his intense gaze. "I've just always liked the barn. It doesn't matter, okay?" She was being defensive, but she couldn't seem to stop herself. "I liked to hide in the loft when I was a kid. I would bring a book with me. Chuck found me up there more than once when I wasn't supposed to be there. Instead of kicking me out, he created a little nook of sorts. I was allowed to read up there as long as I didn't walk through the woods after dark."

Griffin moved his lips silently, as if trying to find words, and sighed. "Okay, take a look. You're the one with cat-rescue experience anyway. You'll be able to tell your friend Sabrina what sort of supplies we need."

"See, now you're thinking." Ava beamed at him and started for the ladder, which was still surprisingly sturdy. Her smile lasted until she reached the loft, then it disappeared. "Well, shit."

"That doesn't sound like a good 'shit.'" Griffin had watched her ascent with the sort of studied worry a father would reserve for a child.

"I think you were being conservative when estimating

thirty cats." Ava shot him a rueful smile. "It's probably more like fifty."

Griffin viciously swore under his breath, the kitten hissing in tandem, then he collected himself. "So what do we do?"

Ava angled herself on the ladder so she could focus on him but still keep an eye on the rabble-rousing kittens playing in the loft. "Here's the thing—the adults are going to be harder to catch than the kittens. We need to focus on them. The kittens will be the easy part. They're not as world weary as the adults."

"Okay." Griffin nodded. "Just out of curiosity, what do you get out of this arrangement? I know what I get—help with cats I have no idea how to catch."

"What makes you think I'm out to *get* anything?"

"Because you're human ... or I'm hoping you are. The jury is still out. It's human nature to get something in exchange for offering services. That's just the way the world works."

"I guess it never occurred to you that I just want to help, huh?" Ava couldn't muster as much righteous indignation as she would've preferred. She couldn't blame Griffin for not trusting her. From his perspective, she was an absolute menace.

"No, it really didn't," Griffin replied. "Since the moment I found you spying through my kitchen window, it's been clear you have an agenda."

"Agenda is such an ugly word," Ava groused.

"That doesn't mean it's the wrong word."

She blinked twice, then blew out a sigh. "Fine. I want access to the barn."

"This barn?"

She nodded. "I have fond memories of it. It was ... a

refuge of sorts when I was a kid. I could curl up with a book and shut out the real world. That's what this farm always was to me. I want to see it saved. If that means I work with you to do it, well, I guess I'll have to suck it up."

"So you want access to the barn. In exchange, you're going to help me catch fifty cats."

"That's the offer," Ava agreed.

"Well, awesome." Griffin grinned. "I agree to your terms."

"Just like that?"

"Yeah. I'm that desperate."

She smiled back and started to make her way down. "It's not going to be as hard as you think," she assured him. "Our biggest problem is checking the litters upstairs. We can't take kittens that are still nursing. We'll have to catch the mothers first and keep track of which litter belongs to each specific cat. Then when we have the mothers, we can gather the kittens and transport them together."

"It sounds difficult," Griffin said as he pressed the kitten to his chest.

"It will be." Ava wouldn't sugarcoat it for him. "But it's the right thing to do."

He handed the kitten back to her.

"Before the rescue gets here, we need supplies. Do you plan on starting construction on the barn right away?" She worried he would say yes.

"Actually, I'm going through the house first," Griffin replied. "Bear is coming out here tomorrow, and we're going to do a walkthrough. We're prioritizing everything. With winter coming, some things are more important than others. We're going to get some work done on the barn, but the house comes first."

Ava nodded. "That makes sense. If I can have a couple

of days, at the very least, we can get the nursing kittens out of here with their mothers. That will be an important step."

"Then that's what we'll do."

Ava shot out her right hand. "Perhaps we should shake on it."

Griffin dubiously eyed her hand, then reluctantly took it. "You're going to be work, aren't you?"

Ava laughed as if he'd told the funniest joke ever. "Oh, you have no idea. You'd better prepare yourself because it's going to be a bumpy ride."

6

SIX

The next day, Ava and Sabrina started the process of capturing the cats. Griffin eyed the open barn door through the kitchen window as they worked.

If Ava weren't such an utter pain in the ass, Griffin would respect her. But she was, and annoyance was his constant companion when she was in close proximity.

"What are you doing?" Nick appeared next to Griffin, almost making him jump out of his skin. Griffin had forgotten Nick, Bear, and several other members of the construction team were present. He'd lost himself momentarily in the cat caper.

"Just checking to see how many cats they've caught," Griffin replied before sipping his coffee. He meant to turn away from the barn, but Ava's appearance with a huge cage in her hands stilled him.

"I thought you didn't like Ava," Nick said after several seconds of watching.

"I can't stand her."

Nick's lips twitched. "Is that why she's on your property right now?"

"She's on my property because we made a deal. Well, kind of." Griffin forced himself to turn away from the window. He had to tamp down his disappointment when he could no longer watch Ava. As irritating as he found the woman—she was like a strange rash that he couldn't quite scratch—for some reason, he couldn't stop looking at her. It was both aggravating and confusing.

"You made a deal?" Nick's eyebrows rose. "I'm almost afraid to ask."

"She wants access to the barn. In exchange, she and her friend are going to trap as many of those cats as possible."

Nick scratched his cheek. "That's weird. Why would she want access to the barn?"

"She says my grandfather allowed her to read in it as a kid, and she's feeling nostalgic or something."

"Do you believe that?"

Griffin shrugged, holding up his palms. "Not really, but she does seem dedicated to helping the cats. I mean ... I don't really consider myself a cat lover, but the idea of all those kittens never having homes feels wrong."

"Basically, you're saying you're a softie." Nick grinned. "I get it."

"I'm not a softie." Why the teasing bothered him so much, Griffin couldn't say. "I just—I don't know—they have such tiny faces. I know they're going to grow up into cats, but if they can have real homes, I don't want to keep them from that."

Nick burst out laughing. "Okay, well, I get it. As I told you, barn cats are necessary in these parts, but I don't blame you for wanting to save them."

"The rescue's going to help me partner with a vet to get older ones checked over and fixed. The ones who can't be socialized and are healthy enough will be returned to the barn. They think I'll still have a good five or six barn cats when they're done."

"Do you want barn cats?"

Griffin hesitated. "I don't know. I read up on them last night."

"You did?"

"On the internet."

"Wow." Nick clapped Griffin on the shoulder. "You know there's other stuff on the internet, right? TikTok has videos, and there's even porn out there, if you're feeling lonely."

Griffin scowled at him. "I just like to research things. And I wanted to make sure Ava wasn't lying about the cats to get what she wants."

"And what is it you think she wants?"

"I notice you didn't deny that she would lie."

Nick chuckled. "I don't know Ava all that well. She hangs out with my fiancée occasionally, but Ava was a year behind us in school. Plus, well, Maya and I were completely caught up in each other. We only had room for a few friends, and Ava wasn't one of them back then."

"Because she's crazy, right? You can tell me. She's batshit crazy, isn't she?"

Nick snorted. "I don't know that I would put it that way. It's more that she's set in her ways." He was quiet for several seconds, then his expression softened. "There were rumors about her parents when we were kids."

Oh, well, now we're finally getting somewhere. "What sort of rumors?" Griffin asked. "Were they grifters? Ooh, I could see her being in a cult."

"Not like that." Nick fervently shook his head. "It's more like … her parents weren't exactly good people. Ava was often on her own."

Griffin stilled. "Like … she was abused?" His stomach constricted at the thought. He told himself it was because he didn't want anybody to be abused—especially a child— but he suddenly felt protective over Ava. Sure, he couldn't stand her, but the idea of her being hurt was almost too much, and he had to prop his hand on the counter to remain upright.

"Not abused," Nick said hurriedly. "If she were being physically abused, somebody would've stepped in. This is a small town. We don't look kindly on stuff like that. It's a 'live and let live' community, but nobody is going to sit back and let someone hurt a kid."

Relief punched through Griffin like a hurricane. "So what are you saying?"

"Her parents were just … absent," Nick replied. "I'm pretty sure they were more wrapped up in each other than her, but they claimed to go on missionary trips from time to time."

Caught off guard, Griffin asked, "Like … religious trips?"

"More like humanitarian trips. Her father worked in medical supply, and he claimed he was taking her mother to Africa for a month more than once to help in the Congo or wherever else."

"Why do you say 'claimed' like that?"

"Because they weren't really missionaries. When they left, it wasn't because they were taking humanitarian trips. They would just take off on the father's motorcycle for weeks, sometimes months, at a time. They assumed everybody believed their stories."

"And they just left Ava behind?"

"She was on her own a lot. There was a rumor her parents set up allowances at the local diner and grocery store so she would never run out of food when they were gone. People thought the work they were doing was so important that nobody ever told them no. At least the people who believed the stories. The others just didn't want to stick their noses into anybody else's business."

"But I still don't understand," Griffin pressed. "What did they do with her when she was little?"

"Oh, I don't know." Nick shook his head. "Bear might know."

As if on cue, the burly construction worker appeared in the doorway. "What might I know?" Bear was the gregarious sort, and Griffin had liked him right away.

"Ava Mason," Nick prodded. "Her parents were missionaries, right?"

"In the loosest sense of the term, if you believe the stories," Bear replied as he headed for the sink. His gaze immediately went out the window, to where Ava and Sabrina were working. "Oh, did you sucker Ava into collecting those cats for you? That was a smart move."

"She volunteered," Griffin replied.

Nick added, "She said she would help collect all those cats if Griffin let her *hang out in his barn*."

He said it so pointedly that Griffin couldn't help going stiff. "She said she liked to read there."

"I think she spent a lot of time over here when she was a teenager," Bear replied. "Her parents' place—which is her mother's place now—is through those woods. It's less than a ten-minute walk. I know she helped Chuck a lot as an adult, and people always mentioned her hanging out here as a teenager."

"But her parents were out of town a lot, right?" Nick prodded.

"They were. They would make up these elaborate lies about all the charity work they were doing overseas. People knew better, though. Sometimes they were seen as close as one town over. They just weren't here, taking care of their kid. But Ava was independent, and she did a good job of taking care of herself. She always seemed fine."

Griffin could see that. He could also see the reality being very different from the persona she likely projected. *Was Ava always alone? Is that why she's so loud and brash?* "What did they do when she was little and couldn't stay alone?" He was stuck on that one little detail.

"I don't know. I think she had grandparents. Once she hit fourteen or so, she stayed here by herself. She was pretty independent. We were all ridiculously envious because she never had her parents breathing down her neck."

"But that also means she never had her parents show up for her," Griffin noted.

"Yeah, well, when you're a kid, you only see the fun side of it." Bear shrugged. "Speaking of grandparents, though, I found some trunks up in the attic. We need to get them out of there so we can patch the drywall by the windows. There are some holes. The attic needs to be completely redone, but that can wait."

Griffin wasn't surprised. "Okay. What's the problem?"

"We opened one of the trunks, thinking that it was probably clothes or something, but they're full of diaries."

Griffin blinked several times as he absorbed the news. "Diaries? Are you telling me that my grandfather wrote in diaries?" He had no idea what to make of that.

"Okay, the word *diaries* makes me picture ten-year-old girls," Bear conceded. "They're journals, though, and they seem like the sort of thing a family member should sort through."

"Okay." Griffin cast one final look through the kitchen window to where Ava stood in front of a brunette. Her hands moved a mile a minute, and whatever story she was telling had the other woman in stitches. Since he knew more about the way Ava had been brought up, he couldn't help looking at her in a different light. Sure, she was bossy and a busybody, but maybe she was those things because she'd had to take charge whenever the opportunity arose or fade into the background when she was growing up.

He didn't like her any more than before. She'd done real damage to him when he was trying to start fresh in a new town. But it was possible she wasn't quite the villain he'd made her out to be.

"Let's look at these journals," he said with a sigh as he followed Bear toward the stairs. "They must've belonged to my grandmother or something. I can't imagine my grandfather keeping diaries."

"How much time did you spend with your grandfather?" Bear asked. "Because—no offense—I knew him fairly well, and he often carried a notebook with him. I just thought he was doing things for the farm, making lists and stuff. I don't think that's what he was doing, though."

His tone set Griffin's teeth on edge. "I loved my grandfather."

"I'm not saying you didn't," Bear replied hurriedly. "It's just... Once I saw the notebooks in the trunk, it kind of jarred my memory. Nobody saw him much over the last few years of his life, but before then, he always had a notebook with him when he was out."

Griffin didn't know what to make of that, so he filed it away to consider later. "I guess I missed the notebooks."

When they emerged into the top floor of the house, the area was gloomy. It should've been stuffy, but it was drafty instead, telling Griffin they needed to plug the holes by the windows. He would go broke trying to heat the place in the winter if all the warm air escaped through the holes.

"Here." Bear led Griffin to a corner, where three trunks were pressed against the walls. "All three of them have journals in them."

Griffin peered inside the one that was propped open, and when he opened the notebook on top of the stack, he was well and truly baffled. "Wow." Griffin shook his head as he flipped through the notebook. "This is definitely my grandfather's handwriting. I had no idea he kept diaries."

"I think if you keep referring to them as diaries, you're never going to accept it," Bear said. "Diaries are girl things. Although never tell my wife I said that. She'll castrate me and enjoy it."

"I don't understand."

"We have a lot of kids," Bear explained. "Probably too many, but once we started, we kind of got into a rhythm."

Nick chuckled but didn't say anything.

"Now I'm fixed, so there's no chance of our getting caught up in that rhythm again. But that's not important." Bear waved his hand. "My wife is determined that our daughter be afforded the same opportunities as our sons. That means the boys can play with dolls, and our daughter can play with Matchbox cars. I'm not supposed to assign gender to inanimate objects."

"What about tampons?" Nick queried. "I mean, those don't really seem like boy things."

Bear shot him a withering look. "Just don't. I've talked to her about this so many times that I've lost count. She knows she's being rigid about certain things, but she's afraid, and I can't stand it when my wife is afraid."

"What is she afraid of?" Griffin asked.

"This is a small town. There aren't a lot of kids to hang

around with. We know." Bear motioned between himself and Nick. "It's harder for girls, according to my wife, because the girls either have to conform to the popular crowd or resign themselves to being isolated individuals. Lindsey wants our daughter to be an individual and not face the sort of pressure that could force her to be something she's not. It's a whole big thing."

Griffin thought of Ava. She was obviously an individual. *Does that mean she suffered when growing up even more than I thought?* It certainly seemed so. "I get it," he said as he focused on the journal. "I'll stop calling them diaries. It's just so weird. I had no idea he did this."

"Is there anything good in there?" Nick asked.

"There's just a lot of talk in here about Ada, how he's worried about her and how he wants to do right by her."

"Ada would've been your grandmother, right?" Nick asked. "Her full name was Adelaide, if I remember correctly."

"Yeah. She died when I was a teenager." Griffin sighed. "I always liked her, but I never felt like I knew her." As he gripped the journal, he realized he didn't know his grandfather nearly as well as he'd thought either. "Can you guys help me move these trunks to the guest bedroom?"

"Sure," Nick replied. "Are you going to find a way to keep them?"

"I don't know. I'm staying in the guest bedroom, though—it felt weird to be in his bedroom—and I want to start going through them. I can't imagine keeping all of them." He glanced at the trunks again. "They would just sit there and collect dust. But I don't want to throw all of them out either. I want to keep some."

"I think that's smart," Bear said. "We can move them

down to your room. You don't have to decide right away. You can spend the winter reading them."

"Yeah." Griffin forced a smile. "I just hope I don't find something I don't want to know."

"Like what?" Nick asked.

"Like ... I don't ever want to know he was lonely after my grandmother passed. I'm afraid that's what I'll find. I know my father wanted him to move south when she was gone, and he refused. I didn't think much about it after that. Maybe I should have, though."

"Oh, I don't know," Bear said. "You might find some good stuff in there. Your grandfather was a crazy old coot, but people loved him. In fact, you should come with us to the bonfire party tonight. I bet people will have a million stories about him."

"What now? Aren't you a little old for bonfire parties?"

Nick chuckled. "We are, but it's a small town. We're technically caught between seasons until it snows. Although then we call them snow parties. It doesn't matter." He waved a hand. "Basically, it's just a bunch of adults hanging out and having a few cocktails without any kids around. You should definitely come."

"Oh, I don't know." To Griffin, that sounded downright painful.

"You need to meet people," Nick pressed. "Bear and I are delightful, but there are other people out there you should get to know. It's going to be a long winter otherwise."

"I'll think about it," Griffin hedged.

"No, you're going," Bear said. "Trust me. It might sound stupid now, but it's going to feel way stupider when we get there. Despite that, it will be fun. You need to have a bit of fun."

Griffin balked. "I'm fun."

Bear barked out a laugh. "Yeah, your brand of fun and mine are vastly different. You'll come around, though. I have faith."

Resigned, Griffin could do nothing but nod. "Sure. Leave me the details when you go. I'm sure I can ... figure out something."

"That's the spirit."

7
SEVEN

Ava dressed in layers for the bonfire party. She regularly attended, even though she recognized deep down that they were a little old to be partying outside. As adults, they were supposed to be throwing dignified parties. But the people in Bellaire didn't care, and neither did Ava. The bonfire parties were a great source of gossip.

With that in mind, even though it was supposed to be the coldest night of the fall so far, she dressed to impress. That meant she put on her thermal L. L. Bean pants, a pretty purple thermal top, her favorite fuzzy coat, and a cute pink hat to tuck over her ears. Then she grabbed a pair of fingerless gloves, shoved her phone into her pocket, and headed out.

The parties might've been juvenile, but they did them right. They'd actually built a cabin on the property to serve as a bar area. They kept a keg inside and a few bottles of liquor that they packed up each week, and the cabin had hidden slider panels to keep out the elements.

The party space was packed when Ava arrived.

"Get your beer now," Lindsey said when she saw her. "They've got two kegs. The first is Sam Adams. The second is Bud Light." The way Lindsey wrinkled her nose told Ava all she needed to know about her opinion on the subject.

Ava waved to acknowledge she'd heard and immediately went to the cabin. When she rejoined Lindsey by the fire, Maya sat beside her, and they were giving commentary on all their former classmates.

"There's Cathy Swan." Lindsey lifted her chin and scowled. "I heard she was trying to seduce Jake Jeffries up at the resort this week. She was going all out and even bragged about squeezing his butt."

Ava sipped her beer as she sat. "Isn't Jake still engaged to January Jackson?"

"Most definitely." Lindsey smiled and waved at Cathy, as if she weren't running her into the ground. "Yeah, keep walking, you troll. Nobody wants your skanky energy over here."

Ava pursed her lips and slid her gaze to Maya, who was much calmer than her best friend. Though Maya liked to gossip as much as the rest of them, she was simply less energetic than her attached-at-the-hip bestie.

"She's in a mood," Maya explained. "She's convinced Cathy is on a mission to steal every man in town."

"It's true," Lindsey snapped. "Have you ever seen Cathy go after a guy who wasn't already committed to somebody else? I mean, you don't get more committed than Jake. He practically has hearts floating around his head whenever he looks at January."

"And I'm proud of it," Jake called out as he breezed past. He was dressed for the party, but his coat was hanging open.

"Where is your better half?" Lindsey yelled at Jake's back. He was clearly heading toward the cabin for a drink.

Jake called over his shoulder, "She'll be here in about an hour. She's finishing up some paperwork at the resort. I wouldn't have left her, but I didn't want to get stuck drinking the Bud Light."

"I heard that!" Bear barked from his spot next to the cabin. "It's not my fault they only had one keg of the good stuff."

"I take it Bear was the one tasked with getting the beer this week," Ava said to Lindsey.

"Yeah, and he's mad." Lindsey smiled. "I pointed out there was more than one place to get a keg around here, but did he listen? Of course not. He might be a beer snob, but he's also lazy. He says by the time the second keg rolls around, nobody will care what's in it."

Bear's belief was likely true.

"I guess we'll find out." She sipped her beer again. "Go back to Cathy. Did she really squeeze Jake's butt?"

"She said she mistook him for somebody else, but nobody believes her," Lindsey replied. "Jake is the hottest guy up there. He's in line to inherit the resort when his father retires. Everybody wants a piece of him. He's practically royalty in these parts."

"Yeah, but he's with January." That was the part Ava couldn't wrap her head around. "Those two don't go anywhere without each other unless there's a specific reason."

"Like bad beer," Maya added.

"Hey, the difference between Bud Light and Sam Adams is significant," Lindsey said. "Don't tell me you don't know that."

"Whatever." Maya waved a hand. "As for January and

Jake, they're clearly dedicated to each other. I can't imagine even thinking for a moment that it's feasible to get between them."

"They've usurped your Couple of the Moment crown," Lindsey mused. "That must be difficult."

Maya gave her a murderous look. "Nobody usurped anybody's crown."

"You and Nick are old news," Lindsey countered. "It's okay to admit it. You guys are boring now. You were the talk of the town when you first got together. Without any drama, though, you've turned into yesterday's news. Just ask Ava. When was the last time she wrote about you on her blog?"

Ava's cheeks heated. She was glad it was dark so that Lindsey couldn't see her blush. "I don't gossip," she countered lamely.

Lindsey and Maya snorted in unison.

"Yeah, right." Lindsey rolled her eyes until they landed on her husband again. "Speaking of hot, has anybody met the new guy? I know I'm happily married and all that, but I would totally take a bite out of his ass. It looks firm."

Ava turned to look in the direction Lindsey had become fixated on and found herself staring at Griffin. He was dressed in a simple North Face coat and seemed to be having a good time as he laughed with Bear and Nick.

"Who invited him?" she blurted before she could think better of it.

"I'm pretty sure Bear did," Lindsey replied. "Why?"

"Nick said they both badgered him into coming," Maya added. "They like him. They say he's a nice guy."

"Oh, well, if they think it, then I guess the rest of us are supposed to follow suit," Ava groused.

Amusement danced over Lindsey's features. "I take it you disagree."

"He's just so ... city."

Lindsey burst out laughing. "Anybody who didn't grow up here is considered city. Remember Keith Davidson? He moved here from freaking Traverse City—population fifteen thousand, I believe—and they kept calling him a big-city boy. He finally gave up and moved back over there."

Ava laughed at the memory. "That dude wore socks under his sandals. He was all wrong for Bellaire anyway."

"You have a point." Lindsey laughed then waved at Bear. "Let's get the new guy over here. I want to get to know him better."

Before Ava could stop Lindsey, Bear nodded and held up a finger.

"What are you doing?" she hissed.

"I said I want to meet the new guy." Lindsey shrugged off Ava's grip. "Why does it matter?"

"Because... Because..." Ava didn't have an answer. She couldn't exactly admit to everything that had happened between her and Griffin.

"I think I know," Maya teased.

Ava narrowed her eyes. *Is it possible Maya knows the truth?* Since Nick had been hanging out with Griffin, it was more than possible. "No, you don't."

"Don't listen to her," Lindsey ordered in her bossiest tone, grabbing Maya's hand. "I want to know."

Maya turned to Ava and grinned. "Sorry, but you're usually the one gossiping about everybody else. I think you've earned this."

Ava let out a pent-up breath, resigned.

"According to Nick, Ava was hiding in the bushes outside the Holden farmhouse the day Griffin moved in."

Maya's eyes sparkled. "Apparently, Griffin caught her, and sparks flew."

Ava's lips curved down. "That's not what happened."

"You weren't caught spying, or sparks didn't fly?" Lindsey demanded.

"I... The second part." Ava's cheeks burned yet again, and it had nothing to do with her proximity to the fire. "There were no sparks."

"Uh-huh." Lindsey didn't look convinced. "What did Griffin say about her?"

Even though Ava was determined that there'd been no attraction, she found she wanted to hear the answer to Lindsey's question.

"Nick is convinced Griffin felt sparks," Maya replied. If she was bothered about gossiping, she didn't show it. "He's still feeling out the situation, though."

"Ugh." Ava rubbed her cheek. "There were no sparks," she said less adamantly. "Just... Don't be weird." She ducked her head as Bear, Nick, and Griffin joined the party.

"There's my favorite girl." Nick swooped in and gave Maya a kiss before nudging her over so he could share the bench with her. "Griffin Holden, this is Maya."

"Your fiancée." Griffin's eyes lingered on Ava, something she could hardly miss, before moving to Maya. "Nick does nothing but gush about you twenty-four, seven. He absolutely adores you."

Maya took the hand he extended and smiled. "Oh, that's sweet. I hope he isn't bothering you with ridiculous tales of our youth. No matter what he says, I was always the better basketball player."

"That's what I told him," Nick promised.

"*Is* that what he told you?"

Griffin averted his gaze and focused on Lindsey. "You must be Bear's better half."

Lindsey nodded. "Actually, I'm the better three-fourths in this relationship. Since he's so good at keeping the kids occupied, though, I keep him around."

"Oh, that's the woman I love more than life itself," Bear said as he sat next to his wife and gave her a tight side hug. "Is it any wonder I fell for you in eighth grade and never managed to get back up?"

"No," Lindsey replied, not missing a beat. "Sit." She gestured for Griffin to take the only open spot, which happened to be the other side of the bench Ava was taking up real estate on.

"Oh, well..." Griffin looked conflicted.

"Sit," Lindsey ordered. Because she had so many kids, she was used to managing chaos. Griffin didn't stand a chance under her watchful eye.

"Okay." Griffin clutched his beer tighter and sat next to Ava. "How are you?" he asked her without making eye contact.

"I've been worse," Ava replied. She steadfastly refused to look in his direction. "How are the cats?"

"You made a real dent in the barn for only a few hours of work," Griffin replied. "Thanks for doing it."

All conversation ceased after that for a full twenty seconds.

"Are we missing something?" Maya asked when she'd obviously grown uncomfortable with the silence. "What cats?"

"It's the barn," Nick replied as he snuggled Maya in at his side. "It's overrun with cats. Apparently, Ava has volunteered to help. She and Sabrina at the cat rescue went in and removed a bunch."

"It's better to get the mothers and their kittens first," Ava explained. "The kittens are still young enough that they can be socialized. They'll all go to foster homes. Then when the kittens are weaned, the rescue will fix the mothers and tip their ears before returning them to the barn."

"Oh, I've heard about this." Maya nodded. "When I was working down in the city, they did it in cat colonies. It's a lot of work, but it really cuts down on the unwanted kittens."

"Exactly." Ava smiled. "Once the kittens are out—and I think there are a few older ones still hanging around that aren't total lost causes—then we'll set to work trapping the older ones. Sabrina is going to take them to a vet for a checkup and fix any that need to be fixed, then a few will be returned to Griffin's barn."

"Supposedly, it's smart to have barn cats," Griffin explained. "They cut down on rodents. My grandfather's barn was completely overrun, though."

"It's still good that you're doing it," Maya insisted. "Some people might not take the time to try to do their best by the animals. They might kill the mothers and leave the babies to starve." She turned to Nick. "If there are a lot of kittens, maybe we could take one or two."

Nick nodded. "We've been talking about pets. They're our trial run before kids," he said with a grin. "A kitten sounds like a good idea. They're even less work than a dog."

"Two kittens," Maya countered. "That way, they won't be lonely because they'll have each other."

"Sure." Nick was the easygoing sort, so Ava wasn't surprised that he agreed so easily.

Bear opened his mouth, likely to suggest a cat for his kids, but Lindsey immediately shook her head.

"No way. I like what they're doing out there, but we can

barely take care of our kids. If you add a cat, the children will fight about it, and the cat will just add to the mess. No."

Bear's lips curved down. "You used to be so adventurous when we first met. What happened?"

"I went to high school, then you knocked me up the summer after graduation."

"Oh, right." Bear smiled. "I think they would prefer a dog anyway. With Christmas right around the corner, perhaps that warrants a discussion."

"Do you want to sleep on the couch?"

"If I have a dog to cuddle with, maybe."

Leaving them to their argument, Maya focused on Griffin. "So, how are you liking the farm so far? Is it an adjustment coming from the city?" She cast Ava a pointed look.

"I don't know," Griffin replied. "It's not so bad. I mean, there's a lot to do in the house and the barn, but I like the idea of fixing up what's old and making it something completely different, something better."

The statement grated Ava. "Why does it have to be something different?"

Griffin shrugged. "I don't know. I mean, I like the framework. I'm not sure there's a lot of flow to the rooms, though. I have some ideas."

"You should take the plans Ava had drawn up when she thought she was going to be able to buy the farm," Lindsey interjected. "They might give you some ideas."

"Plans?" Griffin's forehead creased. "I'm not sure I understand."

"Ava had her heart set on buying that farm," Lindsey continued obliviously. "She's always been in love with it. She was going to turn it into a bed-and-breakfast and use her blog to leverage it. Heck, she was making plans right up until it came out in the paper that you'd paid the taxes. That changed everything for her."

"Is that a fact?" Griffin asked, his eyes boring into Ava.

She wanted to find a hole and crawl into it.

"I guess you didn't tell him that part, huh?" Lindsey asked.

Ava shook her head. "No. There didn't seem to be a reason. Thank you so much for sharing it on my behalf, though."

"You're welcome," Lindsey replied, unbothered. "That's why she was spying on you, in case you were wondering. She's been holding out hope that you would be overwhelmed by everything that needs to be done with the house and barn and put it back on the market. I guess that's not going to happen, huh?"

"Not this week," Griffin replied. When Ava managed to find the courage to look up, she found him staring into her eyes. "You could've mentioned it."

"What does it matter?" Ava stood, and her legs were a lot shakier than she'd anticipated. "It's done. You're renovating, and I'm looking for a different property. It's not a big deal."

"Are you sure? I didn't realize anybody was even considering buying the farm."

"Oh, that's been Ava's dream since she was a kid," Lindsey replied. "All she's ever talked about is that farm. You crushed her."

Ava had had enough. "Thank you, Lindsey," she gritted out. "I think he gets the idea."

"I was just trying to help." Lindsey acted innocent, but she had a glint in her eye.

"It's not a big deal," Ava said to Griffin. "I had a plan.

Yours is hardly the only farm in the area, though. I'm sure I'll find something else that will work."

Griffin didn't look convinced, but he nodded. "Well, here's hoping." He raised his beer.

"Yes, here's hoping." Ava downed the rest of hers. Her excitement for the party disappeared with the amber liquid. Things were not going her way, and she had to change that. *But how?*

8

EIGHT

The next morning, Griffin stood at the kitchen sink, drinking coffee and watching Ava work in the barn through the window. She'd arrived with the sun, alone, and quickly began collecting cats.

She was tenacious. He had to give her that. But she was also an enigma.

She wanted the farm? It made sense. *Why else would she spend all her time spying on me? Who would agree to catch cats simply because they wanted to hang out in the barn?* He'd been suspicious, and though he had answers, he remained uneasy.

He couldn't figure her out. She had a sassy mouth—something he normally liked—and was unbelievably beautiful. She didn't even try to be fancy. He'd only seen her wearing makeup once since they'd met, which meant she was self-assured. What he didn't like were her busybody tendencies. He'd been hoping to ingratiate himself with the community and not have to explain his past. She'd made that impossible.

Despite that, Bear and Nick seemed open to being

friends. They'd been pleasant without being overbearing, volunteering their opinions on various things, and he liked their significant others a great deal. Maya and Nick were like a Hallmark couple come to life, and even though some people might find Lindsey abrasive, she made Griffin laugh. She didn't care what anybody else thought and said whatever came to her mind but also had a heart of gold. She was loyal to her friends, and it was obvious she and Bear were built to last, despite all the banter. Griffin had enjoyed hanging out with them the previous night. But Ava kept throwing him.

He sighed, then drained the rest of his coffee and grabbed his coat. Bear wouldn't arrive until after lunch to start some of the attic patching. That meant he had time on his hands, and there was no reason he couldn't help with the cats. If he was being completely honest with himself, which wasn't easy, he was also interested in talking to Ava. He found her fascinating. He just hadn't figured out whether that was a good or a bad thing yet.

He stepped lightly because he wanted to take a gander at what Ava was doing before she realized she was no longer alone. When he reached the open double doors, he cocked his head to listen and wasn't disappointed.

"I get that you're used to ruling the roost, Captain, but I think it's best if you cede just a little bit of control and get in the cage," Ava said.

When Griffin peered around the corner, he found her talking to a huge Maine Coon. The cat had to weigh at least twenty pounds. His coat was fluffy and gorgeous, and his paws were big enough to cause a mouse apocalypse. He only had one eye, though, which gave him a demented look.

"I promise I'll bring you back once the vet checks you over," Ava continued. The cat was a good ten feet from her, his tail lashing back and forth, and he looked less than impressed with the offer. "I can tell you're not fixed. You've got some big cojones there. I bet you've fathered at least three of the litters we found in the loft. I need to make sure that doesn't happen again."

Captain—*why did she decide to name him that?*—didn't move. Instead, he continued to glare at Ava.

"Do you want your children to grow up surly?" Ava asked. "I would think that as a parent, you would want your offspring to have warm homes. Also, no offense, but you've procreated enough. It's just a quick little thing for men. You're big and strong. You should be volunteering to take one for the team."

Captain's response was to yawn.

"Come on," Ava prodded as she motioned to the trap. "There's Fancy Feast in there. Who doesn't want a fancy feast?"

When the cat didn't fall for her machinations, Ava sighed. "You're going to be trouble, aren't you?"

As if to prove it, the cat lifted a leg and started licking the cojones Ava was so impressed with. Even Griffin did a double take.

"That can't be normal," he blurted and instantly regretted it when Ava practically jumped out of her skin. "Sorry. I didn't mean to frighten you. I was just caught off guard by his big ... cojones."

Ava gave a hollow laugh as she pressed a hand to her chest. "You need to learn to make a noise. I could've killed you."

Griffin blinked quickly. "You could've killed me?"

"That's what I said." Ava shot him a testy look. "I've seen movies. I know how to protect myself from a psycho killer. In case you're wondering, I would be the final girl."

Even though Griffin found her odd—and annoying—he couldn't stop himself from grinning. "The final girl?"

"That's what they call the girl who survives at the end of the horror movie. Sidney in *Scream*? She was the final girl. Alice in *Friday the 13th*, Nancy in *A Nightmare on Elm Street*, Laurie in *Halloween*... They're all final girls."

"I get the reference. I'm a big horror movie fan. I just think it's funny that you assume you would be the final girl."

Ava's forehead creased. "Um ... who else would it be?"

"Maya," Griffin replied without hesitation. "She's got final girl written all over her."

Ava planted her hands on her hips as she stood. "No way. I love Maya—don't get me wrong—but she would be the first girl to die. Do you want to know why?"

Griffin found he was enjoying the conversation, so he nodded.

"Because she would never leave Nick. She would be the one wandering around outside with him, smelling the roses and crap, and Jason would swoop in and machete them because they would be too wrapped up in each other to recognize the incoming danger."

"That's ... an interesting take on things. What about Lindsey?"

"She's the mouthy sidekick. She'd make it to the third act because she's the funny character, but she can't be the final girl. Too much snark ruins the end of the movie."

Griffin wanted to argue—he was a big horror movie fan—but he couldn't because he didn't disagree. "You're pretty snarky," he pointed out finally. "How do you know you wouldn't be the mouthy sidekick? Maybe there's another woman in town who would be the final girl."

"No. It would be me. Anyway, what are you doing out here?"

He had to admire her directness. She didn't beat around the bush when digging for information. She just said whatever came to her mind. "This is my barn, last time I checked."

"Oh, right." Ava turned, but Griffin could still make out her eye roll. "I don't think Captain over there is going to be cooperative."

Griffin slid his gaze back to the cat, who was steadfastly cleaning his private area. He didn't appear to have a care in the world and certainly wasn't worried about the humans who had invaded his space. "Why did you name him Captain?"

"Because he only has one eye. That makes him a pirate."

"I thought the patch made a pirate."

"If you think you can get a patch on that cat, more power to you. Being a pirate is a state of mind. It's not a patch."

"Ah." Griffin smirked and shook his head as a white cat up in the loft caught his attention. She—at least, she looked like a she—was fluffy and seemed to be flirting with Captain from above. "How many do you think are left?"

"At least fifteen," Ava replied with a grimace. "I'm waiting for things to settle before heading up to the loft again. I want to make sure we didn't overlook a litter of kittens. Just in case."

"You have a good heart."

"I wouldn't go that far."

"No, you do. You're out here volunteering your time to save feral cats. I don't know a lot of people who would do that."

"I can't stand the idea of an animal suffering," Ava admitted.

"I can't either. That's why I decided to come out here and help you. Bear isn't going to be here until after lunch. Then I'll be up in the attic."

"What's up in the attic?"

"Holes."

"Oh." Ava made a face. "I haven't been up there since I was a teenager. Once, Chuck asked me to help him donate some of your grandmother's old clothes. I thought he might want to hold on to some of the stuff, but he said love was more important than things, and your grandmother would want to help those in need."

"I don't really remember her all that well," Griffin admitted. "But I've heard stories and that does sound like her. I didn't see many clothes up there, so I guess you got most of them out."

"I'm pretty sure I did." Ava smiled. "What else did he have up there?"

"Mostly journals. Did you know he kept journals?"

"Yeah." Ava's smile diminished a bit. "He told me it was something he started when he was a teenager. He started filling a journal a year. That was his goal. As he got older, though, he began filling in more. I had theories but didn't want to press him."

Intrigued, Griffin asked, "What sort of theories?"

"I don't want to speak ill of the dead. I loved him. I was ... just worried toward the end."

Her expression told Griffin she meant it. "It's okay. What did you think he was doing with the journals?"

"Trying to remember. I think he was having trouble with his memory. Like, I think he was writing stuff down from day to day—the more mundane stuff compared to what he used to write—then he would read through the previous day's entries when he woke in the morning."

Griffin hadn't considered that, but it made sense. "Bear and Nick helped me move a couple of trunks into the bedroom I'm using, and I'm going to go through the journals. I won't keep all of them, but I figure some of them might be important."

"You're going to throw them away?" Ava looked horrified at the thought.

"That was the plan. Is there a reason I shouldn't?"

"I don't know." Ava squirmed under his probing gaze. "It's just ... those were his private thoughts. Once they're gone, they're gone."

"Yes, but what good are they? If they're just sitting in a trunk, and nobody reads them, they won't be serving much of a purpose."

"I guess." Ava didn't look convinced. "If you find anything about me in there, can I have it?"

Griffin's eyebrows rose. "You think he wrote about you?"

"Not in a gross way." She made a disgusted face. "I used to help him a lot, though. He always said I was funny. I wouldn't mind having something to remember him by."

Though Griffin was determined to keep her at arm's length—she was a menace, after all—the naked emotion on her face touched him in a way he hadn't realized was possible. "I think I can do that. I plan to go through them here and there over the winter. I'm not doing it in a night or anything."

"No, I don't blame you." Ava brightened. "The more recent ones are probably going to be filled with mundane details. Like, I bet he was keeping track of when he went to the grocery store and stuff. He wouldn't want people catching on that he was slipping, so he would've covered to the best of his ability."

"That sounds like him."

"Yeah." Ava let out a breath. "So, do you want to talk about what Lindsey said yesterday?"

Griffin wasn't expecting the shift in conversation, and he couldn't help laughing. "I'm not sure what you're referring to."

"Oh, don't do that." Ava wrinkled her nose. "It's disingenuous. I hate disingenuous people. I know you're curious about what Lindsey told you. For the record, I did have plans to buy this place."

"How come you didn't tell me that right away?"

"Would it have mattered?"

"I don't know. Probably not. But it would have been better to admit you were spying because you wanted the farm than all the other stuff I was imagining."

"What were you imagining?"

"Well, you did say the word *pervert* a lot. I was starting to think you were covering for your own dark impulses."

Ava gave him a withering glare. "Oh, you wish," she groused.

He laughed, which only served to deepen her scowl. "Why do you want this farm so badly?" he asked when he'd sobered.

"Because every good memory I have from my childhood revolves around this place." Ava's face took on a far-off expression as she looked around the barn. "I used to spend a lot of time here when I was a kid. My parents were ... different. They didn't want me daydreaming. But Chuck used to say that life wasn't worth living if it didn't include a fair amount of daydreaming. I just really love this place."

"And you had plans to turn it into a bed-and-breakfast?"

"The house," Ava replied. "I was going to update the attic into a huge master suite and use the rest of the house as a bed-and-breakfast in the summer and fall. Well, that was the first idea. Then I considered converting the barn. But that's a whole other conversation."

"Why in the summer and fall but not winter and spring?"

She shrugged. "Golf and skiing are big deals in this area, thanks to the resort. The skiers want to be at the resort, though. It's just the way they are. You might get some snowmobilers in the winter, but I've found most snowmobilers aren't B and B types. Summer tourists love B and Bs, though, and fall-color-tour people are the same.

"My theory is that you can make a full-time living by only opening the B and B half the year," she continued. "I had an accountant run the numbers for me, and he thinks it's more than feasible."

"And you just happen to have the money to buy a farm lying around?"

"I have some money tucked away," she replied, averting her gaze. "It's not going to keep me rich for the rest of my life, but it's a solid chunk, and I believe that if I use it to fix up a place to use as a B and B, that investment will fund my needs for the rest of my life."

Griffin couldn't help being impressed. "That's quite the goal."

"It's more like a dream right now." Ava managed a smile. "I'll make it happen, though. Somehow."

"I'm sorry you'll have to find another property."

"What makes you say that?" Ava asked slyly.

"Because this property is mine."

"For now. Are you sure country living is going to be your cup of tea?"

"I'm not much of a tea drinker."

"Then are you sure country living is going to be your cup of coffee?"

He grinned. She was fast on her feet. He really did like that. "I guess I can't say that with any degree of certainty, but I'm not unhappy so far. Yeah, I have a lot of work in front of me, but I like the quiet. I think when I get everything done, I'll be more than happy here."

Ava's smile didn't change. "Or perhaps you're deluding yourself."

Griffin's suspicious nature reared its ugly head yet again. "Are you just hanging out here because you're biding your time? Do you think I'm going to change my mind and sell this place to you?"

"Is that a possibility?"

"Not from where I'm standing."

"Yeah, but maybe after a tough winter, you'll decide you want to stand somewhere else."

She clearly wasn't going to back down. As much as he didn't want to disappoint her—truly—he refused to give her false hope. "My life in the city isn't something I expect to go back to. At least anytime in the foreseeable future. If I were you, I would adjust my dreams. I'm sure there are other farms you can buy."

"Yeah, I've decided to just wait on this one." Ava gave a cheeky smile. "That doesn't bother you, does it?"

"I honestly don't care what you do." He glanced at Captain, who had moved to the corner and looked to be readying for a nap. "As long as you collect all these cats, I mean. That was part of the deal."

"Oh, I'm going to take care of the cats."

"Good."

"I'm also going to wait you out."

"If you say so."

"I know so."

"Yes, well, I guess we'll both have to wait and see how it works out."

"Gladly."

9
NINE

Three days later, Ava was frustrated. Even though they'd managed to capture the bulk of the cats—and some were getting treatment, while others were finding new homes—a few cats remained, and she was convinced they were the devils in the group.

"Well, this is just lovely," she said to a mangy-looking black cat. He sat on a workbench and eyed her with endless loathing. "You've managed to get the food out of the traps how many times now? You would think just once you would screw up and spring it."

The black cat merely blinked at her.

"I need a butterfly net or something," she groused, looking around for something she might be able to use against her current nemesis.

When her eyes fell on Griffin, who had appeared in the open doorway, she practically jumped out of her skin. "Make a noise," she snapped.

Griffin just smiled. "How many are left?" he asked as he stepped forward.

"I think about ten." She sighed and went back to staring

at the black cat. "I think this one needs medication." She inclined her head toward the beast in question. "Cats are prone to kidney problems when they get older, and he's been eating well but is still thin."

"You know a lot about cats." Griffin edged closer, but the look the feline shot him promised retribution if he got too close.

"I've read up, and I volunteer my time at least twice a month in the spring. That's kitten season. The thought of kittens growing up to be feral when they could have loving homes makes me unbelievably sad."

"It sounds like it." Griffin narrowed his eyes at the cat. "Well, I think he's too worked up to trust us right now. We can put a new can of food in the cages and leave them for a few hours before coming back."

Caught off guard, Ava asked, "And do what?"

"I was thinking you might like to head to the attic with me."

"Oh, really?" Ava crossed her arms. "And what do you want to do in the attic, Romeo?"

"I was thinking you might be able to help me pick out the things my grandfather would've wanted me to keep so I can start donating and dumping the rest."

"Oh." Ava uncrossed her arms. "I guess I could do that."

Amusement lit Griffin's eyes. "Did you think I had something else in mind?"

She shrugged. "I've known my fair share of perverts."

"How many times do I have to tell you I'm not a pervert?"

"It doesn't matter how many times you say it. That's exactly what a pervert would say."

"Don't I have a trustworthy face?"

Ava surveyed him for a moment, then shrugged.

"Maybe. I'll help you in the attic. It's raining like crazy, and it's not as if I can sit outside the barn at a safe distance and wait for them to get in the cages."

Griffin gestured for her to follow him. "Come on. Let's leave the cats to do their cat business."

Ava glanced over at the black cat one more time—she really was worried—then followed Griffin into the rain. They scampered across the driveway, and when they made it inside, they were both laughing.

"It's really coming down," Griffin noted as he kicked off his boots and shrugged out of his coat. Then he reached over to help her out of her jacket. "I forgot what it was like on a farm when it rains."

"And how is it?" Ava asked.

"Muddy."

She laughed despite herself. "True story. I take it that mud isn't a thing in the city."

"Gawd, why are you so obsessed with life in the city?" Griffin shook his head as he led her into the kitchen. "I was going to make some tea first. If you're interested, I mean."

"I could use something to warm me up. As for living in the city, I don't know." She held out her palms. "It's always been this mystical place to me. I can't help being fascinated."

Griffin paused with his hand on the faucet handle. "Are you about to tell me that you've never been to a city before?"

Ava snorted. "Of course not."

"A city other than Traverse City," he countered. "Just because it has 'city' right in the name, for the record, that doesn't necessarily mean it's a city."

It felt as if he was talking down to her. "I've been to a city. Detroit, in fact." She said it like it was a big deal.

"Oh yeah?" Amusement flitted across Griffin's face. "How long ago was that?"

Ava thought about making something up so that she wouldn't look like a country bumpkin. Instead, she sighed and said, "My grandfather took me to Detroit when I was a kid. We went to Belle Isle. He was going there to meet some old friends and didn't want to leave me behind. That's the one time I've ever been south of Bay City."

"Seriously?" he asked with disbelief.

"Don't even think of making fun of me."

"I'm not. I just... It's hard for me to imagine." He filled the kettle and moved it to the stove before gesturing toward the counter stools. "Did you like Belle Isle?"

"I remember liking it a lot," she admitted as she hopped onto a stool. "But I was young, so my memories are fuzzy. I remember this place with a ton of flowers."

"The conservatory."

"And there was an aquarium."

"That's still there."

"And I think there was some sort of beach park."

"That could be the yacht club, though it could just be one of the beaches too." Griffin grabbed a package of cookies and handed them to her. "I guess Bay City is technically a city," he hedged after a beat.

"Not the sort of city you're used to."

"No, but ... it's kind of a city."

Ava laughed. "You can say it. I'm not exactly worldly."

"That's not necessarily a bad thing," Griffin argued. "I grew up in the city, but I always thought it was better up here."

"Did you spend a lot of time up here?"

"Not much."

Griffin looked so sad that Ava wanted to offer him some sort of solace. She didn't know how, though.

"I came up sometimes in the summers. Not when I was a teenager or anything. I was too cool for that." Griffin gave a rueful smile. "I'm sorry my grandfather was alone so often toward the end. I didn't think. Or maybe I was just too self-involved to even try to think."

"Would you have come up if you knew he was sick?"

"Yes."

After a moment, she blurted, "What happened with the building that fell?"

Griffin's eyes widened. "Nobody has ever called you subtle, have they?"

"I can be subtle."

"Not so far as I've seen." Griffin shook his head as he reached for the box of tea bags. "There was an error in the plans. Nobody noticed it. The error was ... catastrophic." A muscle worked in his jaw as he tried to hold it together. "People lost their lives."

"Is it something that could've been fixed? Like, if you'd caught it the day the building fell, could you have done something to go in and stop the building from falling?"

"No."

"That sucks." Ava didn't know what to say. "Obviously, you didn't get arrested or anything."

"No, I didn't." Griffin handed her a tea bag. "It went down on the rolls as an error. Prosecution wasn't recommended—it rarely is in these instances because there's no motive attached. I didn't want it to fall down, but I still feel guilty."

"I'm sorry." Ava meant it. "That's a lot to take on." Since she was there and had been feeling guilty for days, she opted to apologize for the rest of it. "I shouldn't have published it on my blog."

"Why did you?"

She shrugged. "I was mad. As you know, I thought I was going to get to buy this place." She glanced around. "Finding out that dream was dead in the water, well, it threw me. I'm not all that graceful in defeat."

Griffin barked out a laugh. "I would never have guessed."

Ava rolled her eyes. "I've just always loved this place. I can't help it."

"Well, I'm sorry I stole your dream. But I'm not sorry I came here. I needed a break, and this was one of my favorite places in my childhood. I always felt safe here. That's what I needed more than anything after what happened."

"I get it." Ava took them both by surprise when she reached over and patted his arm. "This place is magical when you're feeling down. That's why I wanted it."

"But you still hate me, right?"

She nodded. "Oh, I'm plotting your death even as we speak."

"Good to know."

ONCE THEY WERE FINISHED WITH THEIR tea, Griffin led Ava to the attic. He'd made a dent in the sorting, but there was so much stuff crammed into the space that he was feeling overwhelmed.

"I just don't know what most of this is," he admitted as he dragged a hand through his hair. Trunks were spread out from one end of the attic to the other. "I don't want to throw away something that was important to him. But I also don't want to keep things that are unnecessary. It's like I'm paralyzed with indecision, which is something that has never happened to me before."

Ava made a clucking sound with her tongue as she moved to the first trunk. "Have you considered that this paralysis has absolutely nothing to do with the contents of this attic and everything to do with what happened when that building fell?"

"That sounds like some interesting psychobabble."

Ava smirked. "I'm just saying. It makes sense from a clinical perspective." She dropped to her knees to get a better look at the trunk's contents. "You shouldn't be too hard on yourself. You're obviously going through something."

"I have you to be hard on me, right?" Griffin teased.

"Exactly." She bobbed her head and held up a book. "These are history books. They cover a lot of the local communities. I've never seen them before."

"I tried to look online to see if they were common, but I couldn't find them anywhere."

"And I'm guessing you don't want to read them."

"Not so much." Griffin gave a small smile. "If I need to know something about the area, I'll probably just Google it."

"Right." Ava opened the book and frowned. "These are nice books, but the bindings aren't mass market. I think someone local put them together and distributed them. That makes them rare. Is this the only trunk with books?"

"No." Griffin shook his head. "There are some in several other trunks. Those books are different from the others, though."

"Well, I wouldn't toss these. I know Laney up at the library. She just took over as head librarian for her mother when she retired. I'll ask her about these. I bet she'll want them. That way, you don't have to worry about tossing them, and they'll be given to someone who knows how to keep them up."

Griffin sighed, relieved. "That sounds good." He eyed Ava as she moved to the next trunk. Oddly, when he'd first invited her into the house, he'd been convinced it was a mistake. She was aggravating, abrasive, and as bossy as hell. But in the cramped attic with bad ventilation, he found he could breathe more easily than he'd been able to in a long time. "You're good at making decisions." He hadn't meant to say it out loud. Once it was out, though, there was no taking it back.

"I kind of had to be," Ava admitted. "My parents were bad at it. In fact, the longer they could put something off, the better. That's why our power was cut off so many times I lost count."

Griffin startled. Like him, Ava obviously hadn't meant to say that out loud, because she appeared momentarily perplexed.

"I guess you were forced to be an adult before you were ready, huh? That had to suck."

"It was fine." Ava's smile didn't touch her eyes. "That's how I learned to be self-sufficient at a young age."

Griffin had questions but knew better than to ask them. Ava had turned defensive without even realizing it upon figuring out she'd said more than she should. "I'm very glad for your decision-making skills because I'm at a total loss."

That time, when Ava smiled, it was legitimate. "Well, I aim to please." She moved to the next trunk and looked inside. The squeal she let out had Griffin's shoulders jumping. "Do you know what this is?" She gestured toward the contents of the trunk, which had been wrapped when

Griffin went through it the first time. He hadn't bothered wrapping it again until he decided what to do.

"That's a tea set," Griffin said. "They're all teapots."

"They're Fitz & Floyd teapots." Ava almost sounded reverent. "Some of these are so rare that you'll be able to sell them for between five hundred and a thousand dollars each."

"For a teapot?" Griffin asked, floored.

"They're not just any teapots. They're special. This one, for example, is from the Twelve Days of Christmas set. It's the French Hens pot ... and it's amazing."

Griffin's forehead creased. He couldn't understand why she was so excited about a teapot. "Those are chickens."

Ava ignored him and carefully returned the teapot to the chest before collecting another. "This is the Ladies Dancing teapot from the same collection. Do you have any idea how rare these are?"

Griffin leaned over to get a better look. "They look like prostitutes."

Ava narrowed her eyes. "They're not prostitutes. This teapot is amazing."

"And that?" He pointed toward another. "That's a big cow with women riding it."

"That's the Maids a'Milking pot," Ava replied, clearly irritated.

"That could be taken in a creepy way."

She glared at him, but he was having too good of a time to stop.

"And that one?" He pointed at yet another teapot.

"That's just a Santa teapot. It's not worth as much as the Twelve Days of Christmas ones, but it's still probably worth a hundred bucks or so. They're all in pristine condition."

Griffin stared at her profile, taken in by the wonder on her face. "You can take them." He made the offer before he realized what he was saying.

Startled, Ava shook her head. "These are valuable."

"Someone loved them." The more he thought about the offer, the better he felt about it. "I'm guessing they belonged to my grandmother, but I don't ever remember seeing them. They're obviously important to you. They should go to someone who is going to love them."

Ava's eyes widened, and her mouth formed an O. "But they're part of your history."

"Except they're not." Griffin crouched next to her. "I have memories of helping my grandfather on the farm. We hung out in the barn and had root beers because my parents didn't want me having pop. That's my history. I've never seen these before, and you obviously love them."

Ava blinked several times, her eyes glassy. "I don't know what to say."

"Just love them." Griffin smiled. "You obviously already do."

"I should pay you."

He waved off the suggestion. "Don't worry about that. I just want to see you happy." He hadn't meant for it to come out that way, so he was as stunned as she was when he said it. Still, as he thought about it, he realized he meant it. He did want her to be happy.

She'd been nothing but a thorn in his side since they'd met, yet he didn't want her to be unhappy, for some reason. When she smiled, she lit up the room. He preferred that to the sadness he'd seen when she mentioned having to make the decisions in her family.

"Take them. I'll help you get them downstairs. We'll wrap them carefully. My only condition is that you take the trunk with you. I'm desperate to get these things out of here and make some room."

Ava chuckled. "I'll take good care of them. I promise."

"I know you will. That much was obvious by the look on your face."

She swiped at a tear. "I'm almost sixty-five percent convinced you're not a pervert now too," she added.

"See? We're making progress." He grinned. "Let's see what other treasures you find, huh? Maybe I can unload the entire attic on you."

"Don't get ahead of yourself."

"It was worth a try."

TEN

Griffin decided that helping Ava catch the cats was in his best interests. He'd assumed it would be easier than it turned out to be, which had him taking a step back. Unfortunately, watching her fail time and time again was getting to him.

It had been weeks, and she was still working. The one-eyed Maine Coon and the black cat seemed to be spear-heading a revolt with the other feral ones along with an orange monstrosity that had joined in to make her life hell, and Ava hadn't caught a single cat in four days. Both she and Griffin were getting frustrated. He simply couldn't decide whether it was because of her or in spite of her.

"What if we try to herd the cats toward the cages?" he asked as he wiped his forearm across his forehead. It was cold outside—the temperature wouldn't rise above the forties, despite the fact that it was only October—but he was sweating up a storm inside the barn.

"Seriously?" Ava glared. "Have you ever tried to herd a cat?"

"We could use a broom or something."

"Oh, well, a broom." Ava rolled her eyes. "Because a broom will work when trying to catch a cat."

"I don't hear you volunteering any ideas."

"I'm thinking."

"Well, let me know when you're done." Griffin stomped over to the bench on the far side of the barn and glared at the black cat five feet away. It hadn't fled when he headed in the cat's direction. If he reached out to grab it, however, he would get a face full of claws. The cat, despite the fact that it didn't look healthy, was quick. "Don't you want to feel better, bud?" he asked the cat mournfully. "We really are trying to help."

To his surprise, Ava didn't offer up a sassy comment. She looked sad when she joined him. "I can't be sure, but I think we're dealing with kidney failure."

"Does that mean he'll have to be put to sleep?" Griffin didn't like that idea at all.

"Not necessarily. There's special food that can extend his life. He wouldn't be able to stay out here, though. He would have to be kept at a place where he would have access to only that food."

"That's sad." Griffin rubbed the back of his neck.

"It is. I don't know what to do, though. He's smarter than us."

"He's quicker than us too." Griffin didn't even realize what he was doing until he'd already slung an arm around Ava's shoulders. "There has to be a way. We need to think. These cages aren't working. Maybe we need to build a bigger one that doesn't look like a cage."

Ava didn't react to him touching her. There was nothing lecherous about the move, but she could've made a scene. That was her way, after all. Instead, she furrowed her brow. "Could you build a different sort of cage?"

"I can at least try." He moved away from her, trying not to dwell on the fact that he already missed the warmth of her body. He sat on the stool at the workbench and grabbed the pencil he'd been using earlier to sketch some ideas for the spring barn refurbishment.

"Would you put a room out here?" he asked as he worked.

"A room?" She furrowed her brow. "There are multiple rooms."

"I know. It's just... You were going to turn this place into a B and B. How were you going to do that? The house is big enough to create four guest rooms—five if you count the attic, which could be easily converted—but I can't imagine wanting to turn one of those rooms into your own bedroom because then guests would be invading your personal space."

She appraised him. "I was planning to make one of the rooms mine to start with but eventually convert the barn into a separate house. How did you know that?"

"Because your personality is too big to share with guests and get repeat customers."

She scowled. "You're a putz. Has anybody ever told you that?"

He chuckled and rolled his neck. "This barn is big enough to be a cool apartment. Yes, it needs work. I think the entire thing is going to take a massive overhaul, but it could eventually be a house. Then the actual house could be the B and B, and you would still have privacy."

"That was the ultimate plan, but it wasn't going to happen overnight."

"Yeah." Griffin smiled "Are you still bitter I stole your farm?"

"Are you asking if I'm mad you stole the dream I've been

harboring since I was fourteen? As a matter of fact, I am. I've decided to temper my anger, however."

"Oh yeah? How come?"

"Because one winter up here is going to be your limit. The city doesn't get the same sort of winters we do. You're going to be out of your element and missing your Starbucks by January."

Griffin snorted. "You haven't even been to the city since you were a kid. How do you know what sort of winters they get?"

"I know things."

He waited.

"I can read a weather app."

"There it is." Griffin chuckled. He found her bravado delightful, although he would never admit that out loud. "The goal is to get this place buttoned up and safe from the elements before the big snows in December. I'll be in the main house this winter. After that, though, I might want to change it up."

Ava's body went rigid. "You're going to turn this place into a B and B?" she asked tightly.

Griffin shrugged. "Maybe. I haven't gotten that far yet."

"But ... that was my idea." She sounded like a whiny twelve-year-old. Griffin had to wonder if she was aware of it.

"I didn't say I was definitely doing it. It's just a consideration."

Ava glared at him. "Well, I'm glad I could be of help." She turned her back to him and focused on the loft.

For a moment, Griffin was amused. He thought she was being purposely salty. Then he realized she was blinking rapidly, and her eyes were glassy. "Hey." He abandoned the notebook and pencil and stepped toward her. "I was just screwing around. I'm not really considering a B and B. I was just messing with you."

"It's fine." Ava refused to look at him. "You know, maybe if I go up to the loft and try to herd the cats toward the ladder, you might be able to hold a cage, and we can get a few that way."

"We can do that." An ache had begun to spread in Griffin's chest when he realized he'd upset her. That hadn't been his goal. Sure, he liked irritating her because she was hilarious when she was angry, but he didn't want to crush her dreams. He already felt guilty enough for taking the farmhouse from her. Even though he couldn't have known her plans, he felt as if he'd done something wrong. That was ridiculous, yet he still felt it. "Hey, are you okay?" He gently tugged on her shirt sleeve to get her to look at him.

Though there was no smile on her face when she turned, there were no tears either. "I'm fine," she said forcefully. "You don't have to worry about me. I'll survive. I always do. I like the idea of putting the cages at the top of the loft. Then I'll go to the far corner and start herding them in your direction. If you're at the top of the ladder, they'll have to go into the cages to avoid you. That will help us snag at least one or two of them."

"Okay." Griffin worked his jaw. "I didn't upset you, right? I was just thinking out loud."

"I'm fine."

Griffin wasn't certain he believed her.

"I'm fine," she repeated. "You should do whatever you want. It's your property."

Griffin hesitated then nodded. "Let's get the cages ready. Then you can go up to the loft. I'll carry up the cages, and you can put them in place."

"That sounds like a plan to me." Ava attempted a smile,

but it didn't reach her eyes. That made Griffin want to kick himself all the more.

They were in the process of arranging the cages at the bottom of the ladder when the sound of footsteps at the open barn door caught their attention. Nick and Maya were decked out in matching cold-weather attire, smiling as they took it all in.

"Oh, how cute. You guys are working together now. You should get matching shirts," Nick drawled as he released Maya's hand.

They were even wearing matching knit mittens. Griffin wasn't sure whether it was unbelievably adorable or vomit inducing.

"You guys are doing enough matching," Griffin replied before he thought better of it. He liked Nick and didn't want to start a fight.

Rather than be offended, Nick grinned. "We went to Traverse City yesterday, and this woman was selling hand-made mittens and hats. We couldn't help ourselves."

"Yes, we're going to be twins all winter," Maya stated as she stared soulfully into her fiancé's eyes and wiggled her butt while doing a little dance.

"Do you guys need something?" Griffin asked with a sigh that was more wistful than agitated. When he saw the couple together, he felt something foreign. He was starting to think it was longing. No matter how ridiculous he found Maya and Nick when they were together, the fact that they were always in sync and cuddled against each other made him think that maybe—*just maybe*—he wanted something similar. He'd never considered it before.

"A kitten," Nick replied. "Maya really wants one, and we thought we would come to the source."

"Two kittens," Maya corrected him. "We don't want the

one to be lonely. We figured if we got two, they could keep each other company when we were at work."

"I don't actually think there are any kittens left," Griffin replied as he dragged a hand through his hair. "We got all the litters, right, Ava?"

Ava nodded. "Sorry. You can contact Sabrina. I think she has more than twenty kittens she's looking for homes for. The kittens were the easy ones to collect. It's the grizzled old-timers we're having trouble with." She pointed at the black cat for emphasis.

"Oh," Maya said, her face falling. "I didn't realize you'd already gotten all the kittens out." She edged closer to the black cat. "Should we be trying to get an adult cat instead of a kitten? Would that be the more humane thing to do?"

The black cat swiped at her hand when she reached over to stroke him. Her mittens and her solid reflexes saved her from harm.

"The problem is that the older feral ones have a harder time adjusting to humans," Ava explained. "That's not to say it never happens. It's just rare. The kittens, though, might have a feisty few days, but then they usually settle. The older ones, well, the odds aren't as great for them. That's why we're trying to get them checked over and fixed by a vet. They would prefer being wild, but this way, we can get a handle on more litters."

"Oh." Maya made a face at the cat. "Who's a big grump? He doesn't look very good."

"He doesn't," Ava agreed. "We're worried. But we're having trouble catching him, and it's frustrating. Griffin says he might try to fashion a new sort of cage."

"What are you doing with these cages?" Nick asked as he gestured toward the ones they'd moved.

"There're about five cats up in the loft," Griffin

explained. "We were going to take them up the ladder, put them in front of the only spot where the cats can get down, then send Ava to herd them toward the cages. We won't get all of them, but if we were to get one or two, that would be a great help."

Nick nodded. "Well, let me help. The cages look heavy, and climbing the ladder with them won't be easy."

"You don't have to do that," Griffin protested.

"I want to do it."

"We really do want to help," Maya insisted. She turned back to the black cat. "Don't you want us to help you, buddy?"

Griffin chuckled. "I've tried talking to them reasonably too. They don't seem to listen."

"It's a bummer." Maya held out her mitten for the cat to sniff and waited. "While we're here, Ava, I wanted to remind you that career day at the high school is right before Thanksgiving break. I'm helping Nick organize it, and we have you down for talking about your blog. You're still on for that, aren't you?"

"Sure," Ava replied as she started up the ladder. She tried to grab one of the cages, but Griffin stopped her. "I thought we were taking the cages up."

"We are, but Nick and I are going to climb the ladder with them," Griffin replied. "They're heavy and require balance."

"And you're saying I'm not strong enough to do it?"

"I'm saying I don't want you to fall and hurt yourself."

"I'm pretty sure you're being sexist."

"And I'm pretty sure this is my property, and I'm not going to have this argument. We'll bring up the cages after you."

Ava let loose a string of curses under her breath as she

climbed. When Griffin glanced over his shoulder to see how Nick and Maya were reacting to the show, he found them sharing knowing looks. "What?"

"Nothing," Nick replied. "It's just … the sexual tension is so thick in here you could cut it with a knife."

Griffin balked. "You're full of it."

"It's the truth, bud. I hate to be the bearer of bad news, but you guys are hot for each other." Nick grabbed one of the cages and started up. "You don't want to tell me to be careful, do you?"

Griffin glowered at Nick once he reached the top. When he glanced at Maya, she looked a little too serene for his taste. "What's career day?" he asked, desperate to change the subject.

"It's when we have booths at the high school and allow the kids to ask questions," Maya replied. "Nick organizes it because he thinks it's important for the kids to know their options, even though they're from a small town. We try to have as many different careers represented as the city schools, so we work overtime to give them a good cross section of possibilities."

"That sounds good."

"Yeah. You could do one. A booth, I mean. You're an architect, right? We don't get a lot of those up here. You would be a big draw."

Griffin immediately shook his head. "I don't think that's a good idea."

"Because that building fell? That was a terrible accident. The kids don't need to know that part. They just need to hear about the job itself. It will be good for them."

"I don't… I mean… Maybe." Panic filled him, and when he looked up to the loft, Ava was watching him with unreadable eyes.

"You should do it," she said softly.

Even though Maya and Nick were in the barn, when he focused on her, it was as if they were the only two people in the world.

"The kids will want to hear about it. Don't let my stupid blog get in your way. People will have forgotten about it by then. It's still weeks away."

Griffin wasn't so sure. Still, he didn't want to disappoint Nick and Maya. He liked them. If he was going to stay in town, they would be a part of his friend circle. He had no doubt about that.

"Mark me down," he said after a beat, resigned. "With pencil. I need to think about it, but I can probably be coerced."

Maya clapped excitedly. "Awesome. The kids are going to love you. In fact, everybody in this town is going to love you before it's all said and done."

He glanced back at Ava and found her smiling. Again, they were the only two people in the world. "I guess that's something to look forward to, then."

11

ELEVEN

Ava was full of energy when she descended on the Holden farm the next day. She'd done a lot of thinking the previous evening—and not all of it had been constructive—but she'd decided she couldn't keep blaming Griffin for her life not turning out the way she'd wanted it to. Being friendly to him in the barn while plotting against him when his back was turned made her feel like a disingenuous person. She wanted to change that.

"You want to do what now?" Griffin's forehead creased as she explained her plan to him.

"I want to take you to one of my favorite B and Bs in Charlevoix. If you're really going to take the winter to decide what you want to do with this place, you should have all the options."

Griffin didn't look convinced. "Why aren't we catching the cats?"

"Because for right now, the cats are outsmarting us. I still need to think on that. You should know all your options for this property."

"Uh-huh." Griffin crossed his arms. "Why does this feel like a trap?"

"Because you're a cynical individual. Also, my behavior hasn't been stellar since you arrived. You have reason to be skeptical. Even if I'm lying, though, what have you got to lose? It's a day trip to a B and B that goes all out for Halloween. I mean *all out*. You'll have fun."

"How do you know I'll have fun? Maybe I hate Halloween. Have you considered that?"

"No, because only an idiot would hate Halloween."

"What's to like about Halloween?"

"Oh, come on." Ava felt exposed, something she wasn't expecting, but managed to hold it together. "Horror movies. Corn mazes. Hot chocolate. Leaves changing color. Ornate lawn scenes. How can you not love Halloween?"

"In the city, people egg you when they're bored on Halloween."

"That happens in the country too. I promise it's not happening today, though."

Griffin didn't look convinced. "Why? Just tell me why."

Ava ran her tongue over her teeth, debating how she wanted to respond. Ultimately, she knew that lying was out of the question. "Remember how I told you your grandfather used to go all out here for Halloween?"

Griffin nodded.

"Well, that's what I thought would happen again." She turned wistful as she looked out at the property. "I wanted to have big Halloween parties and thrill all the kids like he thrilled us when we were little. Escaping to this farm was all I had for a while, but around Halloween, it was more than a refuge. It was an adventure."

Griffin looked as if he wanted to ask questions, but the look on her face likely turned him off, something she was grateful for. Ultimately, he nodded. "Fine. I'm driving, though. I'm not going to risk you leaving me behind in a town I don't know because you think it will be funny."

Ava made a face. "Why do you think I would do that?"

"I have no idea. But your sense of humor is sometimes weird. I'm covering my bases."

"Fine. You can drive. I expect a nice dinner while we're over there, though, and the Charlevoix restaurants are expensive."

"Like ... a dinner date?"

"No, not like a date." Ava wrinkled her nose in disgust. "Are you kidding me with that? It's just a scientific outing."

"You're the one inviting me to a B and B."

"Yes, but only because I want you to see what's possible. You're selling this property short, and I don't like it. If you're going to take my dream, I want you to have the option of creating a new one for yourself. You might not like it. I think if you see it, though..."

"I can buy dinner. Wherever you want. I just... What are we going to do all day?"

Ava gave a mischievous grin. "You'll see."

Griffin was obviously still skeptical, but he nodded. "Okay. Let's do it."

AVA WAS FAMILIAR WITH CHARLEVOIX, SO she navigated for the drive. The trip only took about forty-five minutes, and the view was lovely the entire way, thanks to the turning trees.

They didn't talk a lot—it seemed to be an unspoken agreement between them—but the atmosphere inside the vehicle wasn't uncomfortable. Instead, it was sort of pleasant. Occasionally, Ava pointed out places of interest. She seemed knowledgeable about the history of the area, something Griffin appreciated, and there was nothing prickly about her demeanor. In fact, she was the exact opposite of the first time they'd met.

Griffin didn't know what to make of it. At first glance, he'd been drawn to Ava's looks. She was beautiful, fresh-faced, and expressive. But that mouth of hers had turned him off in an instant. *What if that was a defensive response, though?* Griffin understood about putting up a wall to protect yourself. If that was what Ava was doing, he could forgive her for that. But he had questions.

For starters, the more she let slip about her childhood, the more he was starting to suspect there was something dark there. *Why would a kid in a small town need to take refuge in someone else's barn?* Griffin had a lot of questions—some were even invasive—but he kept quiet, telling himself it was none of his business.

Yet when Ava showed signs of vulnerability, something inside him reacted. He felt protective, as if he wanted to shelter her from the terrible outside world. Of course, Ava wasn't the only one who needed protecting. Griffin felt vulnerable too. Maybe that made them a good match. They were two damaged individuals trying to move forward. *Do I even want us to be a match?*

He'd convinced himself he didn't. Sometimes, when they were in the barn together, he was certain he still didn't. Other times, though, she disarmed him. She was smart, funny, and god, was she beautiful. He caught himself looking at her when he should've been working, and her face was starting to drive him to distraction.

"That's where we're eating later," Ava said as they passed a restaurant, drawing him out of his reverie.

Griffin read the sign. "The Weathervane. It looks fancy."

"It's beautiful inside," Ava said with a wistful sigh. "It's got this great balcony looking out on the water. I could sit there every night. We won't be able to eat outside today because it's cold, but the inside is just as charming."

"Oh yeah? What sort of food are we talking about?"

"Are you picky? You look picky."

He frowned. When she said things like that, his back went up. He held it together, though. "I'm actually not picky. I'll eat almost anything."

"What's your favorite?"

He'd never really considered it. "Middle Eastern, I guess."

Her eyebrows rose. "Really? I think I've only had that once or twice. I remember it being good. A lot of meat."

Griffin chuckled. "They do like their meat ... and hummus. There's this stir fry dish that's heavy on the tomatoes. It's my favorite."

"I like tomatoes too."

Ava smiled, and he was back to wondering if they might be a good fit. *Why does it always happen when she smiles?*

"As for the Weathervane, there's a little bit of everything. They have fancy stuff like escargot—which I've never tried—and whitefish fingers, but they also have this pork chop thing that's made with maple bourbon sauce that's just amazing."

Griffin blinked quickly. "We're coming here so you can have a pork chop?"

"Don't judge." She shot him a quelling look. "I happen to think pork chops are delightful. I ate them a lot as a kid. I could make a package of them last an entire week if I was careful."

Griffin's brow furrowed. *Another tidbit from her childhood.* He wanted to ask questions and get to know her better, but he was afraid. She was already talking him into going out to B and Bs on adventures. He would never have seen himself doing that before. But they were going on an adventure, and he was looking forward to it. *How did this even happen?*

"What else do they have?" he asked, forcing himself to remain on topic.

"They have good steaks and ribs, if that's your thing. Oh, and they have this amazing morel-and-leek macaroni and cheese." Ava pressed her fingers to her lips in a chef's kiss. "It's amazing."

"Morels are mushrooms, right? Are they good?"

"Morels are a state of mind up here, my friend," Ava said with a laugh. "You either love them or hate them. In the spring, you have to be careful when driving because everybody will be out in the woods, looking for them. They park willy-nilly and pop out of the woods so close to the road that it will give you a heart attack. You'll drive into a ditch if you're not careful."

"I take it that's happened to you."

Ava shrugged. "Maybe once or twice. Anyway, you should definitely try the macaroni and cheese if you're on the fence. It will change your life."

"I'll keep that in mind."

AVA WAS BURSTING AT THE SEAMS WITH EXCITEMENT when they arrived at Claridge Farms. She danced from foot to foot as she waited for Griffin to zip up his coat.

"Come on." She grabbed his arm when she felt he was taking too long.

"Calm down." Griffin appeared out of his element as he

glanced around. Despite his reticence, he managed a flash of bemused enchantment when he saw all the fake cobwebs in the trees and the adorable ghosts hanging from the branches. "This is kind of over-the-top, huh?"

Ava shot him a dirty look. "Or absolutely perfect."

"I guess it depends on the way you look at it."

"Definitely." She kept a firm hold on his jacket sleeve and practically dragged him. "Come on." She didn't let go even when they reached the fence of the paddock. Instead, she linked her arm through his and stared out at the horses cavorting in the field. "Isn't it amazing?"

"I've never been much of a horse person," Griffin replied.

Irritation bubbled up, but Ava managed to hold back a snarky comment—just barely. "Have you even been around horses?"

"Not really. When I was in New Orleans, I accidentally stepped in a huge pile of horse shit on Decatur Street. I was focused on the street performers—they were doing a Michael Jackson set in front of the riverwalk—and I ruined a perfectly good pair of shoes. Since that day, I've decided horses aren't my thing."

Ava rolled her eyes. "So because a horse did what horses do, you're writing the entire species off as stupid. I see how it is."

"I didn't say they were stupid. Just that they weren't my thing. If you're going to try to convince me that I should have horses at the farm, that's not going to happen. They're too much work."

"They *are* too much work," Ava replied, causing him to do a double take. "I wouldn't take on horses either. Feeding them is expensive. They crap all over the place, as you've noticed. And taking care of them in the winter is a bitch."

"So ... why are we here again?"

"Because some companies offer horses at B and Bs for specific events. Like, you can rent them—and the people who take care of them—for a week at a time. If you were doing a special summer festival or a winter one, for that matter, that would be the way to go. Someone else is responsible for the vet bills and food. You just enjoy the fun part for a week."

"And what about the shit? Who deals with that?"

"That would be the handlers."

"Well, it doesn't sound terrible." He sniffed as he went back to staring at the horses. "I still don't know."

"Come on." Ava tugged on their linked arms. "We're barely inside yet. You have to see it to understand it." She inclined her head to the huge field to their right. A sign touted a haunted corn maze that was open daily for children and nightly for adults. "We're going to that after dinner."

Griffin's pace slowed. "What now?"

"We're going to that. But we have to wait until it's dark. The day showing is adorable—the workers are dressed in cute and fuzzy costumes—but it's the nighttime showing that always gets me."

Griffin cocked his head as he regarded the maze. "I don't think I understand," he said finally. "What happens in there?"

"Monsters." Ava giggled, her eyes sparkling. "It's totally freaky. They go all out. I love it."

"You love being scared?" Griffin looked as if he was having trouble wrapping his head around it.

"I love being scared over make-believe stuff." Ava led him toward the pumpkin patch. "I don't care how terrifying that corn maze is—it's still better to play at the fake stuff than be overwhelmed by the real stuff."

When Griffin didn't respond, Ava turned to find him staring at her. "What?"

"Ava…" He stepped toward her.

"Is there something on my face?" Ava quickly moved her hands over her mouth.

"It's not that." Griffin lightly grabbed her wrist. "It's just … you're a constant surprise," he said finally. More bubbled under the surface, and for a moment, Ava wanted to know what he was thinking.

She'd found herself wondering what was going on inside his head more often than she was comfortable with over the last week. She'd wanted to write him off as the guy ruining her life, but he was more than that. Well, of course he was more than that. Vilifying him had been easy. Accepting that he was an individual with emotions and needs—and dreams that might've been crushed somewhere along the way just like hers had been—was difficult. But it was impossible to ignore.

"What?" she asked.

"You just never do what I think you're going to do," he said. "You don't conform to norms or follow a pathway to a set destination. You're the sort of person who doesn't know where she's going when she leaves for a road trip."

For some reason, the description delighted Ava. "I guess that's true. What about you?"

"I've always known where I was going." Griffin didn't look happy about the admission. "Until now." He stepped closer. "You know those apocalypse movies where the world ends, and somehow, the people in the movie are left to navigate themselves somewhere without the technology we've become accustomed to, like GPS and maps on our phones?"

Ava nodded.

"I feel like I'm in one of those movies lately. I don't know where to go or what to do. I've always thought I would be the first person to die in an apocalypse, and now I'm living it every day. That's not my scene."

Ava just stood there for several seconds, then she burst out laughing.

"It's not funny," he grumbled.

"It's a little funny." She linked her arm through his a second time. It felt natural. No, it felt right. "Stick with me. I'm the one you want on your side in an apocalypse. I'm going to survive."

"Doesn't that mean I'm deadweight in your book?"

"No." Ava shook her head. "It just means you have a separate skill set. You might not realize what that skill set is yet, but you will eventually. I'm betting that when you finally get your head around it, everybody is going to be impressed."

"Even you?"

"I won't be as impressed as the others." Ava registered the disappointed slope of his shoulders and felt the need to bolster him back up. "I already know you can do great things."

Griffin's eyes filled with an emotion Ava couldn't quite ascertain. "Thank you," he said in a gravelly voice. "I think you're capable of great things too."

"When I'm not gossiping on the internet, you mean?" she asked, trying to lighten the mood.

"Doesn't that go without saying?"

"I always say everything, even the parts I shouldn't say."

"Yeah, I'm starting to figure that out."

"Just wait until you have dinner with me." Ava resumed tugging him toward the pumpkin patch. "You're going to find out just how much inane chatter one taciturn man can put up with over the course of a single meal."

Griffin chuckled. "You know what? I think I'm looking forward to that."

"Yeah, talk to me again in a few hours."

"Gladly."

12

TWELVE

Ava's cheeks were flushed with excitement when their meals arrived. Griffin was still unsure why she was so excited about the pork chop, but he'd gone with the leek-and-morel macaroni and cheese just to make her happy.

He realized that was why he'd done all of it, because he liked seeing her smile. When she was happy, she lit up the entire room—or pumpkin patch, if that was where she happened to be. She'd collected ten pumpkins to take home, studying each one a long time before making her selection, and she seemed to be firing on all thrusters as they prepared for the corn maze.

"How is it?" she asked after he'd taken his first bite.

"It's really good." He grinned at her. "Do you want some?"

"Maybe a little." She edged her plate over and let him put some of his pasta there. "Do you want to taste my pork chop?"

Griffin's mind immediately went to a dirty place. "Um, sure." He watched as she cut off a section and moved it to his plate. He immediately dug in, making noises of pleasure because they seemed to be expected. The food was ridiculously good, but he was more interested in her. "Can I ask you something?"

"Sure." Ava was completely focused on her food and didn't even bother looking up.

"Why did you need to escape to my grandfather's farm as a kid?"

Ava froze with her fork halfway to her mouth. "I ... don't... What makes you think I had to escape?" She refused to meet his gaze.

"Just some things you've said. If you don't want to talk about it, you don't have to. It's okay."

"No, it's fine. I just ... don't know what to say."

"Okay." He went back to his food.

An uncomfortable silence descended over the table and had him wishing he'd kept his mouth shut.

"My house was just difficult when I was a kid," Ava volunteered after a few moments. "My mother and father fought—at least what I remember of them being together—and when my dad left, my mother didn't have anybody to fight with but me."

Griffin's stomach constricted. "Did she hurt you?"

"Of course not." Ava responded a bit too fast for his liking. "She just yelled a lot. I liked to escape, and your grandfather's farm wasn't all that far away. It was always quiet there. I just wanted a place to unwind. He figured that out and let me read in the barn. It's not some big, sordid story."

Griffin knew there was more to it but didn't press her. He didn't want to ruin what had been a good day so far. "I'm sorry I brought it up. You seemed to have a close bond with my grandfather, though."

"I loved him." Ava's eyes were clear when she finally raised them. "He was an amazing man. I miss him every single day."

"I miss him too." Griffin sighed. "Even though I always complained about having to leave the city when I was younger, I had fun when I got here."

"I don't remember you hanging around during the summers."

"That's because once I hit the age when girls were a thing for me, I stopped coming. I didn't want to leave my friends. That turned out to be an utter waste, though."

"Meaning what?"

"As soon as my name was attached to the Peck Building disaster, all the friends I thought would stick by me disappeared into the woodwork. It happened overnight."

"That doesn't seem fair." Ava's brow furrowed. "It's not as if you were in there, building it yourself. You just made a mistake. We all make mistakes."

"Yeah, but this mistake resulted in two deaths and was all over the news. All anybody wanted to talk about was me and what I'd done. I knew it would be bad, but I guess I didn't realize how bad."

"It's not fair."

He arched an eyebrow and chuckled. "As my father always says, life isn't fair. I just need to suck it up. I'm still dwelling on it, and it's a waste."

"It's okay to feel what you feel," Ava insisted. "That's what your grandfather always told me when I was giving myself grief about some of the stuff I was feeling. He said feelings were to be explored, not shuttered."

"That sounds like him."

"Maybe you should allow yourself to wallow so you can get over it faster," Ava suggested.

"Maybe." Griffin went back to inhaling his food. "Come on. Let's bulk up on protein and carbs then hit this haunted maze. I have no idea what to expect, but if it's lame after all this buildup, I'm going to hold it against you."

"You're going to love it. Trust me. It's one of those experiences you'll never forget."

For some reason, Griffin believed her. The sparkle in her eyes told him everything he needed to know. She was excited about it, so he would be excited too. He just wanted to see that smile again and was angry with himself for chasing it away.

"There'd better not be clowns," he said, then sipped his wine. "That's my line in the sand. Evil clowns are a bridge too far."

"Aren't all clowns evil?"

"Pretty much."

"You'll be fine." Her smile was back and bigger than ever. "Trust me."

GRIFFIN PAID FOR THEIR ENTRANCE TO the corn maze shortly before seven o'clock. Ava was zipped up tightly in her coat and wore a hat but had forgone gloves. He noticed when he dug into his pocket for his.

"You're going to freeze," he chided her. "I don't want to be responsible for your fingers falling off. You're going to need them to catch cats."

Ava laughed as she danced from one foot to the other. "I'll be fine. I need my hands free in case I need to fight off an enemy."

Griffin arched an eyebrow. "What enemy do you expect to be fighting off?"

Ava gave a one-shoulder shrug. "You never know. What

if the real zombie apocalypse hits in the middle of our corn maze run? I'm not going to have time to waste shedding gloves when I need to throw an evil clown into the path of a zombie to make my escape."

Griffin laughed so hard that it seemed to take him by surprise. "I'm glad to see you've given this some thought."

"I think about the zombie apocalypse all the time," Ava admitted ruefully. "*The Walking Dead* started airing at a time when I thought I might be a writer. I even started a book about zombies and worked on it diligently in the barn one summer."

"Oh yeah?" Griffin eyed his gloves for a beat longer then shoved them back into his pockets. "Now you've got me thinking about zombies," he groused. "If I get frostbite, I'm going to blame it on you."

"That seems fair."

They headed into the maze together. The first two turns were quiet, which was to be expected. By the third turn, however, Griffin had become tense.

"You just know that something is waiting to jump out at us. It had better not have a chainsaw. I've seen those haunted houses on the news when they're starting to hype the season, and nobody needs a chainsaw."

As if on cue, a man dressed as a monster—complete with fake entrails hanging off his shirt—jumped out from the darkness and caused Griffin to practically come out of his skin. Instead of cutting Ava off so he could save himself, however, he shoved her ahead of him and put his back to the man.

"Don't touch her," he warned him.

Ava didn't know what to make of that. She'd been through the maze every year for the past ten years and knew what to expect. The jump scares were over-the-top, and the costumes were ridiculous. The screams gave her a headache. But Griffin's protective nature was not something she'd built into her expectations.

"You know they won't hurt us, right?" she prodded as they made another turn. "They wouldn't be able to stay in business if we got hurt. It's all harmless fun."

"I know." Griffin pouted. "I just don't want them touching you. That's invasive."

Ava studied him a beat longer, then extended her hand. Even she didn't know she was going to do it until she was already midreach. "It's okay," she promised in a low voice. "I've got you."

Griffin stared at her hand for what felt like a really long time. Ava would've loved to know what was going through his head. Rather than give voice to his thoughts, however, he slid his hand over hers and linked their fingers.

The air sizzled.

They might've been in a corn maze, surrounded by people who were being paid to jump out and scare the bejesus out of them, but in that moment, they were the only two people in the world.

Griffin smiled. "Maybe you should protect me. This is more your scene than mine."

"I can do that." Ava had no idea what had caused her to say it. She meant it, though. In that moment, she wanted nothing more than to protect him. She'd seen the look on his face when he mentioned his friends abandoning him. He was hurt and trying to recover. Since she'd spent the bulk of her childhood in exactly the same place, she wanted to help him.

Sure, he'd stolen her farm—and that wasn't something she could just get over—but he was a good man. It had been easier when she hadn't known him. Talking about him in her blog when he'd been some amorphous shadow bent on ruining her life wasn't a big deal. But since she'd met him, she didn't want him to feel any sort of hurt. *How did that even happen?*

"Stick with me." She cracked a smile and took the lead.

"This feels wrong to me," Griffin grumbled as he followed her around another turn. "You're tiny. How are you going to protect me when the zombies come? You're not a big enough meal to tempt them."

Ava giggled. "You're so funny."

"I am. I missed my calling. I should've been a stand-up comedian."

"Or a Chippendales dancer."

His fingers flexed around hers. "Is that a good thing or a bad thing?" he asked after a moment. "Like, do those dancers turn you on?"

Grinning wickedly, she said, "Wouldn't you like to know."

His voice was hoarse when he answered ... about five seconds after what would've been considered normal. "Yeah, I'd kind of like to know."

"Well, I'm not telling you. You'll just have to suffer. I—" Whatever she was going to say died on her lips as a hulking man wearing a hockey mask and carrying a machete jumped out of the corn and rushed her. "Oh, holy hell!"

Griffin released her hand but only to grab her around the waist and pick her up. "I can't believe you think this is fun!" he bellowed as they turned another corner.

Ava peered over his shoulder to make sure the masked killer wasn't following them. When she realized they were at eye level, their faces close together, her heart threatened to beat out of her chest. More than that, they were at mouth level.

She'd noticed how attractive he was before. Ava hadn't been able to ignore that little tidbit even from the start. But she'd told herself it didn't matter. In that moment, though, with his warm body pressed to hers and untold dangers lurking in front of and behind them, all she could focus on was that mouth.

His lips looked soft. His breath smelled like macaroni and cheese. His eyes were fierce.

Their hearts pounded in tandem, and their eyes were fixed on each other. All either of them had to do was lean forward and ... well, their relationship would be irrevocably changed.

Neither of them made the move.

"Are you okay?" Griffin asked after what felt like thirty years.

"I'm good," Ava promised him, disappointment rocketing through her. *Why am I disappointed?* "Are you okay?"

"Yeah." Griffin nodded. "I'm good. Are you sure you want to finish this?"

"Half the fun is making it to the end," Ava promised. "It will be okay. I'll protect you."

"Then let's do it."

GRIFFIN WAS CONVINCED WHOEVER HAD SET up the corn maze wanted to kill him. As far as he could tell, there was no discernible pattern as to when the people in masks would jump out. Most of them were armed with what looked like real knives and machetes. At least so far, there had been no chainsaws, and the knives looked dull. Still, he was over the entire thing.

"How much longer?" he demanded. He hadn't pulled out his phone to check the time, but they'd been inside for at least twenty minutes, and he was ready to call it a night ... and only part of that was because there had been a moment when he'd thought about abandoning his wits and kissing her.

There she'd been, soft and pliant in his arms, both of them gasping into each other's faces, and all he'd wanted to do was say "screw this," and kiss her. That would've been a mistake—the last thing he needed at the moment was a romantic entanglement—but the wild look in her eyes and the feeling of her breath on his face was more than he could take.

He was attracted to her. Griffin might not be able to admit that out loud, but he was brutally honest with himself when it mattered. He couldn't deny what he felt, what he had been feeling for days. He wanted her.

But he didn't want to have a relationship with her. Or well, it wasn't just her. He wasn't in a place where he could give his all to a relationship, and that wasn't fair to her, so he had to take a step back.

Only he couldn't do that in the blasted maze. Yes, he understood they were in no real danger. But the jump scares had amped him up to the nth degree, and he couldn't ignore the protective instincts that kept rearing their ugly head.

Griffin didn't want her hurt. He wanted her tucked in at his side, safe and laughing. Sure, she was having way more fun than he was, but the furtive looks she kept shooting him had his heart pounding. She wasn't scared—she was intrigued.

When yet another individual—that one dressed like a clown—jumped out of a corner, Griffin hit his limit.

"That's just wrong!" he snapped as he grabbed Ava and scurried to get to the next barrier. He was so worked up that he didn't notice a piece of wood on the ground, and he tripped, taking them both down.

Ava was under him, his large frame completely covering hers, and she wasn't moving.

"Ava! I'm so sorry." He flipped her over, prepared to give her mouth-to-mouth if she wasn't breathing.

But Ava was laughing so hard that tears were leaking from her eyes. Her breath hitched, and a peal of laughter escaped, echoing in the air.

"You're not funny," he groused. "I could've really hurt you."

"You're such a whiner," she shot back. "It's just a corn maze."

"I could've crushed you."

"Okay." She rolled her eyes.

Frustrated, Griffin slid his arm under her waist. He planned to pull her to her feet. Instead, he only managed to get her to a sitting position. Given their proximity, their mouths were on top of each other when he tried to shift again and stand.

That time, there was no stopping either of them. He had no idea whether she was the one who leaned forward to erase that final inch or if he was. Ultimately, it didn't matter. Their lips met in an explosive kiss, all the screams from the other parts of the maze turning into a low buzz as they lost themselves in each other.

Griffin cupped the back of her head and tilted her so that he could take the kiss deeper. He wanted to devour her. Whatever he was feeling in that moment was infinitely better than anything he'd felt in months. Warmth suffused him as she melted into his arms.

He had no idea how long they went at each other. It could've been seconds or even minutes. All he knew was that their tongues kept playing a game of tag, and he had no interest in stopping. When he finally pulled back, her eyes were wide, and she looked as if she was about to panic.

"Sorry about that," he said gruffly as he pulled her up. Once he broke eye contact, he couldn't make it again. The spell was over, and he felt completely out of place. "That was an accident."

Breathily, Ava asked, "An accident?"

"Yup. I'm not sure how it happened. I'm sorry, though."

After a moment of quiet, she replied, "Okay. I think the exit is right over there. We should take it."

"Absolutely," Griffin agreed. "Let's get the hell out of here."

13
THIRTEEN

The ride back to Bellaire had felt ridiculously long. That she and Griffin opted to embrace awkward silence rather than talk about things only made the ride longer. When they pulled into his driveway, she hopped out of the vehicle before it had even pulled to a stop, and the haphazard wave she gave him was right out of a slapstick comedy. She'd even churned up gravel in the driveway in her eagerness to get away.

She'd thought things would be better when she got home, but she tossed and turned all night. Whenever she closed her eyes, all she thought about was that kiss. Her lips felt numb with the memory.

That meant when she woke, she was exhausted. She took a long shower to try to shake off the fatigue. When that didn't work, she headed straight for Maya's coffee shop to overdose on caffeine. One way or another, she would forget that kiss.

Maya and Lindsey were at one of the tables, drinking coffee and laughing, when she walked in. She only realized her lack of sleep was obvious to others when Lindsey's eyebrows nearly popped off her forehead.

"Sex hangover?" She grinned.

Ava narrowed her eyes. "Why would you even ask that?"

"Because I heard you went on a trip out of town with Griffin Holden yesterday," Lindsey replied. "What else could it be?"

"There was no sex." Ava felt the need to make that very clear. "There was absolutely zero sex."

"Uh-huh." Lindsey didn't look convinced.

"Do you want a latte?" Maya asked as she got up.

Ava nodded. "A big one. If you can throw some bourbon in it, I won't complain."

Maya smirked as she passed, stopping long enough to give Ava a once-over. "You do look like you're suffering from a sex hangover."

"It must have been bad sex, if you're frowning like that," Lindsey noted as Maya carried on behind the counter.

Ava threw herself into the booth across from Lindsey. "Listen up. I know you like to have your fun with people—it's only fun for you in case you're wondering—but I'm not in the mood."

"Oh, that sucks." Lindsey made a face. "Is he bad in bed, or is it the other thing? If it's the other thing, cut your ties now. If he just needs some lessons, I can help you with that. I'm good at teaching."

Ava frowned. "What's the other thing?"

"You know."

Ava blinked and waited.

"*You know,*" Lindsey insisted.

"I wouldn't have asked if I knew," Ava fired back.

Lindsey gave a long, drawn-out sigh. When she held up her pinkie and fixed Ava with a pointed look, it still took her a full ten seconds to realize what she was saying.

"Oh, knock that off." Ava slapped Lindsey's pinkie away. "Why would you even assume that?"

"Because what else could it be?" Lindsey replied. "He's too hot to be totally worthless in bed. He would've at least watched a little porn during his youth, and while those movies send a bad message, there are some tricks in there to be found. That means he has to be hung like an infant. It's the only explanation."

"I have no idea whether he's hung like an infant," Ava barked back. But that wasn't entirely true. She'd felt his excitement during the kiss, and he definitely wasn't hung like an infant. But she didn't feel like talking about that. "We didn't have sex. We went over to Claridge Farms so that he could get some inspiration for his grandfather's farm."

Maya wrinkled her nose as she returned to the table with Ava's latte. She used her hip to nudge Lindsey over, then sat down to stare at Ava. "Why would you give him hints for the property? I thought you were still holding out hope that he would decide it was too much work and sell it to you."

Ava averted her gaze and focused on the wall. "No reason."

"Oh, there's a reason," Lindsey countered. "We want to hear it."

"There's no reason. I just... Maybe... Um..." She didn't know what to say.

"You feel bad for writing the blog entry, and you were trying to make it up to him," Maya surmised. "You've figured out he might not be such a bad guy after all."

"And you're hot for him," Lindsey added.

"I am not hot for him!" Ava yelled.

Maya glanced around as if checking to make sure nobody had snuck in when she wasn't looking. "Something happened. You can deny it all you want, but it's written all over your face. You might as well tell us. You'll feel better for it, whatever you think right now."

Ava stared for several beats, then buried her face in her elbow on top of the table. "We went through the corn maze. You know the haunted one at Claridge Farms? We did that together after dinner."

"Wait, you had dinner? Was it a romantic dinner?"

"It was at the Weathervane."

"So it was a romantic dinner. Things are progressing much quicker than I anticipated." Lindsey looked smug when Ava raised her eyes.

"I just wanted the pork chop."

"They do serve some good pork there," Lindsey agreed. "Bear and I go there every year on our anniversary. That's a total date restaurant."

"We weren't on a date." Saying it didn't make it true, but Ava was determined to convince herself, even if she couldn't convince the others. "I don't know what I was thinking. We talked and had a good time, then we went to the maze."

"Also a date activity," Lindsey noted.

"How is that a date activity?" Maya asked. "I thought the maze was for kids."

"Not *that* maze," Lindsey replied. "It's a horror maze. People jump out at you and try to scare you. That's where people go when they want to touch one another without it being obvious. How many times did you throw yourself at Griffin?"

"I'm starting to regret coming here," Ava lamented and sipped her latte.

"That means it was a fair number of times," Lindsey informed Maya.

"He was more frightened than me," Ava insisted. "It's just ... he was also protective. He might've picked me up to move me out of harm's way a few times."

"See?" Lindsey shot Maya a knowing look. "Total date."

"It was fine until we got close to the end. Then—and I still don't know how it happened—his face was right in front of mine, and there was a lot of heavy breathing. Somehow, we ended up kissing."

Lindsey waited expectantly.

"That's it," Ava snapped when nobody filled the silence. "We kissed, and that was it."

"Well, that was a letdown," Lindsey muttered with a sigh.

"It wasn't a letdown," Maya shot back. "It was a great first step." Her eyes were a bit too sparkly for Ava's comfort. "Was it a good kiss?"

Ava wanted to downplay the incident, but she believed in being brutally honest, especially with herself. "It was the best kiss of my life." She squeezed her eyes shut and buried her face in her arms again. "What a freaking mess."

"No. It's not a mess," Maya said. "It's a good thing. You guys clearly have chemistry. Nick and I talked about it all the way home when we stopped by the barn the other day."

"You talked about our chemistry?" Ava asked, horrified. "Why would you do that?"

"Because it's off the charts. You guys clearly like each other."

"We do not." Ava refused to entertain that for even a

second. "It was just the heightened emotions of the moment."

"Uh-huh." Lindsey made a face. "Everybody in town is talking about you guys. Those blondes who always hang around in a gang—you know, the bottle blondes with the bad haircuts, right?—they all set their sights on Griffin, and they've already dropped out of the race without trying because word has spread about the two of you."

"There is no word to spread," Ava insisted.

"Okay. You keep telling yourself that. We'll talk again in a week. We'll definitely know about this by then." She held up her pinkie again.

Maya shoved the pinkie away. "Why won't you at least entertain the possibility of this?"

"Because... Because..." Ava had to think hard. "Because I'm not in a place for a relationship. And he's definitely not. Plus, he stole my farm."

"Yes, but if you guys were to make things work, then you could build your dream farm together."

Ava froze. She hadn't considered that. Almost immediately, she shook off the idea. "No. I'm not getting involved with him simply because I want that farm. That's not how it works."

"I'm not suggesting you get involved with him *because* of the farm," Maya replied. "I'm suggesting you get involved with him because your heart—and clearly your lips—want you to."

"No. That's not true. It only happened because of where we were."

Maya didn't look convinced, but she let it go. "Okay. It's up to you."

"It *is* up to me, and I say there's nothing going on between us. It was just a fluke."

"I guess you know best."

"I most definitely do."

GRIFFIN STOOD IN THE DOORWAY TO THE BARN, glaring at the black cat. The feline kept avoiding the traps they'd set, and he was growing increasingly smug about the situation—well, if cats could be smug.

"Can't you just get in the cage?" he whined.

The cat sat ten feet away and shot his leg up so that he could lick his balls.

"You're definitely smug," Griffin muttered, swiveling quickly when he heard the sound of footsteps on the gravel behind him. His first thought was that Ava was coming to catch some cats. Why he was so excited about that prospect, he couldn't say. Disappointment washed over him when he realized it was Nick and Bear. "Oh, hey."

"I don't think he's excited to see us," Bear noted, his eyes twinkling. "I'm hurt, dude."

"No, I'm thrilled to see you," he insisted. "I'm still waking up." Even to Griffin, it sounded like a lame excuse.

"Of course you are. You're waking up." Bear winked before focusing his attention on the black cat. "What's up, big guy?"

The cat barely looked up from his grooming.

"I wish I could do that," Bear said wistfully. "Life would be so much easier."

"Oh, don't be gross." Nick gave Bear a shove while laughing.

"Like you don't wish you could do that." Bear shook his head then flicked his eyes back to Griffin. "Who were you hoping we would be?"

"Nobody," Griffin replied automatically. "I'm glad to see

you guys. I'm surprised too. Are we supposed to be doing something today?"

"I'm avoiding my wife," Bear replied. "As for Nick, he's just along for the ride. Also, we don't believe you. We know who you were hoping to see."

Griffin's cheeks burned, but he was determined to pretend that was a result of the cold and not the way Bear was pushing him. "I have no idea what you're talking about."

"We heard you went on a date with Ava last night," Nick volunteered as he shifted closer to the cat. He wasn't close enough to grab the animal, but if he inched just a little bit closer, it might be possible.

"I'd be careful," Bear warned him. "Look at the way he's watching you. Cat scratches and bites can be nasty. They're full of bacteria."

"That shows what you know." Nick plopped down on the ground. "We're just being friendly. Don't get weird."

"Whatever." Bear turned back to Griffin. "How was your date with Ava?"

"How do you even know about that? Also, it wasn't a date."

"Didn't you guys leave town together? How is that not a date?"

"She wanted to show me some bed-and-breakfast in Charlevoix."

Bear arched an eyebrow.

"We didn't stay there," Griffin snapped. "We just ... looked around."

"And didn't come home until long after dark," Bear noted.

"Seriously, how do you know that?"

Bear chuckled. "Edna Graves lives one house down.

Gossip is her trade. She saw you and Ava leaving together early yesterday, and she was watching when you got back, and she said it was well after dark."

"Well, Edna needs to find a hobby."

"Oh, most definitely," Bear agreed. "*Grey's Anatomy* is on its fall hiatus now, though, so she has precious little to do. You're her new favorite show."

"You and Ava," Nick corrected him.

"There is no me and Ava." Griffin swallowed. That somehow felt wrong. "She's just helping with the cats."

"And going on day trips with you," Bear pressed. "What's up with that?"

Griffin was a big believer in body language setting the tone, so he crossed his arms and jutted out his chin. He hoped he looked strong rather than defensive. Bear's expression told him he'd missed the mark.

"She wanted to show me what was possible if I decided to turn the farm into a bed-and-breakfast. We had dinner while we were over there, then we went through the world's worst haunted corn maze. Seriously, why are those things allowed to be made? They're terrible."

"You have a back seat full of pumpkins," Bear argued.

Griffin swore mentally. He'd forgotten about the pumpkins. Ava had been in such a hurry to leave after the kiss—that stupid, stupid kiss he both wanted to repeat and incise from his memory—that she'd left her pumpkins behind. He would have to find a way to get them to her, one that he hoped didn't involve their being within five feet of each other. Despite his best efforts to tell himself that the kiss had meant nothing, his heart was putting up quite the impressive fight.

"Ava picked those out," Griffin explained. "She was

tired last night, so she'll come back to get them today." At least he hoped that was true.

"Uh-huh." Bear cocked his head. "Where did you guys have dinner?"

"Um ... someplace called the Weathervane."

Bear nodded. "That's a date restaurant. I know. Lindsey and I go there every year for our anniversary. That stupid leek-and-morel pasta puts her in the mood for romance, although I have no idea why."

"It was just dinner," Griffin insisted.

"So nothing else happened?" Nick pressed.

"Nothing," Griffin replied decisively. He couldn't meet Nick's steady gaze, though.

"Nothing?" Bear tried one more time.

Frustration grabbed Griffin by the throat. "There may have been a kiss." He regretted it as soon as he admitted it. "It was only because of that stupid maze. I had to protect her from one of the clowns, and we were on top of each other. It was just a biological thing."

"Uh-huh." Bear beamed at Nick. "You owe me a beer. I told you."

Griffin balled his hands into fists at his sides. "What exactly did you tell him?"

"That you and Ava were hot to trot for each other."

"Well, that's not true." Again, Griffin couldn't be entirely certain he meant it. "I am not in a place for a relationship," he added. That, at least, was entirely true. "It's not the right time."

"So you're saying that after you get settled and decide what you're going to do, then you'll be in a place where you can date Ava?" Nick prodded.

"I ... don't ... know." Griffin wanted to be anywhere but

inside the barn with the busybody men. "I just know I'm not in a place for a relationship right now."

"If you say so." Bear didn't look convinced in the least. "Do you mind if I head up to the loft? I want to come up with some plans for you in case you want to convert the barn into living quarters in the spring and make the house a bed-and-breakfast."

"Why would I want that?"

"Because that's what Ava wants, and you guys are clearly on a crash course for love," Bear replied with an impish grin.

"Ugh." Griffin squeezed his eyes shut. "I can't stand you right now."

"You'll get over it." Bear clapped him on the shoulder. "Eventually, when you're not feeling so raw emotionally, you're going to be glad I did this. Mark my words."

Because Griffin needed the conversation to end, he simply nodded. "Do what you want. There is no me and Ava, though. It's not going to happen."

"Yeah, you keep telling yourself that."

14

FOURTEEN

va avoided the barn for two days. She figured that was enough of a cooling down period. When she returned, fresh food and traps in tow, she found Griffin sitting on the barn floor about five feet from the black cat.

"I get that you're intrinsically mistrustful of humans," he said. "The thing is we really are trying to help. If you would just open your heart a little bit, you'll see that we're good people."

The cat, of course, didn't respond.

"How about we strike a deal?" he suggested. "I'll get you one of those heated cat houses I saw on Chewy for the winter, and you'll allow us to take you to the vet. I promise to bring you back."

Ava's heart pinched. He wasn't a bad guy at all.

Dammit! Why does he have to be a good guy? All her resolve to pretend the kiss hadn't happened was starting to flee.

Perhaps finally sensing her, he shifted his gaze to her, and her spine stiffened. He peered at her with soft eyes as a million unsaid things passed between them. The air seemed somehow thicker.

This can't happen. This can't happen. This can't happen. She smiled, although it felt unnatural. "Are you guys buddies now?"

Griffin matched her smile. "I don't know that I would call us buddies. We have a healthy respect for each other. I don't try to touch him, and he licks his balls directly in front of me in thanks."

Ava's lips quivered. "Well, that sounds nice." She put the new cage on the floor and eyed the cat in question. "When I was little, your grandfather had a cat give birth in here. She had five kittens. There was a little black one that hung out with me when I was reading in the loft. I desperately wanted to bring it home but ... well, that didn't work out."

Griffin didn't make a move to get up. "Why not?"

"My parents didn't think I was responsible enough to take care of a cat." Ava shifted her eyes to the loft. "I could have taken care of it. They felt otherwise. Their stuff was always more important than mine. But it was probably for the best. Chuck found homes for them."

"Meaning you lost your cat."

"It was never my cat."

"I think maybe it was." Griffin rubbed his hands on his knees. "You haven't been around much."

"Yes, I've been doing some stuff." Ava didn't want to look at him—she constantly got lost in his eyes lately—but she couldn't seem to help herself. "That's a lie," she admitted after a beat. "I've been afraid to see you."

Griffin smiled. "I know. I'm a little unsure how to respond too. I guess I should apologize."

"For what?"

"For kissing you."

"I kind of kissed you back."

"You did, but I was trying to be a gentleman and let you off the hook."

"That's not necessary. It happened. I think we both agree it was a mistake. I don't want to get hung up on it."

"It was definitely a mistake."

Ava didn't want to focus too much on why his confirming what she had said bothered her so much. But it did. She pushed forward anyway. "We're adults. We should just suck it up and make a pact or something."

"I didn't know adults made pacts."

"Of course they do. That's a regular thing ... that I just made up." She sighed. "I just meant that we could make a pact that we'll be friends. That's it. If we say it out loud, we'll have to follow through."

"Is that how that works?" Griffin chuckled. "I'm fine with making a pact. I didn't realize we were friends, though."

The rebuke stung more than Ava anticipated. "Forget it." She averted her gaze.

"Wait." Griffin scrambled to his feet. "I didn't mean that how it came out."

"It's fine." Ava kept her eyes on the cat, who stared back at her, unblinking. If she didn't know better, she would say he was mocking her.

You like him. He sees it. Now you look like an idiot, she imagined the cat saying.

"It's not fine," Griffin countered. He moved in front of her, and Ava registered the heat emanating from his body.

Why does he have to look so warm? Why do I remember how his body felt against mine, how we fit so well together, as much as the kiss? Why can't I forget the soft touches and finger brushes?

He was driving her insane. Perhaps that was his goal. They weren't friends after all.

"Ava, that came out wrong," Griffin insisted. "We *are* friends. I'm not sure how it happened—given how all this started, you should be in jail—but I had fun with you the other night."

She narrowed her eyes. "We made a pact."

"Not that. Although I guess I know where your mind is. I just meant that I liked seeing the bed-and-breakfast. You're a fount of useless information. You watch way too much television—as do I—and you can talk on almost any subject.

"If I had to do the corn maze over again, I would," he continued. "I do not like being frightened. I can watch horror movies sometimes—although clearly not as often as you—but that maze was not fun."

"I had fun."

"That's because you're clearly not frightened of anything."

Oh, if only he knew. Ava kept her smile in place, even though the dark pit of despair she managed to hold at bay most days reared its ugly head out of nowhere. *Don't make me come in there, girl!* Ava let out a puff of air when the memory invaded but managed to keep her face neutral. She was good at that.

"You might be surprised," she said when she was reasonably certain she could speak without squeaking.

"No, you're fearless, and I've never understood that," Griffin said. "I like hanging around you because of that. The other stuff, though, it's not appropriate. I have no idea what I'm doing with my life, and I don't have the mental bandwidth to give a relationship the energy it would need to thrive."

Ava stilled. "I don't want a relationship from you."

"I know. Hell, I'm doing this all wrong." He dragged a hand through his dark hair. "I'm just saying we're friends. We're at least friendly. That's a new thing for me. I was trying to tease you earlier. I wasn't trying to hurt you."

Ava regarded him, then sighed. "I get it. Our initial meeting was less than auspicious."

"That's putting it mildly."

"Maybe I shouldn't have sprung the outing on you so quickly. Perhaps we should get to know each other as friends first. That way, the pact will stay intact."

"I can see you're serious about this pact stuff. But I'm all for it. Whatever you have in mind."

Ava cocked her head, considering, then nodded. "Okay, then. We'll ask each other questions when we work today. Nothing too personal." She extended a finger in warning. "You don't have to answer the question if it's too uncomfortable. You can pass. Before we know it, the day will be over, and we'll be friends."

Griffin looked dubious but still nodded. "I'm game to try."

"Awesome. Let's get our gloves on then get going. I'll start."

"That sounds like a perfect way to spend a day to me."

"WHAT FOOD WILL YOU NEVER EAT AGAIN?"

Griffin stood in the loft, his hands on his hips, and eyed the cyclops Maine Coon with a great amount of displeasure. He'd managed to chase all the cats in the loft down except for that one. They were going to try to close off the area so that the cats couldn't take it over again. Of course, that was easier said than done.

He couldn't see Ava, but he could hear her below him. She was trying to entice the black cat into a cage. It didn't sound like it was going well.

"Liver," Ava replied without hesitation.

Griffin made a face. "Who eats liver the first time?"

"My father used to like it, so my mother cooked it whenever they got into a fight. That means it was on the table at least once a week when I was growing up, and I still have flashbacks. I think I might have PTSD."

Griffin smirked. "I can see that. I'm grossed out just thinking about it."

"What liquor will you never drink again?" Ava queried. She made a scuffling sound, and Griffin had to wonder if she'd launched herself at the cat. The way she cursed in the aftermath told him she hadn't caught the smug pain in the ass, regardless of how she'd approached it.

"I'll drink anything now, but I went through a phase when I wouldn't drink tequila," he replied. "I went to Cancun with some buddies when I was eighteen. We overdid it, as eighteen-year-olds are known to do, and when I threw up the worm a few hours later, I was traumatized."

"Sounds like me and the liver."

"It does." Griffin narrowed his eyes and inched on his knees toward the fluffy cat. "You have to have a blind spot, right? I mean, you have one eye. So maybe if you look over here..." He held out his hand to the right. "You won't be able to see over here."

He lunged for the cat and missed ... badly. He hit the wood with an *oof* and grimaced when the straw on the floor ended up in his nose.

"Oh gross." He slapped at his face. He could only imagine the sort of germs living in the straw.

"What's wrong?" Ava's voice was much closer than it had been, and when Griffin shifted to look at the top of the ladder, he found her entering the loft.

God, she was beautiful. Even without makeup, her skin radiated health. Because she was trying not to laugh at his predicament, she looked even prettier. Happy Ava was a sight to behold.

"He hates me," Griffin lamented, jutting his lower lip out. "He's never going to let us catch him."

"He is. We just have to wear him down. We're smarter than him."

"All evidence seems to point to the contrary," Griffin muttered as he struggled to a sitting position. He had straw stuck in his hair. "Why can't we do this?"

Ava held out her hands. "This is their terrain. They know all the ins and outs of the barn and have the advantage. We can catch them, though. Have a little faith."

Griffin made a disgruntled sound and eyed her. "Have you ever been in love?" Even he didn't know he was going to ask the question until it had already escaped.

Her shoulders jerked. "I thought I said no personal questions."

"Right." Griffin averted his gaze.

"The answer is no," Ava said after a beat. "I've never been in love."

Slowly, he turned back to her. "Why?"

"I don't know. I just haven't. I don't think most men can handle me."

"Because you're mouthy?"

"Pretty much."

"There are a lot of guys who like mouthy women. But

up here, it's probably more difficult. Down south, you would've already been snapped up."

"Basically, you're saying I'm wasting myself on the country," she said dryly.

He scratched his cheek, considering. "No. I guess I phrased it wrong. I know you love it up here. But I didn't get it until I saw you at Claridge Farms. You love everything about living in the country. You should definitely be in the place that makes you happy. What I meant was that the guys up here have probably been raised with certain expectations when it comes to their mates. Television and history tell them that their wives should be demure, happy home-makers. You have other ambitions."

He couldn't read the expression on her face. "What?" he asked defensively, his hand automatically going to his hair. "If it's a spider, just kill me now."

Rather than laugh, she managed a small, heartfelt smile. "You're good at reading people. As for a potential spider, let me look."

Griffin's heart pounded when she moved close enough to touch him. Gently, she combed through his hair. Warmth suffused him at her proximity, and when he inhaled, the heady scent of cloves, which he'd started to associate with her, filled him to the brim with an emotion he didn't want to identify. He was fairly certain it was desire.

Her presence ran roughshod over him. His mouth went dry, and his fingers itched to touch her. All he could manage was saying her name on a strangled rasp. "Ava."

She dropped to her knees next to him, her eyes full of yearning, and he was positive he had the same look in his eyes.

"We made a pact," she said in a low voice. Her face was only inches from his. He appreciated that she didn't deny they were having a moment, but that didn't make things easier for him. His trance might be impossible to shake off.

"I haven't been able to think about anything but kissing you for days," Griffin growled, his hand going to her waist. "Can I touch you?" he asked after he'd already closed the distance.

"It's a bad idea," she said.

"It's a terrible idea," he agreed. "I can't think, though."

"Yeah."

When she exhaled, her breath hit him in the face. Whatever he was feeling, whatever emotions she was stirring up in him, he wanted more. He couldn't deny it.

"I shouldn't have come back."

"You had to. I have your pumpkins."

Her cheeks turned red. "I forgot all about them."

"So you didn't come back for your pumpkins?" He flexed his fingers, then aimed them at her waist again, stopping short before touching her. "Ava, may I touch you?"

"Yes," she replied without hesitation.

His hands hit her waist at the same moment their mouths collided. Ava landed on him with enough force that they both flopped back into the straw. That time, Griffin didn't care. If there was a spider crawling through the mess, it would have to wait its turn. He had bigger things on his mind.

Their tongues touched tentatively at first then with determination. She grabbed clumps of his hair, and he squeezed her ass, groaning at how it felt in his hands. She'd been driving him crazy with that thing for weeks. Since he'd gotten to touch it, he couldn't imagine ever letting it go.

They rolled so that Griffin was on top, and he pulled back far enough to stare into her eyes. His head kept screaming, *This is a mistake!* over and over again. His heart, though, disagreed. As for his body—it would go on strike if he didn't give in to his needs.

But he wasn't so far gone that he couldn't ask the obvious question. "Are you sure you want to do this?"

"I don't have much of a choice," Ava admitted in a husky voice. "I can't think either. I just want to take. Fill myself with you. I can't explain it. I've never felt this way before."

"Maybe we just need to do it," Griffin suggested. "Then we'll have scratched that itch, and we can go back to the pact."

"Sure." Ava moved her hands down to his rear end and squeezed as hard as he had. "That sounds like a great idea to me."

"Are you just saying that because you can't fathom the idea of stopping this?"

"Yes."

Griffin grinned. "Me too."

He put his mouth on her again. There was no turning back. If they were making a mistake—which was likely— they would have to deal with the ramifications after the fact.

"Don't stare," he ordered, extending a finger toward the curious Maine Coon. "Mind your business."

15
FIFTEEN

"There's straw poking my ass."

That wasn't the most poetic thing to say after a round of gritty sex in the loft of his grandfather's barn—with multiple cats watching from various perches—but Griffin had no idea what else he should say.

"You hope it's straw," Ava replied. Her head was nestled in the crook of his arm, and her hand rested on his chest. "What if it's a spider or something?"

Griffin didn't immediately jump to his feet and start flapping his arm to displace the offending arachnid, although he kind of wanted to. In truth, he was comfortable. The feel of Ava's body against his and her warmth suffusing him were too good to let go of just yet. But that didn't mean he wasn't feeling awkward. "Did you have to put that in my head?" he demanded.

"If it's in my head, then you have to worry about it too."

He chuckled. "You are ... a lot of work."

"Have you been talking to my mother?"

"Not last time I checked, although that does bring up an interesting question. Are your parents still around?"

Ava averted her gaze. "I think there are other things to talk about, don't you?" She propped herself up on an elbow and stared down at his face. "This was a mistake."

"Oh, baby, you say the sweetest things," Griffin drawled. He didn't bother to mask his smile. "I believe we knew it was a mistake when we were doing it." He dragged a hand through his hair.

"Yes, we both agreed that we're not relationship people. Yet here we are." With a dubious expression, she scanned the loft. "Why are all the cats up here watching us?"

"We're their new favorite television show," Griffin replied. He trailed his fingertips over her shoulder, marveling at how soft her skin was. "This is probably the most action they've seen in years."

"You saw the kittens. They've hardly been bored."

"True." Griffin moved his fingers to her hair and stroked it. She was beautiful, to the point that she made something inside him ache with yearning, making him uneasy. He shouldn't be thinking about that again so soon after the first round—or, well, ever again.

"What are we going to do?" Ava lamented. Either she hadn't noticed how distracted he was, or she didn't care. "Now that I've seen you naked, it's all over."

Griffin frowned. "In a good way or a bad way?"

"Bad for me. Good for whoever you decide to sleep with next." Ava looked him up and down. "How often do you work out? I mean, you have eight abs. That should be impossible."

A chuckle escaped before Griffin could stop it. "I used to work out all the time when I was in the city. After the accident, I didn't want to go anywhere, so I bought a couple of pieces of machinery and never left my house."

"Where is the machinery now?"

"What do you mean?"

"You obviously didn't bring it with you. You only took like twenty things off that truck the day you moved in, and half of them were boxes of clothes and shoes."

"Not that you were watching or anything," Griffin said dryly. "You were lost in the bushes, if I recall correctly."

"Yes, well, I'm nothing if not diligent when observing. You didn't move any workout machines into the house."

"They're in storage down south along with the bulk of my furniture. I didn't want to take the time to move them if I wasn't going to like it up here. I figured I could pay for six months of storage and then decide."

"That makes sense." Ava lightly glided her fingers over his chest. He didn't have a lot of chest hair—even though he didn't consider himself vain, manscaping was one of those things he couldn't avoid—but she seemed fascinated with it. "Which way are you leaning?"

"I honestly don't know," Griffin replied. "Talk to me after the first big snow."

"Are we still going to be talking then?" Her voice was a bit shriller than normal.

"Do you want to be talking then?" Griffin had no idea how to approach the situation. Even though he'd understood what a bad mistake he was making in the moment, he couldn't regret what had happened. It had been too magnificent. First-time sex rarely went so smoothly, especially in a barn loft. Of course, he'd never done it in a barn loft before, so for all he knew, that could've been the norm. But it felt different—almost magical.

"I asked you first," Ava said in a low voice.

"Yes, but since you brought it up, it seems to me you should be the one answering."

"Maybe I don't want to answer."

Griffin wrinkled his nose as he stared into the fathomless depths of her eyes. She was a pain in the ass. But the memory of the way she'd felt under him refused to dissipate. All he could think about was how she would feel on top of him. The need was overwhelming.

"Let's talk about it," he said finally. "I'm not sorry it happened." He hadn't realized he was going to blurt it out like that.

"Weirdly, I'm not sorry it happened either," Ava admitted. She didn't meet his eyes. "But that doesn't mean it was a good idea."

"Oh, it was a terrible idea. We definitely shouldn't have done it."

"Now what happens?"

"Well, I've been thinking—it would still count as one time if we did it again before getting dressed."

Ava's jaw dropped. "Are you being serious?"

"I am. You can be on top this time. If there's a spider flattened beneath me, I don't want to let it up. Maybe it will suffocate before it can launch its revenge attack."

The way Ava giggled warmed Griffin to the very tips of his toes. *Why does she have this effect on me?* He couldn't explain it. He'd dated before, but none of those women's smiles made his insides feel as if they were liquefying.

"We both agreed that we can't be in relationships right now," Ava said after a few seconds. "Having sex once might be something acquaintances do. Having sex twice, though —even if you want to link it to the first round—is not something acquaintances do. If you do it twice, you need a label."

"Friends with benefits?"

"Are we friends?"

"We're friendlier than we were."

"Yes, but we're not exactly friends." Ava flopped down on the straw next to him. "What about more than friends?"

"Married people are more than friends."

"Let's not go there."

"I'm just saying." He took a breath. "We could be sex buddies. You know, people who see each other occasionally, climb each other like trees, then go about their normal lives. No emotions are involved. It's just sex."

You're already emotionally involved with her, his inner voice warned him.

Griffin ruthlessly pushed the voice away. "It was just a thought."

"Weren't sex buddies a thing in the nineties or something? I swear they had an episode of *Sex and the City* that talked about sex buddies."

"Weren't you a little young for *Sex and the City*?"

"I saw it in reruns."

"Did you like it?"

"I liked Miranda. I hated the others."

"Interesting." It wasn't all that interesting, but Griffin didn't know what else to say. "Where did we land on the sex-buddies thing?"

"I don't know," Ava replied. "I think we need to test it."

"Does that mean we're having sex again?" Griffin couldn't contain his hope.

"Yes. This round is purely scientific, though. If we can have sex again and feel nothing, I might be up for exploring the sex-buddies thing."

A hot ball of pleasure sparked in Griffin's stomach, accompanied by a pang of something else—fondness. But he refused to focus on it. All he knew was he wanted more of Ava. If he had to cover up the fact that he might be feeling something more than buddyhood with her, then he would do what needed to be done.

"You get to be on top this time," he said. "You're going to end up with marks on your knees like me. That straw hurts more than you might think. It's a fair trade-off, though."

"So much for chivalry," Ava teased as she leaned in to kiss him.

Griffin cupped the back of her head so he could stare into her eyes. "Sex buddies aren't chivalrous." His breath hitched at her proximity.

"Then I guess it's good that you're not being chivalrous," she murmured as she climbed on top of him.

"Yes. Chivalry is dead. Long live ... whatever this is."

AVA COULD BARELY BREATHE WHEN SHE landed in the straw next to Griffin a second time. Even though it was cold outside, the barn was steamy, and she was a sweaty mess.

"No feelings, right?" she asked when she could form words.

"No feelings." Griffin's eyes were closed, as if he were preparing for a nap. That allowed Ava to study his profile without his staring back.

Why does he have to be so hot? His skin was like satin, and his dark hair felt like silk when she ran her fingers through it. His body was both soft and hard, thanks to his muscles. And that lowdown squirming feeling that threatened to knock her over whenever she was in close proximity to him —that was another problem entirely. They were definitely in more than a sex-buddies situation. Yet she couldn't say those words out loud. If she did, everything would be over.

As hard as it was for her to admit, she didn't want it to be over.

"You're basically a sex toy to me," Ava lied. "Actually, I have more feelings for my vibrator than you because he's been around longer and has come through in a number of difficult situations."

Griffin smiled, lacing his fingers with hers as they synced their breathing. "I'm glad you don't have feelings for me."

"You're no different from some random stranger on the street."

Griffin arched an eyebrow. "That fills me with concern. Do you do this with random people on the street often?"

"No, but they're not as hot as you. They don't have eight abs."

"Good to know that my hard work is what put me over the top."

"Yeah." Ava could've released his hand to scratch the itch on the side of her nose, but she didn't. She used her free hand and kept contact with him. "We need to come up with rules," she decided.

"Rules?" Griffin opened one eye. "What sort of rules?"

"Well, this isn't a relationship." Even though her heart screamed in protest, Ava refused to back down from that assertion. She wasn't in a place mentally where a relationship made sense. She was supposed to be able to buy the farm, renovate it, then find the perfect boyfriend once all that hard work had been carried out.

"We both agree it's not a relationship," Griffin said stiffly. "Don't suddenly get weird. I haven't changed my mind on that."

"I know. It's just ... we have to be careful. If the people in town get wind that we're doing ... well, this, then we're never going to hear the end of it. We're going to start getting pressure on all sides. They're not going to understand the sex-buddies thing."

"Yeah, Nick and Bear already think there's something going on."

"That's because Maya and Lindsey think there's something going on," Ava replied. "They're the ones who filled their significant others' heads with nonsense."

"I think Bear and Nick think for themselves on that stuff, and they've made more than a few comments to me."

"Well, then we have to make sure they don't get the wrong idea on that," Ava insisted. "That means no dating."

"I'm pretty sure sex buddies don't date."

"I'm just getting the rules straight. Sex buddies do not go for coffee together. They don't see movies together. They don't do anything together outside of sex."

"We've never been to a movie or to have coffee together," Griffin replied.

"No, but we have been to a haunted maze together."

"Fair point."

"Some people might consider that date behavior." Ava thought back to how Lindsey and Maya had reacted when she'd told them about the event. "We should probably refrain from mentioning each other in anything other than clinical terms going forward."

"Okay." Griffin bobbed his head. "I can live with that."

"Do you have rules you would like to share with the class? Now would be a good time."

Griffin cocked his head as he considered it. "Not that I can think of offhand. Do I assume we're just going to do it here whenever the mood strikes? I mean, are we allowed to call each other if we're in the mood?"

"Oh, I don't know." The question threw Ava. "Do you want to be able to call me?"

"It might be nice to be able to arrange a time. Otherwise, I'll be stuck waiting for you to show up here, and with the weather changing soon..."

"Right. So we can call each other to set up specific times for interludes. Just because we call, however, that does not mean the other party has to drop everything for sex."

"I believe that goes without saying."

They fell into silence. It should've been awkward. But it wasn't.

"Is there anything else you think we should cover?" Griffin asked.

"Just that we should both agree now that, whenever somebody gets bored or finds someone they really want to date, they can walk away without a lick of guilt."

"No questions asked," Griffin agreed. "This is a temporary thing. We scratched an itch we probably shouldn't have scratched, but it's okay because we're both adults and know the score."

"Right." Ava beamed at him as she rolled to her side. "This was a very mature discussion."

"It's the most mature discussion I've ever had while naked. Do you want to see what else we can figure out to do while naked?"

Ava's jaw dropped. "Again? Shouldn't that be impossible?" She glanced down at Griffin's crotch. "Apparently not." A giggle escaped. "Is this you calling me?"

"This still counts as the first time, Ava," he replied with mock severity. "I think we should take advantage of the situation."

"Okay, but next time, I expect some blankets out here. I really am worried a spider bit my butt or something."

As if to reassure her otherwise, Griffin gave her butt a pleasant squeeze as he rolled her on top of him. "Next time, we won't do it out here, in front of our audience." He glared at the black cat, who had ventured close enough that Griffin could hear him purring. "We'll do it in the house, in an actual bed."

"Would sex buddies do it in a bed?"

"Doing it in a bed just means we're not animals," Griffin replied. "I don't mind the barn, but if the temperature drops another three or four degrees, it's going to be way too cold for my friend to want to play."

Ava nodded. "Good point. A bed, it is."

"I thought you would see things my way." He caught the back of her head and switched their positions so that Ava was the one with her back pressed into the straw. "I have to say this might be the best idea I've ever had," he mused as he rubbed his lips against hers. He wasn't exactly kissing her, but he was gearing up to start.

"I'm pretty sure it was my idea," Ava argued.

"No. It was mine."

"Mine."

"Mine."

They glared at each other.

"We'll argue about that later," Griffin said then slammed his mouth against hers.

Ava had the distinct impression he was trying to shut her up.

He pulled back. "For now, we should just explore our new understanding."

"You read my mind."

"Funny how that worked out."

16
SIXTEEN

Being friends with benefits turned out to be fun. Every day, Ava came to the farm to catch cats. The remaining few were wily, though, and she grew frustrated after a few hours. After that, she and Griffin went through the barn or the garage, and she told him what she'd had planned for the farm before he claimed it. With each passing day, Griffin could see her vision all the clearer. And it sounded nice, something he wouldn't have been able to admit—or perhaps feel—weeks before. That was why he decided to have a sit-down meeting with his attorney on a Zoom call to hash things out.

"You're actually thinking of staying there?" Jim Reynolds was a former classmate of Griffin's, and they'd kept in touch over the years. When Griffin went into business with his father, he'd felt as if he needed his own representation. Jim slid in seamlessly and had become a friend as much as a lawyer.

"Maybe," Griffin replied. He found it hard to make eye contact with Jim.

"No offense, Griff, but you've never struck me as the

sort of guy who thrives when there's not a Starbucks on every corner."

"There's a very good coffee shop here. The eclairs are amazing too."

Jim just sat there, looking skeptical.

"I like the quiet," Griffin volunteered. "I don't have to be something I'm not here."

"You mean Gerald Holden's son?" Jim asked softly, and sympathy practically rolled off him in waves. "Do you want to hear how things have been going here since you left?"

"Probably not," Griffin muttered.

"I'm going to tell you anyway. The gossip has died down, Griff. People aren't calling for your head any longer. I talked to the prosecutor the other day, and he thinks you'll just have to pay a fine when the dust settles."

"Am I supposed to celebrate that?" Griffin demanded. "Two people are dead, Jim."

Jim blinked rapidly but held it together. "I'm well aware. Everybody feels sorry for those people. But they were in an area they weren't supposed to be in."

"They were homeless and trying to survive."

"Well, yes, but nobody is claiming them, Griff," Jim insisted. "Nobody is threatening to come out of the woodwork and sue you for their deaths. That's a good thing."

"How?" Griffin's stomach was threatening to revolt. *Is that supposed to make me feel better?* It certainly wasn't.

"Even the reporters have forgotten about this. They've moved on to other stuff, like the trouble at the Ambassador Bridge, and all the money they're threatening to spend on the Belle Isle Zoo renovation. Your little mishap is falling off the radar. In fact, I think if you stay there for the winter, it will be okay for you to come back in the spring. By summer at the absolute latest."

Griffin worked his jaw. "And what if I don't want to come back?"

"Then I'm going to have to drive up there and check your temperature. Not in a gross way. I won't stick a thermometer up your butt or anything."

"Thank the maker for small favors," Griffin drawled. "I'm being serious. What are my options if I want to stay here?"

Jim blinked again. "And do what?"

"I don't know." Griffin averted his eyes again. "Say I wanted to convert my grandfather's property into a bed-and-breakfast. Do I have the money for that? Can I make it happen?" When he risked a glance at Jim, his mouth was hanging open.

Jim was not the sort of person who could keep his opinion to himself, so he said the exact words Griffin was expecting. "Are you kidding me right now?"

"No." Griffin had known there would be pushback, and he hadn't even told his father about his potential plans yet. Not that they were communicating much lately. "I'm serious. Do I have the money to not only update this place but also run it without making a profit for a year?"

"Unbelievable," Jim muttered. "Um ... let me look." He started tapping on his computer. "How much do you think it will cost to renovate the farm?"

Griffin thought back to the estimate Bear had given him. Then he doubled it. "We're talking a good five hundred grand to do absolutely everything."

"Really?" Jim's forehead creased. "That's not as bad as I was expecting."

"It's not like building a hotel down there or anything," Griffin explained. "We're talking six rooms overall. I'm considering converting the barn into a space for me and using the house as a bed-and-breakfast. During peak season, I'd have full occupancy—and that's more often than you might expect—and if I rent the rooms for between a thousand and fifteen hundred for a week, that's like seventy-two hundred to nine thousand a week."

"Yeah, but you can make six figures off one design down here."

And shake with anxiety the entire time, Griffin silently added. "It's less pressure to do the bed-and-breakfast."

"Yeah, but you're not going to make that every week," Jim insisted. "What happens when it snows?"

"Actually, the rooms would be full when we have snow because this is a huge area for snowmobiling and skiing. There are snowmobile trails directly across the road, and I can even build some here on what used to be the fields. People would love it."

"So wait, you're saying you could keep those rooms filled in the winter too?" Jim looked baffled. "When would the downtime be?"

"Well, summer is for golfing and vacations." Griffin had given the project a great deal of thought, and it wasn't hard to lay it out. "Fall is for color tours. It's a big deal up here. The leaves are mostly gone by Halloween, though. Then it's drab until the snow starts flying. That's the window we're in now.

"I expect I would have about two months of downtime in late fall, heading toward early winter," he continued. "That's a worst-case scenario, though, because I still think I would be selling out some of the rooms during that time."

Jim nodded, taking it all in.

"Then in the spring, I'd run into the same problem as fall," Griffin explained. "Once the snow goes, and the ground is too wet to golf, there's another six-to-eight-week stretch when people don't visit as much."

"So on bad years, that's four months downtime," Jim replied.

"Yes, but I still think there will be visitors during that time."

"Okay, but let's talk about staff. You have to feed the guests, right? That means hiring a cook."

Griffin rubbed the back of his neck. Ava was the one who had explained that part to him, and it had only made him more eager to consider the bed-and-breakfast. "Actually, I would just have to arrange to have doughnuts and sticky buns delivered in the mornings. That local coffee shop I mentioned could handle it. They don't expect food at bed-and-breakfasts. They handle all that themselves. They would have access to the kitchen to make whatever they wanted, if they cared about that—and I have it on good authority that they don't care about that—so my biggest expenses would be upkeep on the property and cleaners," he said.

"That's it?" Jim looked baffled.

"It's not like a hotel," Griffin stressed. "The people I've been talking to know a lot about the bed-and-breakfast industry up here. I think it could be a good investment."

"Yes, well, it doesn't sound horrible," Jim grudgingly admitted. "You're going to need grounds crews, too, to handle the snow, because we know you're not going to do that."

"True." Griffin managed a smile. "Shoveling is never going to be my thing."

"Are there any other prospects for bringing in money?" Jim asked as he started writing on a pad of paper.

"A few things," Griffin replied. "During the Halloween

season, those corn mazes are popular. I was thinking maybe we could do small crops, like corn and pumpkins. This woman I met took me to one in another city the other day, and it was packed. They're clearly raking it in, although that would be seasonal."

Suspicion filled Jim's eyes. "This woman you met?"

"Don't," Griffin warned him, extending a finger. "She's just a friend." Even saying it made him feel guilty. Ava was more than that, although he couldn't admit it to her.

"If you say so. Who is going to plant these crops?"

"I was thinking I would figure it out." Griffin averted his gaze.

"You're going to grow corn? Do tell."

"My grandfather did it. I helped him some summers. I'll need someone to help, but I think I can manage it. I'm not trying to feed the town or anything."

"Fine." Jim held his hands up in supplication. "I'm not going to argue about the corn. The thing is your finances are in pretty good shape. You still have a decent amount invested. If I were you, though, I wouldn't risk those investments on this little endeavor. I would keep them separate. That's your retirement and risking it on a whim is not a good idea."

Griffin wanted to tell him it wasn't a whim, but even he wasn't certain that was true. "Just ballpark it for me."

"You need to sell your house down here. You can get the five hundred grand you need for the renovations from the house, and you have more than enough money in your other accounts for whatever incidentals you might need. Even if I go low end and completely cut off income from those four months you mentioned, you're still looking at bringing in three hundred grand during the other weeks. You should easily be able to take care of your taxes and hiring a grounds crew and maids and still have plenty to live on up there. The cost of living isn't high."

"So I can do it." Griffin didn't know whether he was happy or sad to hear it.

"You can. The question is are you going to do it?"

"I don't know. I need to think on it a bit. I just wanted to know if it was even possible."

"It is."

"Great."

"Uh-huh." Jim didn't appear to be in a hurry to end the call. "Tell me about the girl who took you to the other place."

Griffin jolted ramrod straight. "Oh, look at the time. I have to be going. I have things to do in the barn."

Jim rolled his eyes. "You're not getting rid of me that easily. We're going to finish this conversation another time."

"Talk to you later." Griffin left the meeting room and let out a breath. The bed-and-breakfast idea that Ava kept bringing up was not only doable but also capable of being a long-term business model. *So what do I want to do with that information?*

"I LOVE WHAT YOU'VE DONE WITH THE PLACE, MA," Ava said dryly, wrinkling her nose as she took in her mother's filthy kitchen. It was the same house she'd grown up in—plus a few extra holes in the drywall—but it seemed so much smaller to her, which should've been impossible because she spent her formative years convinced she was about to suffocate as the walls closed in on her.

"Yeah, it's coming along." Darla Mason lit a cigarette as she sat at the small table on the other side of the island and fixed Ava with a shrewd stare. "How come you're here? I can't remember the last time you stopped in for a visit."

Why am I here? Ava wasn't certain she could answer. Griffin had been asking her questions about her childhood, though. He was understandably curious about why she'd constantly hidden out in his grandfather's barn just so she could read. So far separated from her childhood, Ava was trying to come up with an answer for herself as much as him.

"I just wondered what you were doing these days," Ava replied, her gaze going to a framed photograph on the wall. It was the only decoration that hadn't come from a bar and the nicest photo of her parents that existed. They were, of course, at a bar. For once, they didn't appear to be fighting. The photo was from before alcohol had ravaged her father's looks and liver.

"When was that taken?" She pointed toward the picture.

Darla beamed at it. "That was 2002. What a great year."

Twenty years ago, Ava mused. "Where was I in 2002, Ma?"

Darla looked baffled by the question. "What? How should I know?"

"That's what I thought," Ava muttered.

Because she couldn't help herself, she retrieved a garbage bag from beneath the sink and started attacking the mess. Her mother had stopped worrying about keeping the house clean when her father died twelve years ago. The house smelled like a landfill, but oddly enough, that wasn't the reason Ava never visited.

"So, I've been spending some time at the Holden farm," she started.

"I heard." Darla looked smug. "Everybody in town is

Griffin teased her. "If you want to dress up, though, I'll be more than happy to give you a treat."

Ava glared at him even as a ripple of desire coursed through her. *What is it about this man that continuously gets me so excited?* She'd never felt anything like it. But she wouldn't admit that to him. "Do you have a big bowl of chocolate hidden under your shirt that I don't know about? That's the only treat I'm looking for tonight."

Griffin shot her a knowing look. "Is that so?"

"Yup."

"Well, I can probably come up with a bowl of candy. I'll have to run to town because I didn't bother stocking up, given I'm so far away from the action."

"You probably would've gotten looky-loos regardless. You're the hot new commodity in town. All the single mothers would've driven their kids out here just so they could have an excuse to see you up close and personal."

"And now you're saying that won't happen because of the rain?"

"All the kids will go to smaller house parties and eat all the candy the parents bought to hand out. That's how it is here."

"You sound pretty sad about that."

"I just love Halloween." Ava rubbed her hands together to ward off the cold. "It's always been my favorite holiday."

"And why is that?"

She shrugged one shoulder. "I don't know. I guess I like the idea of being able to venture outside your comfort zone and be someone else for a night. It's not realistic over the long haul, but if I want to be a sexy nurse for a night, then it's allowed."

"You can be my slutty nurse if you want."

"I said sexy."

"I... Huh. So you did." Griffin gave a sheepish smile. "You can be my sexy nurse."

"I was going to be a cow this year. I had an adorable costume."

Griffin's expression was hard to read. "You were going to be a cow? You just said you were going to be a sexy nurse."

"No, I said I could be a sexy nurse if I wanted to be. That doesn't mean I wanted to be. I was a sexy nurse three Halloweens ago. This year, I was going to be a cow. I had a bell and everything."

Griffin touched his tongue to his top lip, seemingly debating, then held out his hands. "Were you at least going to be a sexy cow?"

"You've seen me naked. What do you think?"

"I think that you would make the sexiest cow ever." He frowned. "That came out way weirder than I thought it would."

"Whatever turns you on."

"Yeah, let's change the discussion. How do you feel about coming over here to watch movies with me tonight? I can pick up some candy and pizza in town, and we can hang out together. You can spend the night."

Ava's shoulders jolted. They'd been together multiple times since they'd come up with their rules. Never once had those instances included a sleepover. "You want me to spend the night?"

"There's no reason for you to go out in the rain when it's unnecessary. If you're going to be here anyway..." Griffin seemed uncomfortable. "I mean, if you're not doing anything else."

Ava considered how she wanted to respond. Part of her thought it was a terrible idea. The more time they spent together, the more "normal" their situation would seem. Neither of them wanted that. On the flip side, watching horror movies, gorging on candy and pizza, and snuggling up with him was pretty much her idea of a perfect night.

"We're still on the same page, right?" she asked. "Like, we're still just friends with benefits."

"We are. I'm not asking you to marry me. I simply don't see a need for you to be on the roads late at night when the temperature is plunging below freezing and the roads could glaze over. If you're uncomfortable with that thought—"

"Who said I was uncomfortable?"

"You're acting uncomfortable."

"I'm acting like my normal self."

"If you say so." Griffin's expression told Ava he was starting to regret extending the invitation. "Forget I said anything."

"I would love to watch movies and eat pizza. Candy wouldn't hurt either."

"Oh yeah?" Griffin arched an eyebrow. "You're not going to get weird on me, are you?"

"That's not the plan, although sometimes when I get hyped up on sugar, I turn weird through no fault of my own. I really can't control it."

"I'll take that under advisement." He licked his lips. "So, does seven work for you?"

"Sure." She bobbed her head. "Can I pick the movies?"

"I don't know. What are you going to pick?"

"I have a few ideas. I'll surprise you."

"Okay, but it had better not be anything gross. I don't like movies where people's insides end up on their outsides."

"I'll keep that in mind."

. . .

GRIFFIN HAD JUST PULLED INTO THE DRIVEWAY with the pizza and candy when Ava parked behind him. He could make out her features under the dome light in her truck and noted that she'd showered, taken the time to do her hair, and had even put on makeup. She looked beautiful.

He forced himself to look away and exited his SUV. He jogged to the front door and only allowed himself to breathe when he was inside. *Why does she have to be so beautiful?* It was making him think the sort of things he shouldn't be thinking, and he was mad at himself.

He shouldn't have invited her for a sleepover. He'd known that as he was doing it. Despite that, he wanted her to sleep over more than he'd ever wanted anything else. The entire thing was dumbfounding.

The sound of her footsteps stomping against the front mat forced him out of his reverie. He had a smile on his face when Ava appeared with a duffel bag in her hand.

"Hey," she said. If he wasn't mistaken, she was nervous.

Well, join the club. But he was also excited. It wasn't just that he wanted to fall asleep with her wrapped around him —although he did—he also wanted to wake up with her. He craved a bit of normalcy in his life because nothing had felt normal or comfortable for a very long time. Even though his skin practically hummed when he was around Ava, and his heart often wanted to pound out of his chest, he was comfortable with her.

More than that, things felt right with her. *Isn't that a kick in the pants?* At a time when he should be lamenting all that had gone wrong, he was marveling at what felt right. She was obviously magical. That was the only thing that made sense.

"Did you say something?" he asked when he realized

talking about you and Old Chuck's grandson. Apparently, he's handsome and drives a 2020 model Ford. You should totally jump on that."

Ava furrowed her brow. "I don't really care what he drives."

"If he has a newer model vehicle, that means he has money," Darla insisted. "I've never been a fan of that farm, but maybe you can convince him to sell it or something."

"I wanted to buy that farm," Ava reminded her mother on a wave of frustration. "That was always my dream."

Darla wrinkled her nose. "Why? Who wants to work on a farm?"

"I don't want to work on a farm. I want to turn it into a bed-and-breakfast."

"Yeah, that doesn't sound much better." Darla shook her head and took a long drag on her cigarette. "Do you know what you should do?"

"No, and I don't want to hear it." Ava purposely made a bunch of noise when sweeping the old fast-food bags into the garbage bag.

Darla apparently didn't care what her daughter did or did not want. "You should stop taking your birth control so you get pregnant. Don't tell him that's what you're doing or anything. When the stick turns pink, just tell him your birth control failed. You'll have him then."

Disgusted, Ava asked, "Isn't that the ruse you pulled on Dad?"

"Yeah, and it worked like a charm." Darla took another drag on her smoke. "We were happy, despite how we got together."

"That's not exactly how I remember it."

"And how do you remember it?"

"I remember you guys screaming at each other. I remember you throwing things. I remember ... other stuff."

Darla gave a dismissive wave. "You were always such a whiner as a kid. You made a big deal over that stuff. That's just how your father and I communicated."

"It was a big deal to me."

"Oh, I remember." Darla made a sound that was half snort and half chuckle. "You were such a baby about that stuff. You would take off in the middle of the night and sleep in that stupid barn. I couldn't understand why you wanted to hide out there by yourself when we had a perfectly good house here."

"No, you could never understand," Ava agreed. The barn had been the only thing to save her as a kid. Anything was better than listening to her father and mother go at each other, even freezing to death.

In the dead of winter, the barn could hardly be considered warm. She still snuck inside to hide from what was happening at home. The first few times Chuck had found her, he'd called her parents, understandably confused. It didn't take him long to figure out what was going on once they showed up to claim her, although he never pressed Ava on the issue. Instead, he decked out the loft with blankets and a small heater. He'd stressed that she had to be careful with the heater so as not to inadvertently spark a fire. Because he'd been serious, Ava was serious when following his rules.

That barn had been her salvation. It bothered her that her mother couldn't see it.

"I just wanted to stop by and see how you were doing, Ma," Ava said blandly as she lowered the garbage bag to the chipped linoleum floor. *This has been a wasted visit.* They were all wasted visits. "I have to get going, though. I have stuff to do."

"You mean get pregnant." Darla gave an exaggerated wink. "I understand. You definitely need to get on that."

"Definitely," Ava replied flatly, hating her mother with every syllable. "That sounds exactly like something I would do."

17
SEVENTEEN

Halloween hit with a monsoon, and Ava's disappointment was palpable.

"There won't be any trick-or-treaters," she lamented as she stared through the open door of the barn and wrinkled her nose. The rain bucketed down, and they hadn't caught a single cat in days. She was starting to despair.

Griffin moved to stand next to her. His presence was unmistakable, even though she didn't look at him. He exuded warmth, and she was starting to get attached to it.

After they went two days without seeing each other—both of them seemingly agreeing that it was best not to make their dalliances a regular thing—they'd immediately thrown themselves at each other. The loft had been their welcome escape yet again. After that, they hadn't even bothered to pretend they weren't meeting in the barn because they wanted to see each other. They'd had sex another four times and were growing more and more comfortable together.

"You're a little old for trick-or-treating, aren't you?"

Griffin teased her. "If you want to dress up, though, I'll be more than happy to give you a treat."

Ava glared at him even as a ripple of desire coursed through her. *What is it about this man that continuously gets me so excited?* She'd never felt anything like it. But she wouldn't admit that to him. "Do you have a big bowl of chocolate hidden under your shirt that I don't know about? That's the only treat I'm looking for tonight."

Griffin shot her a knowing look. "Is that so?"

"Yup."

"Well, I can probably come up with a bowl of candy. I'll have to run to town because I didn't bother stocking up, given I'm so far away from the action."

"You probably would've gotten looky-loos regardless. You're the hot new commodity in town. All the single mothers would've driven their kids out here just so they could have an excuse to see you up close and personal."

"And now you're saying that won't happen because of the rain?"

"All the kids will go to smaller house parties and eat all the candy the parents bought to hand out. That's how it is here."

"You sound pretty sad about that."

"I just love Halloween." Ava rubbed her hands together to ward off the cold. "It's always been my favorite holiday."

"And why is that?"

She shrugged one shoulder. "I don't know. I guess I like the idea of being able to venture outside your comfort zone and be someone else for a night. It's not realistic over the long haul, but if I want to be a sexy nurse for a night, then it's allowed."

"You can be my slutty nurse if you want."

"I said sexy."

"I... Huh. So you did." Griffin gave a sheepish smile. "You can be my sexy nurse."

"I was going to be a cow this year. I had an adorable costume."

Griffin's expression was hard to read. "You were going to be a cow? You just said you were going to be a sexy nurse."

"No, I said I could be a sexy nurse if I wanted to be. That doesn't mean I wanted to be. I was a sexy nurse three Halloweens ago. This year, I was going to be a cow. I had a bell and everything."

Griffin touched his tongue to his top lip, seemingly debating, then held out his hands. "Were you at least going to be a sexy cow?"

"You've seen me naked. What do you think?"

"I think that you would make the sexiest cow ever." He frowned. "That came out way weirder than I thought it would."

"Whatever turns you on."

"Yeah, let's change the discussion. How do you feel about coming over here to watch movies with me tonight? I can pick up some candy and pizza in town, and we can hang out together. You can spend the night."

Ava's shoulders jolted. They'd been together multiple times since they'd come up with their rules. Never once had those instances included a sleepover. "You want me to spend the night?"

"There's no reason for you to go out in the rain when it's unnecessary. If you're going to be here anyway..." Griffin seemed uncomfortable. "I mean, if you're not doing anything else."

Ava considered how she wanted to respond. Part of her thought it was a terrible idea. The more time they spent together, the more "normal" their situation would seem. Neither of them wanted that. On the flip side, watching horror movies, gorging on candy and pizza, and snuggling up with him was pretty much her idea of a perfect night.

"We're still on the same page, right?" she asked. "Like, we're still just friends with benefits."

"We are. I'm not asking you to marry me. I simply don't see a need for you to be on the roads late at night when the temperature is plunging below freezing and the roads could glaze over. If you're uncomfortable with that thought—"

"Who said I was uncomfortable?"

"You're acting uncomfortable."

"I'm acting like my normal self."

"If you say so." Griffin's expression told Ava he was starting to regret extending the invitation. "Forget I said anything."

"I would love to watch movies and eat pizza. Candy wouldn't hurt either."

"Oh yeah?" Griffin arched an eyebrow. "You're not going to get weird on me, are you?"

"That's not the plan, although sometimes when I get hyped up on sugar, I turn weird through no fault of my own. I really can't control it."

"I'll take that under advisement." He licked his lips. "So, does seven work for you?"

"Sure." She bobbed her head. "Can I pick the movies?"

"I don't know. What are you going to pick?"

"I have a few ideas. I'll surprise you."

"Okay, but it had better not be anything gross. I don't like movies where people's insides end up on their outsides."

"I'll keep that in mind."

. . .

GRIFFIN HAD JUST PULLED INTO THE DRIVEWAY with the pizza and candy when Ava parked behind him. He could make out her features under the dome light in her truck and noted that she'd showered, taken the time to do her hair, and had even put on makeup. She looked beautiful.

He forced himself to look away and exited his SUV. He jogged to the front door and only allowed himself to breathe when he was inside. *Why does she have to be so beautiful?* It was making him think the sort of things he shouldn't be thinking, and he was mad at himself.

He shouldn't have invited her for a sleepover. He'd known that as he was doing it. Despite that, he wanted her to sleep over more than he'd ever wanted anything else. The entire thing was dumbfounding.

The sound of her footsteps stomping against the front mat forced him out of his reverie. He had a smile on his face when Ava appeared with a duffel bag in her hand.

"Hey," she said. If he wasn't mistaken, she was nervous.

Well, join the club. But he was also excited. It wasn't just that he wanted to fall asleep with her wrapped around him —although he did—he also wanted to wake up with her. He craved a bit of normalcy in his life because nothing had felt normal or comfortable for a very long time. Even though his skin practically hummed when he was around Ava, and his heart often wanted to pound out of his chest, he was comfortable with her.

More than that, things felt right with her. *Isn't that a kick in the pants?* At a time when he should be lamenting all that had gone wrong, he was marveling at what felt right. She was obviously magical. That was the only thing that made sense.

"Did you say something?" he asked when he realized

the silence had stretched on for longer than could've been considered comfortable.

Ava smirked. "I asked what kind of pizza you got."

"Oh." Griffin shook his head to force himself to focus. "I got one with meat and one without because I wasn't certain how you felt about sausage."

Ava's eyebrows rose in a suggestive manner, causing him to grin.

"I heard it as I was saying it. There's no reason to comment on it."

"Who said I was going to comment on it?" Ava dropped her bag onto the kitchen floor and sauntered over to check out the boxes. "This is more than two pizzas."

Griffin's nerves came out to play again. "Yeah. I got pizza, wings, breadsticks, and one of those huge cookies."

"And that's the candy?" Ava pointed toward the grocery bags.

"It was already on sale. I made sure to get the bag with the Snickers."

"That's definitely the best bag." Ava studied him. "So, um, do you want to eat in here or in the living room?"

"The living room is good." Griffin moved to the cupboards. "Are you okay with paper plates? It makes for easier cleanup."

"Sure." Ava gathered several of the food boxes and looped the grocery bag around her wrist. "I'll meet you in there."

"Okay." Griffin watched her go, his eyes automatically lowering to her ass. The way she swung it did ridiculous things to his stomach—and other parts of him. By the time he'd gotten himself together and grabbed the other boxes as well as the plates and utensils, she was cueing up the first movie.

"I just logged in to my account. That's okay, right? I saw that you'd brought a television with you the day you moved in. All of Chuck's TVs were older, so this wouldn't have been possible if you hadn't done that."

"It's fine," he assured her. "What's up first?"

"Well, it might be a bit on the nose, but I was thinking we would go with *Halloween*."

Griffin frowned. "What did I say about people's insides ending up on their outsides?"

"That doesn't happen in this movie. Sure, the sequels are bloody gorefests, but there's no blood in the original. I like all horror movies, even the bad ones. I like gory ones, too, but I made a promise to you. Everything I picked lacks gore, and you have veto power."

"So if we get into it, and I don't like it, you'll change the movie?"

"Yes." Ava bobbed her head. "I'll pull up *Hocus Pocus* and call it a night."

Griffin scowled. "I'm not seven."

"You haven't seen *Halloween*. That tells me you're a horror movie virgin. You can never be too careful when dealing with a virgin."

Griffin choked out a laugh. "Is that so? Just so I know, what other movies have you picked for this evening?"

"Well, I figured we would go with *The Ring* after. That's also bloodless and has terrifying ambiance. I kind of want *The Shining* for the big finale, but you're likely not ready for that."

"I know there's blood in *The Shining*."

"Yes, but it's not gory blood. Blood flows out of the elevator, and there's some on clothes in quick flashes, but in general, it's a psychological movie."

"What if I'm not ready for that?"

"I promise to sleep close and protect you." Ava gave a winsome smile.

Sighing, Griffin nodded. He had no idea why he was even pretending to put up a fight. "Fine. If I'm afraid, though, you're going to have to do dirty things to make me forget. We're talking sweaty, sexy, dirty things. No cows allowed."

Ava laughed, the sound suffusing the room with warmth. "I think I can manage that."

GRIFFIN LEARNED QUICKLY THAT JUST BECAUSE a movie wasn't gory, that didn't mean it wasn't scary. By the time they finished *The Shining*, he was at his limit.

"I cannot take another second of this." He tugged the blanket they'd been cuddling under—*how did that even happen?*—over his face and cringed when the movie score built to a crescendo.

"It's almost over," Ava whispered. Her warm breath hit the side of his neck, and when Griffin looked up, he found that her mouth was extremely close.

They hadn't made out during the movies. They'd cuddled, sure, but there hadn't been any excessive groping. Small touches, some accidental, had led to a heightening of his senses throughout the evening. Now, shortly before midnight, as Jack Nicholson was stalking his movie son through a creepy hotel, Griffin was so worked up that he felt like an exposed nerve. The entire date—because that was what it had been, even though neither of them wanted to admit it—had been leading up to one thing.

Griffin didn't care if the kid died. He didn't care if the ghosts won. All he cared about was that Ava's mouth was tantalizingly close to his, and they weren't yet kissing. "We should go to bed," he rasped.

Ava's eyebrows rose. "Don't you want to see how the movie ends?"

"I'm pretty sure the screaming wife and kid somehow escape," he replied. "That old cook brought them a vehicle to escape in. That's how they get away, right?"

Ava nodded. "There's a maze chase, though."

Griffin blindly searched for the remote. "We can watch it over breakfast tomorrow." He clicked off the television and then captured her face in his hands. "Let's make our own movie."

Ava laughed. "That came out more perverted than you thought it would, didn't it?"

"Maybe a little. I still want to switch to a rom-com."

"Yeah. Horror movies are overrated."

"I've been trying to tell you that."

TWO HOURS LATER, WITH AVA CURLED INTO HIS SIDE, Griffin was sated and ready for sleep to claim him. The sound of her steady breathing lulled him, and even though he wasn't used to sharing a bed with someone, he felt unbelievably comfortable with her next to him.

It seemed almost as if she belonged there. No, it was more than that. They belonged together—touching, falling to sleep together, and waking up together. He was becoming more and more attached to the idea of it.

How would she feel if I brought it up, though? Even if she felt the same way, and he was starting to think she did, that didn't mean she would be open to the idea of a relationship. They barely knew each other. The start of their interaction had been less than ideal, and they had very little in common.

You're not thinking about marrying her, his inner voice reminded him. *There's no harm in dating.*

If they were to date, they would have to do it publicly. Hiding a potential relationship could irreparably harm both of them. He needed time to think.

Ava let out a soft whine. At first, he thought it was a sigh. The second time, however, he realized it was a whimper. She was having a bad dream.

Determined to shift her out of it without waking her, he tugged her close. Her head landed on his shoulder, her hand on his heart, and that time, the noise she made was definitely a sigh.

"You watch too many horror movies," he muttered as he stared down at her face, which was just barely visible, thanks to the old clock on the nightstand. "We need to start branching out with the things you watch."

She didn't respond, of course. But she didn't whimper again either. She was dead to the world.

After what felt like a really long time of staring at her—he was convinced he would never get tired of looking at her face—he followed her into dreamland. No nightmares waited for him.

18

EIGHTEEN

Ava woke before Griffin the next morning and was shocked to find she'd somehow wrapped herself around him in sleep. That wasn't normal for her. Of course, she didn't have a trail of serious relationships in her wake to use for comparison's sake, but she'd had a few mildly serious relationships that included regular sleepovers. But she'd never woken up that way with any of them.

"Hey," Griffin said with a husky voice as he stirred.

Ava held her breath and waited for him to realize not only had she drooled on his chest, but also their legs were so entangled that it was impossible to ascertain where she began, and he ended. Instead, he hugged her tighter and sleepily pressed a kiss to her forehead.

"What time is it?" he murmured.

"A little before eight o'clock," Ava replied. He had to still be waking up. That was the only explanation for why he hadn't pulled away from her as if his hair were on fire.

"It's early," he chided her. He traced a lazy pattern over her spine with his fingers. "Go back to sleep."

She blinked. *Is he really not going to say anything?* "I drooled on your chest," she blurted.

"That's okay." Griffin kept his eyes closed as he stroked a hand over her hair. "It's good to keep hydrated."

Ava furrowed her brow. "Is that all you're going to say?"

"What else should I say? Also, shh." He put his hand back on her back. "If you allow yourself to relax, then maybe you'll go back to sleep."

Is he joking? They had a serious problem. It was supposed to be a friends-with-benefits situation. Waking up the way they had proved they were straying into dangerous territory—relationship territory.

She took a breath, then thought again. *It is relationship territory, right?* She wasn't making that up in her head. She didn't have a lot to compare it to. Maybe she was wrong, and it was innocent. She would feel like a moron if she made a big deal about it, and it turned out that there was nothing to complain about.

"Um..." Her stomach picked that moment to growl so loudly that it echoed throughout the room.

Griffin arched an eyebrow and opened one eye. "Are you hungry?"

"I shouldn't be," Ava admitted. "I ate more calories last night than I normally eat in a week."

"Join the club." Griffin stretched his arms over his head.

That would've been a perfect time for Ava to make her escape. But she didn't. He was too warm and cuddly to roll away from.

"How did you sleep?" Ava asked, trying to drag things out so she could continue doing ... whatever it was they were doing.

"Pretty good," Griffin replied. "I had a dream about Jack Nicholson chasing me with a chainsaw, but I'm pretty sure that was just a hodgepodge of stuff that's been building since the corn maze."

"Young Jack Nicholson or old Jack Nicholson?"

"Does it matter?"

Ava shrugged. "Well, I'm willing to bet that young Jack Nicholson would have an easier time catching you. Old Jack Nicholson is in his eighties now, so you could outrun him."

"Good point." Griffin's cheek landed against her forehead. It should've felt as if he were invading her personal space, but it didn't. It felt right.

Dammit! This isn't supposed to feel right.

"Who is your favorite horror movie killer?" Griffin asked.

Ava was convinced he was only asking the question because he felt awkward. They were in uncharted territory, and they were both grappling with how to get themselves out of the mess they'd made. Since she didn't know what else to do, she opted to play along.

"Are we talking single movie or franchise?"

"Does it matter?"

"Yes."

"Um ... single movie."

"Then Jack Torrance would be my favorite. *The Shining* is a classic for a reason. Some people don't like it because they say it doesn't follow the book close enough, but I happen to love it. I'm not really a book purist."

"Who is your favorite franchise killer?"

"That would be Jason Voorhees. I like the setting of Crystal Lake, and even though there are some duds in the franchise—don't even get me started on *Jason Goes to Hell*— the tone of most of the movies is uniform. You don't always have that. Take the *Halloween* franchise, for example." She was babbling, but there was no stopping her. "The first movie is way better than any of the *Friday the 13th* movies. However, subsequent sequels were a hodgepodge, and I hate when a franchise rewrites timelines more than once. I'm willing to accept it once, but after that, it can't happen again."

"I see."

Ava barreled forward, needing to keep talking so that the conversation didn't turn to anything serious. She wasn't worried about Griffin saying something stupid. No, that honor went to her. She would say something moronic. If history had taught her anything, it was that she couldn't keep her mouth shut under pressure.

"So, the original *Halloween* timeline included Halloweens one, two, four, and five," she explained. "The third one doesn't fit in anywhere. There's no Michael Myers, and everybody hates the movie. It's just floating in the middle of the series.

"Anyway, Jamie Lee Curtis is killed off after the second movie, and they move on to her daughter, Jamie Lloyd, who is an orphan and living with another family when Michael comes calling. They do two movies of that before they switch things up with the Paul Rudd debacle."

Griffin dragged a hand through his hair. "I'm so lost."

Ava didn't blame him. She also didn't stop talking. "It was one of his first movies. They aged up Jamie, got her pregnant, killed her off, then had Paul Rudd take care of the baby. There was a cult angle. It was not good. It was so bad, in fact, that it basically killed the franchise for a bit."

"I can see that."

"Then they convinced Jamie Lee Curtis to come back. They made a great movie where she was in hiding and raising her son at a prep school. She was the headmistress.

She'd been hiding from Michael for years, and that whole daughter thing never happened."

Griffin nodded. "Okay, I'm starting to get it. That was the first retcon."

"Yes. The movie was amazing. Laurie cuts off Michael's head with an axe. There was no possible better ending."

"I'm guessing they didn't stick with that."

"No." Ava scowled. "The movie made so much money that they did another one, and Jamie Lee Curtis was done, so they killed her off in the opening minutes. Then they did a reality show movie with Michael killing people. It was freaking terrible. Tyra Banks should not be allowed to act."

"True story." Griffin's smile loosened up some of the angst that had been building inside Ava.

"Am I boring you?"

"No, I'm actually fascinated by the amount of knowledge you have on this subject. Please finish."

"Awesome." Ava shot him a thumbs-up. "*Halloween Resurrection* was a big flop. People were mad, and *Halloween* died again for a bit. Then they managed to entice Jamie Lee Curtis out of Laurie Strode retirement again. This time, they retconned the story about them being siblings as well as everything that happened at the prep school. They erased the son she had in that movie. The only movie that existed in this universe was the first one."

"This is where you get angry, right?"

"The first movie was good enough that I was willing to give it a shot," Ava replied. "People were excited. It was a solid movie. The problem was that they should've ended it with that movie. Did they?"

"I'm guessing no."

"Next was *Halloween Kills*, which was essentially a *Friday the 13th* movie instead of a *Halloween* movie. I didn't hate it, but it didn't do the things that a *Halloween* movie was supposed to do. Still, the actors looked like they were having fun, and there were some good kills."

"We're close to wrapping this up, right? I had no idea one person could talk so much about *Halloween* movies."

Ava didn't take offense. "I'm almost done. We're now at the final Jamie Lee Curtis *Halloween* movie. All the advertising billed it as the final showdown between Laurie and Michael. Do you want to know what happened?"

"I'm sitting on pins and needles."

Ava ignored the sarcasm. "They brought some new character in named Corey, turned Michael into a decrepit moron living in the sewer, and spent exactly ten minutes with Laurie and Michael. Fans melted down."

"And you think this has something to do with the second retcon?"

"I think that everybody would've been way better off if they'd ended things at the prep school. That was the perfect ending."

"Huh." Griffin looked at the clock on the nightstand. "You just did ten minutes on *Halloween* movies. Are you feeling less awkward now that you've gotten all that babbling out of your system?"

"You... I... You..." She didn't know what to say.

Griffin waited.

She gulped to center herself. "How did you know?"

"Because I've picked up on a few of your personality quirks over the past week or so," Griffin replied. "When you're feeling awkward and vulnerable, you start talking. You don't stop until the moment has passed."

Ava thought about denying it but didn't. "I had a moment when I wondered if we were crossing the friends-with-benefits line," she admitted.

"Yeah?" Griffin considered it. "I think we're fine. It's not as if we're going to start having sleepovers every night."

"Definitely not," Ava agreed. "It's just... I can't remember the last time I slept so hard."

An odd glint came to Griffin's eyes, but he nodded. "I'm glad. I slept pretty hard too. Maybe it was the sound of the rain. That always knocks me out."

Unconvinced, Ava replied, "Maybe. What are we going to do about breakfast? I don't really want Halloween candy or leftover pizza."

"Why do you assume that's all I have to eat?"

Ava waved a hand.

"Well, I'll have you know that breakfast is my favorite meal of the day. I sometimes eat it for dinner."

"Me too."

"That's good to know. I have eggs, toast, hash browns, and bacon in the kitchen. How about I cook for you, and you tell me more fascinating facts about horror movie killers?"

"You don't want to know more slasher killer facts."

"You might be surprised."

Ava considered it for all of two seconds. "That sounds good to me. I could do a whole rant on the things they did to Freddy Krueger. He was terrifying in the first movie, then they turned him into a caricature. It's sad, really."

"It sounds it." Griffin gave her a playful slap on her naked rear end. "Come on. I need to stop that stomach from growling, or I'm going to start having sympathy pangs."

"We can't have that."

"Definitely not."

. . .

GRIFFIN WATCHED AVA CLEAN UP THE LIVING room as he prepared breakfast. He'd recognized from the first moment he opened his eyes that she was feeling out of sorts. He'd been surprised when he realized she was plastered against him, their legs twined together. But he hadn't been upset by the development. It somehow felt right.

That realization made him feel awkward, so he was more than happy to let her babble about Michael Myers. Though he would have to get her to branch out on what she watched. He couldn't sit through an endless stream of slasher movies. He needed substance too.

What are you even saying? You're acting like this is going to be something you have to grapple with for the rest of your life. This is temporary.

He kept telling himself that over and over, but he wasn't certain he believed it. Even though Ava had given him an opening, he didn't walk through the door to broach the subject with her. He just wasn't there yet, and part of him wondered if it was because he was fearful that she would end things if he acknowledged there was more going on between them than just sex.

"Can I ask you something?" he blurted.

In the living room, Ava straightened. She had a garbage bag in her hand and was picking up all the candy wrappers they'd been too lazy to dispose of properly the previous evening. "I guess." She looked nervous. "If this is about that birthmark on my butt, I can't help that it looks like a pair of lips."

Griffin chuckled. "Actually, I think it looks more like a strawberry. But I don't care about the birthmark. Well, I care because it's so cute, and I have questions. That's not what I want to ask about right now, though."

"Okay. Shoot."

"You were whimpering in your sleep last night. Did you have a bad dream?"

The look on Ava's face made him immediately regret asking. She looked as if she needed a hole to crawl into.

"It's probably all the junk food I ate. You shouldn't have let me eat that last handful of candy."

"Yeah, but you seemed to be dreaming about something specific." Griffin had no idea why he couldn't let it go, but he'd felt protective when tucking her in at his side. Sure, she was a pain—and he would never think otherwise—but she also felt tiny and vulnerable in that moment. Griffin had wanted to stand as her shield. He'd never experienced anything like it.

"I'm guessing I dreamed about being trapped in a hotel, because I often dream that after watching *The Shining*. I can't remember though." She held her palms out. "Sorry."

"You don't have to apologize." He could tell she was lying and simply didn't want to tell him. The problem was that he didn't know whether she was reticent to share because she wanted to keep him at arm's length or she was embarrassed. The latter option intrigued him. It also frightened him. *Is she hiding something big?*

"I'm sure it was nothing." Ava went back to picking up garbage. "Don't worry about it, whatever it was. How is that breakfast coming?"

He had hash browns in a frying pan. They were the frozen kind but still good. The bacon was in a smaller pan, and he'd put bread in the toaster. That just left the eggs to tackle. "Seven minutes. Time me."

"If I'd known you could cook on top of everything else, I might've taken advantage of your culinary abilities before this. You're going to be in trouble when I'm over here catching cats from now on. If you don't give me food poisoning, I'm going to expect certain things going forward."

Griffin answered without thinking. "I'm sure that can be arranged."

Ava held his gaze for a long beat, the air between them swirling with emotions. Then she let out a breath. "I'm almost done with cleaning up."

"Meet me at the table when you're finished and prepare to be amazed."

"I'm looking forward to it."

19
NINETEEN

Relationships were funny. One second, they were comfortable and predictable. The next, they were edgy and surprising. Griffin had slowly come around to believing he was in a relationship. When he'd first met Ava, he was convinced she was an adorable mischief-maker who might be worth a good flirt. That opinion had only lasted several minutes, until he realized she was trouble.

Throughout the weeks of working together, however, he'd come to realize she was so much more.

More than a month after they'd met—and almost three weeks since their dynamics had shifted, and they'd ended up in bed together—they'd settled into a comfortable routine. They started in the barn, checking the humane cages set to catch the cats. They hadn't caught one in weeks, and between the One-Eyed Wonder and the Black Megalomaniac, they were starting to believe they never would. Five cats were left, and while the rescue was still helping, they were getting antsy about holding the cats that were supposed to return to the barn. They were running out of room. Ava had promised they would figure something out—mixing the cats who hadn't been vaccinated and tested with the cats who had seemed like a bad idea—but she was running on fumes.

After finishing in the barn, they moved into the house. Chuck hadn't been a hoarder, but he also wasn't the sort of guy who threw much away. That meant they had a lot of old treasures to go through, and Ava was better than Griffin at identifying things that should be kept.

The conversations they had when sorting varied. Some were light and fluffy, some were of no consequence whatsoever, and all were full of flirty innuendo. Every single sorting session ended with their tongues in each other's mouths. More often than not, they moved to the bedroom —well, as long as one of them didn't have an appointment to keep. Even then, sometimes, they made up an excuse on the phone. It was happening more and more frequently, and more importantly, it was starting to feel more and more real.

At least to Griffin, that was. He sometimes caught her looking at him in the reflection of an old mirror or out of the corner of his eye, and he thought things might be changing for her too. *What am I supposed to do about that, though?* He hadn't even decided if he was going to stay in Bellaire for the foreseeable future. If he planned on staying in architecture—which he didn't want to think about too much—there wouldn't be many opportunities in the area. He would have to return to the city.

Do I want that, though? Watching Ava swing her hips and dance to the music on her phone as she cleaned out the pantry made him believe that the country offered more than the city ever could. *What about Ava?* If he did want to explore having something serious with her, he couldn't see her living in the city. Her life was in Bellaire, where she knew everybody and had a plan for her future.

And what about that future? He'd taken the farm she wanted. In the back of his head, he was starting to imagine what it would be like if they turned the farm into a bed-and-breakfast together. Whenever he started going down that route, the little voice inside his head told him he didn't live in a romance novel. Things never worked out that perfectly for people. Destiny wasn't at play.

Yet part of him—a part that was growing each and every day—thought maybe it was possible. *If it is, do I want to chase that life? Do I want to settle down on a farm with Ava, run a bed-and-breakfast, and eventually chase kids across the fields and bed down with her in a barn for the rest of my life?*

The old Griffin would've scoffed at the notion. Bellaire Griffin, however, didn't think that sounded all that bad. When he allowed himself the luxury of considering that future, the flash of images that followed weren't terrible. In fact, they filled him with warmth and caused his chest to expand. He liked the idea, although that wasn't easy to admit, even to himself. On the flip side, when he thought about going south, dread settled in the pit of his stomach like a pound of undigested Brussels sprouts.

"What's with that face?" Ava demanded, emerging from the pantry with an armful of spices that looked as if they'd seen better days. "Did you get a whiff of something bad in there? Did it turn your stomach? Ugh. Please tell me Chuck didn't leave potatoes or onions in there." She dropped the spices onto the counter and returned to the pantry. "I don't smell anything, but sometimes I think my sense of smell is dead. It's probably from that time my head got shoved into the wall when I was a kid."

Griffin's brow furrowed as he tried to digest what she was saying. "I didn't smell anything. I was just thinking."

"Oh." She looked relieved when her face appeared again.

"When was your head shoved into a wall?" he asked. "Is that some weird Bellaire High School initiation thing?"

Ava's face paled before she plastered on a fake smile. "Of course not." She laughed. "I was just being funny."

She wasn't, though. She was covering. *Was she really hit in the head as a kid?* Over the course of their time together, he'd started to get a sinking suspicion that something very dark had happened with Ava and her parents. Occasionally, she brought up her mother. Her father, however, was never a topic of conversation. When Griffin had asked, she'd shut down that line of questioning quickly. That had only made him more suspicious.

In truth, Griffin wanted to protect Ava. He was convinced her father had, at the very least, verbally mistreated her. He was starting to think physical abuse had been involved too, and he didn't like it, not one bit.

"Seriously, why do you keep making that face?" Ava whined. "What do you smell?"

"I don't smell anything," Griffin assured her, pulling himself together quickly. If he'd learned anything, it was that the fastest way to get Ava to shut down was to push her about something she wasn't ready to talk about. He needed an opportunity to ask his questions in a closed environment where she had no opportunity to flee.

"There is something, though." He'd been putting a conversation off for as long as possible, but he was just about out of time. "You know I'm selling my place down south so that I can afford all the renovations here, right?"

Ava nodded. "You mentioned it. You said you had things

in storage that were going to have to stay down there, but you were dumping the house."

"Yeah." Griffin exhaled heavily. "I have to empty the house this weekend. It's being put on the market next week. That means I have to get all my personal stuff out of it—not that there's a lot—and sign some papers. I also need to grab a few more things from the storage building. I didn't think ahead when packing clothes, and I want the rest of my wardrobe. Well, other than the suits. I don't want those."

"You're definitely going to want layers this winter," Ava agreed. "This house is drafty, and they're not starting the construction until after the first of the year."

Griffin had a joke ready about how she was going to be the one keeping him warm throughout the winter but kept it to himself. "I have to go down south this weekend. Like ... tomorrow."

"Oh." Disappointment flashed across Ava's face. "That's a bummer. I thought we could watch them decorate downtown. They do it before Thanksgiving every year, but it's awesome."

"I thought you didn't want to go anywhere in public together." Griffin didn't like how accusatory he sounded, but he couldn't help himself.

"I wasn't suggesting we go as a couple," Ava shot back. "I'm not an idiot. I just thought it was something you would want to see." She turned to look inside the pantry. "I wanted you to see it. Forget about it. It was a stupid idea."

Griffin wanted to kick himself. She was so enthusiastic sometimes that it was contagious, and he wanted to see the stupid decorating team work their magic downtown, even though he hadn't known it was a thing five seconds ago.

"I would like to see the decorations with you," he

blurted. Her smile when she turned made him go warm all over. "I have to go down south, though." He hated himself for snuffing the light in her eyes. "I was actually kind of wondering if you wanted to go with me."

He hadn't known he was going to extend the invitation until the words were already out of his mouth. Well, that wasn't entirely true. Part of him had known—the excitable part he was constantly trying to tamp down. Still, he usually had some idea of when he was going to upend his entire world. His plan had been to tell Ava he was going, then have a proper goodbye in bed. But the idea of saying goodbye to her, even for a few days, was apparently too much for him to bear.

What is going on? Griffin's internal judgment patrol elbowed him in the gut. *Since when is a couple's trip a good thing?*

Griffin ignored the voice. "I mean, if you want. Down there, we wouldn't have to worry about anybody figuring out that we're messing around. We could get a few meals at some of my favorite restaurants and maybe head out to Belle Isle so that you can see it again as an adult." He was starting to feel goofier and goofier by the second.

"You want me to go with you down south?" Ava asked blankly.

"You could help me pick the right clothes," Griffin replied. "You could take a breath and relax. Those freaking cats have proven they're not going anywhere."

Ava made a noise somewhere between a snort and a laugh. "That's true. Are you sure you want me to go?"

He'd wanted her to go before he asked the question, even if he didn't realize it. "I really want you to go."

"Then I guess I can manage a weekend away. I haven't

been to the city in forever. Will you protect me from muggers?"

Griffin made a face. "It's not going to be like a movie. There aren't muggers on every corner."

"Cool. So I can wander around downtown Detroit wherever I want, and it will be totally fine?"

"No. There's just not a mugger on every corner."

"Well, I still want to go, even though you're not making it sound very exciting. Ooh, can we eat at Mexicantown? I've always wanted to go there. Greektown too."

"We can do both of those things," Griffin promised, his lips curving up at her excitement. "We need to leave first thing in the morning. I was thinking maybe you could go home and pack now, then come back. We can leave from here together."

"That would be convenient, huh?" She arched an eyebrow.

"I just thought it would be practical," he insisted. "You know, we can wake each other up in the morning and not worry about an alarm."

"I do like it when things are practical," Ava teased, rolling her eyes. "I can totally make that work. Are you okay if I leave the pantry for you to finish?"

"Yeah, that sounds good." Griffin grinned at her as she leaned in to give him a kiss.

She surprised him when she slapped her hands against his cheeks and planted a huge wet one on him. "This will be like an adventure."

Griffin's heart ached as he took in the earnest excitement on her face and realized that he wanted to go on all of her adventures. "Then you'd better get packed, huh?"

"It's going to be amazing."

"It's definitely going to be something."

. . .

AVA USED TWO SUITCASES FOR THE TRIP. She wasn't sure what to bring, so she packed for every contingency. She'd left the suitcases in her car overnight, so Griffin didn't see them until the following morning when it was time to pack and head out.

He scratched his chin as he studied the suitcases. "Just out of curiosity, what's in these?" he asked.

"I just wanted to make sure I was covered," Ava replied. She had two travel mugs of coffee in her hand and was in no mood for an argument. "I also took the time to put together a road trip song list for us to listen to for the drive. We can sing the whole way."

"Awesome."

His tone made Ava narrow her eyes. "Are you about to be difficult?" She wasn't really annoyed with him. She'd decided she liked him when he was persnickety. Actually, she liked all of his moods. Even his bad ones were somehow comforting. But she wouldn't admit that to anybody else.

"Absolutely not." Griffin grunted as he hefted the first suitcase into the back of his SUV. He had to shove his duffel bag aside to make room. When he lifted the second and found it was even heavier, all he could do was shake his head. "You know we're only going to be down there for two nights, right?"

Ava pinned him with a warning look. "I like choices. Don't be weird."

Griffin laughed. "I don't think I'm the one being weird." He secured the suitcases and shut the hatch. "Are you ready?"

"I am. Here." She handed him his mug. "Did I mention the road trip song list I made?"

"You did." Griffin sipped his coffee. "Do you really expect me to sing?"

"You have to sing on a road trip. That's the rule."

"I don't believe I've ever heard that rule." He walked her to the passenger door and opened it for her. "Just out of curiosity, what's on this song list?"

Ava gave a mischievous smile. "You're going to love it."

When Griffin returned the smile, Ava's heart turned into a fluttering mess. Despite her best efforts, she was starting to feel things for him she'd had no intention of feeling. Her first instinct when he'd asked her to go south with him had been to flee. It wouldn't end well because she was becoming too attached to him. But she hadn't been able to stop herself from saying yes. The alternative, well, it wasn't something she could even fathom.

So am I making a mistake? Am I going to end up with a broken heart because of this arrangement, even though we've gone into it determined to make sure that didn't happen for either of us? Probably, but she still couldn't help making the leap.

"The drive is going to be about four hours," Griffin said as he fastened her seat belt for her. "If Nickelback is on that playlist, you're in trouble." He gave her a friendly kiss on her mouth.

"Do I look like I have bad taste in music?" Ava demanded. "There's no Nickelback. Give me a break."

"I guess we'll have to wait and see. I'm reserving judgment until I hear this music."

"You're going to love it. I already told you. Have a little faith."

"Okay, but be prepared for endless whining if I don't like it."

"I'm always prepared for that when I'm with you."

"Oh, you're so funny." He closed the door and held her gaze as he circled the front of the vehicle.

When Ava's heart stuttered like an engine trying to catch, she knew she was in too deep to dig herself out. *But do I even want to?*

20
TWENTY

Ava didn't know what she'd expected when seeing Griffin's house, but the adorable Cape Cod near Lake St. Clair certainly wasn't it.

"Huh." She stared at the house from the driveway.

"What?" Griffin asked, looking between her and the house.

"It's just... The house is classic," Ava replied. "For some reason, I thought you would have some modern monstrosity. You kept the charm of this house, even though it was older. I ... didn't expect that from you."

Griffin eyed her for what felt like a really long time. "I happen to think you can respect older architecture while still making it safe. The electric in here has all been updated, and I had the plaster removed in favor of drywall. But I tried to keep the charm of the original house."

"You did a good job." Ava marveled at the adorable gray shutters. "Aren't you sad about letting it go? It looks as if you put a lot of time and love into it."

Griffin cocked his head. "This place doesn't have the magic of the farm, or Bellaire, for that matter. I like the house, but I think I may be done down here. I'm not certain yet, but that's the way I'm leaning."

Ava studied his profile. That had obviously been hard for him to admit. "I think you'll do a great job renovating your grandfather's house. You'll turn it into everything I always knew it could be."

Griffin blinked rapidly as he regarded her. "I don't know what I'm going to do yet. I'll start on the renovations, but I don't know that I'm staying there. I need to think on things. I just know I'm likely done down here."

Ava swallowed hard, recognizing his warning. *Don't get too attached to me.* Unfortunately for her, it was probably too late for that.

"Well, I'm still excited to see what you're going to do with the house. I bet it's going to be amazing."

"There's nobody I would rather share my ideas with." Griffin turned toward the back of the SUV. "I guess we'd better get your suitcases into the house. Then I thought I would give you a tour before taking you to Greektown for dinner."

"Greektown first?" Ava couldn't contain her surprise. "I thought it would be Mexicantown first, for some reason."

Griffin chuckled. "I love how much thought you've put into this." He opened the hatch and removed his duffel bag first and handed it to her. Then he grunted as he lifted out the first suitcase. "The reason we're not hitting up Mexicantown until tomorrow is because they have dollar margaritas tomorrow, and I couldn't get a reservation at my favorite place until then. I thought we would Uber over there so we can really enjoy it."

"Oh," Ava said, taken aback. "That's smart. What about packing up your place, though? Don't we have to put some work into that?"

"We do. But I don't have a lot of stuff. I think it's going to go faster than you think."

"Okay, well, I'm all for seeing Greektown."

"I think you'll be pleasantly surprised."

GRIFFIN WAS HAPPY ACTING AS TOUR guide, something he hadn't expected. Ava's enthusiasm for trying new things was contagious. He always knew what he wanted when it came to food and drinks and had never much considered branching out. But she so desperately wanted to try everything she possibly could, so he decided to order things she wanted, just so she wouldn't feel wasteful if she tried something and didn't want to finish it.

They went to Greektown because even though it was newer, it was one of Griffin's favorites, and she would love the atmosphere. Once there, they ordered three appetizers, two entrees, and one dessert to share. They ate so much that Ava complained the whole way home that she was going to have to unbutton her pants the second they got inside the house if she wanted to breathe.

It turned out that wasn't a problem. They were both out of their clothes and in his bed in record time. The amount of food they'd eaten was quickly forgotten as the room filled with moans and whispers. Neither said "I love you" or went for the mushy stuff. All the interaction was of a sexual nature, yet there was an added edge to it.

They couldn't get enough of each other, and it wasn't just infatuation. Griffin enjoyed the sex, but he loved listening to her take on everything. From food to music to movies to random people walking down the sidewalk, she had an opinion about everything and wasn't afraid to express it. And surprisingly he was eager to hear it.

Her mind was a marvel. She hopped from topic to topic with the same energy she had when rolling around with him. Even though he'd initially thought her a pain in the ass, he'd started to realize that there was more to her than met the eye, and he wanted to know all of it.

They passed out after doing it a second time, woke the next morning and had breakfast delivered, then dove in to packing. Ava realized quickly that Griffin was right about not having a lot of stuff, and she was affronted.

"You're going to have to decorate when the house is turned into a bed-and-breakfast," she warned him as she searched through his kitchen cupboards. "People like looking at stuff. You're going to have to get rooster statues."

Griffin, who was pulling glasses out of one of the top cabinets, shot her a sidelong look. "Rooster statues?"

"They're a thing, and people love them," Ava insisted. "They represent the country, for some reason." She shoved a pot into a bin. "I have some, if you want them." She was focused on the pot, not Griffin, but he could hear the sadness in her voice. "I bought them with your house in mind. You should have them."

Griffin's heart panged. He hated how sad she looked but didn't know how to fix the situation. He didn't want to give up the house—at least not until he was certain what he truly wanted—so there was very little middle ground to be found. "How about you hold on to the roosters until after the winter, huh? I think that's the smart way to go."

"Because you still think you're going to get tired of Bellaire and move on to bigger and better things once spring hits?"

Griffin hesitated then held out his hands. "I'm not sure. I just know that I need to get through the winter. It might be an arbitrary mark in my head, but winter in Bellaire freaks me out when I think on it too hard. I can't explain it."

"It's not going to be as bad as you think," Ava promised. "It's like anything. You get used to it." She plopped down on the floor and kept rummaging through the pots and pans. "I have a theory about people and weather events."

Griffin chuckled as he finished wrapping the last glass —other than the two he'd kept out for them to drink out of —and moved on to the next cupboard. "Why am I not surprised? You have a theory about everything."

"I do, and they're all good theories." Ava shot him a cheeky grin. "When it comes to weather, though, I think every person gets used to their specific weather event, and it's not a big deal."

"I'm going to need an example."

"For example, take Florida. I like the idea of a tropical climate, but I cannot imagine dealing with a hurricane. I mean, how would we pack up all the cats in the middle of a hurricane? We couldn't just leave them, either, so we would have to suffer through the hurricane, and I would totally freak out if there was a shark swimming in the barn."

Griffin cocked his head. "Why would we have the same barn in Florida?"

"It was just an example."

"Okay, well, I get what you're saying, and I think you're probably right. People get used to snow, hurricanes, tornadoes, monsoons, and the like. But I think you have to *want* to get used to those things."

With a thoughtful expression, she replied, "And you don't know if you want to get used to those things."

"I feel as if I've been hiding from anything real, or substantial, for a very long time. I'm just now starting to sort it all out. That's going to take time. I don't want to make a mistake."

Ava considered it for several seconds. "That makes sense." She went back to sorting. "You might figure it out before you even realize it, though."

Griffin's heart constricted as he studied her profile. "Yeah. I think that's a definite possibility."

WHEN THEY WERE FINISHED PACKING FOR the day— they had very little left to do—they showered and got dressed for dinner. True to his word, Griffin called for an Uber so that they wouldn't have to worry about how much they drank.

They actually went to Mexicantown, a name that made Ava giggle like an idiot as they settled into a cozy booth.

"You would think they could've shown just a little bit of imagination," she whispered. Her heart fluttered a bit when he planted his feet on either side of hers under the table, the contact making her go warm all over.

"Or perhaps this was just the start of it all, and the neighborhood was named after the restaurant," Griffin replied as he opened the menu.

"Is that true?" Ava sat up straighter.

"I have no idea." Griffin chuckled when she made a face. "I just know that the food is great. We should order like we did last night and get several options. I want to make sure you get your fill."

"Probably so you can fill me up with something else later," Ava teased him.

"That's a definite possibility."

They ordered blue margaritas on an endless loop, three appetizers, and huge plates of tacos for entrees. By the time

Ava was on her third taco, she was a little drunk and a whole lot gossipy.

"You don't ever want to talk about that building falling," she noted. She had salsa at the corner of the mouth, something she was aware of, but she didn't care. "How come?"

"There's not much to say," Griffin replied and forked refried beans into his mouth. He waited until he was done swallowing to speak again. "It is what it is."

"You carry around a lot of guilt over it, but something is off," Ava insisted. "I want to know what it is."

Griffin arched an eyebrow. "What do you mean, 'something is off'?"

"I mean nothing you've said about that accident sounds like something you would've done. I want to know what you're hiding."

Griffin clicked his tongue. "What makes you think I'm hiding something?"

"Because you get this look on your face when I bring it up. You look like a wounded puppy. When you actually do something wrong, you get defensive. But you don't get defensive when the building comes up. You get resigned. That tells me something else is going on."

Griffin didn't immediately respond, which Ava took as further confirmation that she was right. She refused to look away from him, methodically chewing on her taco.

He broke eye contact first—which was what she was expecting—and sighed. "It wasn't me," he said finally. His voice was so low that Ava had to strain to hear it.

"What wasn't you?"

"The building. I did come up with the design, but I wouldn't agree on the contractor because I knew he would take shortcuts. That was his reputation, and I refused to work with him. He was an old friend of my father's, though, so my father made the ultimate decision. The Peck Building was his project."

Things finally slipped into place for Ava. "You got blamed for something that wasn't your fault."

"It was my design," Griffin insisted.

"Yeah, but your design would've been fine if the contractor hadn't taken shortcuts. That's what you're telling me."

Griffin gulped, not meeting her gaze. "My name is on the project sheets. I'm the one who initially signed off on things."

"But who signed off on them after the fact?" Ava wasn't an expert on construction, but she was starting to get the gist of things. "It was your father, right?"

"Actually, they used my original plans as a defense and never filed the amended plans with the city like they were supposed to," Griffin replied in a low voice. "They lied when we were questioned, and because my father has been around forever, nobody really pushed him on it."

"But you know," Ava argued. "Why didn't you say something to whatever inspector came around?"

"Because my father could go to prison if I tell the truth."

Ava touched her tongue to her top lip, debating. "Are you close with your father? Because—and I'm sorry if this is too forward, but that's who I am—you've never said anything about your father that suggests you even like him, let alone love him."

Griffin balked. "He's my father. Of course I love him."

"I don't love my father." Ava made a face. "But that's neither here nor there. You're not the one who made the mistake, yet you're the one who is listed in the newspaper articles. Most people get that it was a terrible accident, but you're still the one being painted as the fall guy. Don't you want to clear your name?"

"My name has technically been cleared."

"Except it hasn't," Ava argued. "There are always going to be whispers. Your father is the one who did the bad thing. He should be the one they're whispering about. Not you."

"How can I throw my father under the bus like that?"

"How could he throw *you* under the bus?" Ava countered. "Fathers are supposed to protect their children." The words were barely out of her mouth before she realized what she'd said. "Well, good fathers."

Griffin narrowed his eyes. "You don't ever say anything nice about your father. Maybe we should talk about him."

"Yeah, let's just focus on one jackass at a time, huh? You should seriously consider telling the truth about your father. It's not okay for you to be the one carrying this burden for the rest of your life. You're a good person. He's the one who made the mistake. You should nail him."

Griffin bit into another taco. "You really need to learn to form an opinion," he said when he'd swallowed. "I'm afraid you're going to be mistaken for a dainty wallflower anybody can walk all over."

Ava snorted. "Yes, that sounds just like me, doesn't it?"

THEY DRANK QUITE A BIT, BUT AFTER a walk through Mexicantown to sober up and the ride back to Griffin's house, they both had their wits about them.

Griffin was still mulling over the things she'd said to him as they walked up the sidewalk to the house, and for the first time since the incident—since his mother had agreed with his father that Griffin should just suck it up and accept responsibility because it would be easier for everybody—he was beginning to wonder if maybe the mistake had been taking on the blame when it wasn't his fault.

He helped Ava out of her coat when they were inside, his hands moving over her shoulders as his chest pressed to her back and his lips found the sensitive ridge behind her ear.

He was infatuated with her. Having her take his side had been the thing he'd most needed to hear. It hadn't been an accident when he volunteered the truth to her. It had been a test, and she'd passed with flying colors.

When he turned her so that they were facing each other, they were both breathless. Sparks flew when their mouths met again, but that time, the intensity was something more than sexual chemistry or pure lust.

They didn't have sex when they hit Griffin's bed. They made love, and not only was Griffin okay with it, but he realized they'd been heading down that path almost from the start.

They might've set up rules for a relationship that could never be, but they were in it.

He just had no idea how it was all going to end.

Because it has to end, right?

21

TWENTY-ONE

Griffin felt lighter when they left the city and returned home. *Home. When did I start thinking of it that way?* He had no idea. Returning to the farm was like opening the windows for the first time after a brutal winter.

Things were different with Ava too. No longer were they pretending they were in some weird friends-with-benefits situation. Instead, they were open and affectionate, and what was most surprising to him was that it didn't feel weird. It felt right.

His only problem was that he had no idea what to do about it. His life was still technically in limbo. He hadn't committed to living in Bellaire full-time and hadn't truly decided he wanted to run a bed-and-breakfast. He'd only allowed himself to dream in the short term. That was something he was going to have to come to grips with.

"What are you thinking?" Ava asked as she appeared at his side in the barn. They'd made a pact that they were going to catch more cats that day, no matter what. The One-Eyed Wonder and the Black Menace were among only a handful they had left. The black ringleader currently sat in the middle of the barn, gazing at them, and practically dared them to try to grab him. His expression said one thing and one thing only: *Come at me, bro.*

Griffin rolled his neck. "I hate that this cat is smarter than me."

Ava laughed and narrowed her eyes as she considered the cagey animal. "What if I move behind him, and you stay here? I can try to crowd him, and maybe he'll go into one of the traps in the openings because he doesn't want to risk getting too close to you."

"I believe we've tried that multiple times."

"Yes, but we'll commit this time."

Griffin's lips curved up at the word *commit*. It had a double meaning, whether she realized it or not. "Okay."

Before Ava could creep around to the spot behind the cat, Griffin snagged her hand and tugged her in for a kiss that was less passionate and more friendly and comfortable. It felt as if they'd been doing it their entire lives. When he pulled back, he found her grinning.

"What?" he demanded.

"Nothing." Ava shook her head. "I wasn't thinking anything."

"Liar." He squeezed her hand one more time before releasing her. "Be careful when you're crossing behind him, okay? I think he might've been an evil Sith Lord in his past life."

"A Sith Lord?" Ava huffed a laugh. "I didn't realize you were a *Star Wars* geek."

"Honey, there's nothing geeky about me. I am a manly *Star Wars* fan."

"I didn't know they existed."

"Keep it up," he warned her in a low voice. "I'll show you my lightsaber if you're not careful. It's impressive."

"Ooh, sexy *Star Wars* threats," Ava trilled. "Now we're getting somewhere." She stepped lightly as she circled the cat, who lashed his tail back and forth as he glanced between her and Griffin. "He knows we're up to something."

"Well, he is the Darth Vader of cats."

Ava laughed as she reached her destination and lowered herself to the ground. "Okay. I'm going to sit here a minute or two then start sliding in and removing his space. If we do this right, he's going to keep edging that way, but he won't want to cross in front of you, so his only option will be a cage."

"Yeah, something tells me he's going to figure out an escape route. Maybe he's the Han Solo of cats."

Ava laughed again, making Griffin think he would never tire of that sound. He wanted to hear it every single day for the rest of his life.

And isn't that a sobering thought?

Griffin's knees suddenly felt weak, and he was glad he had a reason to drop to the barn floor. He got as comfortable as possible, then he waited for Ava to work her magic. Because she was indeed magical, he'd decided. Sure, she was impulsive, and she didn't think before she spoke. But she cast a spell wherever she went, and he was growing more and more enchanted with her. *But what if I'm not cut out for country life after all? What if I allow myself to fall in love with this woman, then hurt us both?* He couldn't stand the thought.

Before he could mire himself too deeply in melancholy thoughts, the sound of voices at the barn door caused him to snap his head in that direction. His property wasn't like the city. People didn't drop in unannounced. Nobody just happened to walk by the barn. But it was only Maya and Lindsey.

"You know, if I were a proper country resident, I would've had my gun out to shoot you for trespassing before you even made it out of your car. Aren't you supposed to call before dropping in? Isn't that proper country etiquette?"

Lindsey made a face. "Please. You don't scare me." She moved farther into the barn and frowned when she realized both Ava and Griffin were on the floor. "Is this some weird mating ritual I'm unaware of? If so, you're doing it wrong. You need to be on top of each other."

Griffin's cheeks didn't burn like they might have a week ago. Instead, he merely raised a shoulder. "We're trying to outsmart the cat."

"Oh." The explanation was apparently reasonable enough for Lindsey to believe because she turned her full attention to the feline. "What's his deal? He looks disgruntled with life."

"We can't catch him," Ava replied. "We need to get the few remaining cats in this barn out so that they can be checked for feline leukemia and vaccinated. Otherwise, it's a waste to have protected the other cats. We can't bring them back until we know everybody is safe and won't infect everybody else."

"You're letting the cats come back?" Maya looked tickled at the prospect. "I thought you were finding them all homes. By the way, Nick and I have two of your kittens, and we love them. We named them Magic and Jordan, and they already have the run of the house."

Griffin's forehead creased. "Magic and Jordan? As in the basketball players?"

"Don't ask," Lindsey said. "Nick and Maya fell in love on the basketball court when they were sixteen, although it took them fifteen years to admit it to themselves. Now they're embracing the basketball theme, and it's giving me a headache."

"What doesn't give you a headache?" Maya demanded as Griffin stifled a chuckle.

"I'm just saying that you guys could spend a little less time dribbling balls and a little more time telling me what a great friend I am," Lindsey replied evenly.

"Yeah, we'll get right on that." Maya turned back to Griffin. "So, we're here for a reason."

"I'm guessing it's not barn theater," Griffin deadpanned.

"Not even a little. We wanted to make sure you guys were aware of the resort party tonight."

"Resort party?" Griffin asked. "I don't understand."

"The resort," Maya pressed. "I know you're new to the area but come on. Everybody up here has heard of the resort. It's our one claim to fame."

"I'm familiar with the resort," Griffin replied. "I've even been there before."

"You have?" Ava perked up. "Since you've been back?"

"No, but my grandfather took me up there when I was a kid. He thought I should get into skiing."

"Did you?"

"No. I always thought it looked cool, but I'm a bit of a baby when it comes to the weather."

"Well, then you picked the perfect place to move to." Lindsey thumped his shoulder. "There's little I love more than someone complaining about the weather for five months straight. Oh, wait, I will hurt you if you turn into one of those people."

"That's good to know." Griffin shook his head. "Just out of curiosity, how does your husband put up with you?"

"We have a unique relationship," Lindsey replied, seemingly unruffled by the question. "We're equal parts sugar and spice. Sometimes, we get off on the spice."

"Interesting." Griffin darted a look toward Ava and smiled. "I'm still not sure why you're here."

"Are you slow or something? I already explained it."

"Yet we're still in the dark."

Maya extended an arm to still Lindsey. "The resort has an annual autumn extravaganza party," she explained. "It's kind of a kickoff for the holiday season, which is their biggest time of year. There are other parties, of course—Christmas and New Year's Eve are biggies—but this is one of their best parties."

"And we thought you would want to mark your coming out as a couple at a big party," Lindsey added pointedly, her gaze fixed on Griffin.

Griffin wasn't an idiot, so it wasn't hard for him to figure out what Lindsey was trying to do. She wanted him to act cagey and deny they were a couple so that she could pounce on them and rip their story to shreds. She got off on that type of thing, like the spice she'd mentioned. But he had no intention of doing that.

"Do you want to go to a party?" he asked Ava instead. He saw no reason to waste time denying they were together. Lindsey might be brash and obnoxious—while also having a heart of gold she didn't want to own up to—but Griffin didn't care to play games with her.

Ava's eyes widened, and he wasn't sure whether she was surprised he'd owned up to their being a couple or it was something else. "Oh, well, I haven't been to the holiday party at the resort in years. I remember it being kind of stuffy."

"That was before Jake and January took over," Maya replied. "Last year's was definitely stuffy, but January is in charge this year, and Jake is helping her. From what I hear, they have a lot of fun stuff planned."

"Yes, I heard Jake wanted to hang mistletoe from every inch of the ceiling and turn it into an orgy," Lindsey deadpanned.

Taken aback, Griffin asked, "What kind of party does he want?"

"It was a joke," Maya replied. "Jake and January are pretty lovey-dovey these days. The running gag is that he's got sex on the brain all the time because a few weeks ago, they were caught in a janitor's closet, and everybody in the resort heard about it. Apparently, he was naked, and everybody got to see his butt."

"I heard he has a great butt," Lindsey supplied. "We're talking Chris Evans's butt here."

Griffin rubbed his forehead. "I think we've gotten off topic."

"Yes, but I happen to think butts are a great topic all on their own," Lindsey replied. "Why do you think I married Bear? His butt is perfection." She gave a chef's kiss.

"Awesome," Griffin drawled.

"Ignore her," Maya said. "She's a pain and gets off on it. We just wanted to make sure you guys were aware of the party—everybody's going—and see if you wanted to meet us up there."

"Oh, well..." Griffin blew out a sigh as he considered it. He'd thought their plans for the evening would consist of watching another bad horror movie—Ava seemingly couldn't get enough of them—then going to bed at a reasonable hour. For some reason, living in the country made him aware of how much sleep was appropriate. But the party wasn't the worst idea he'd ever heard. He needed to feel Ava out on the topic first. "What do you think?"

"It might be nice," Ava hedged. "I haven't dressed up in forever. But I don't even know if I have a dress."

"I have extra dresses," Maya volunteered. "I needed them for when I was working at the Renaissance Center because occasionally, I had to double as a hostess for swanky parties, so I have like ten cocktail dresses. I'm sure at least one of them will strike your fancy."

"That sounds good." Ava's eyes moved to Griffin, and he was surprised to find a mixture of emotions there. She looked excited, worried, and angsty all at the same time. "It's up to you, though. If you don't want to go someplace so public, I get it."

He appreciated that she wanted him to be comfortable and was willing to put her wants and needs on the back burner because of it.

"I brought a few suits with me when we came back from my place last weekend," he announced. "I think it sounds fun."

Ava's face brightened, confirming he'd made the right decision. "Really?"

Warmth filled him at the earnestness he found reflected back at him. "Really."

"Oh, so cute." Lindsey interrupted the moment by grabbing his cheek and giving it a jiggle. "You guys are freaking adorable. Go back to your trip last weekend, though. Is that why nobody saw you two?"

Caught off guard, Griffin asked, "Why does it matter?"

"Because there's a bet going, and I think I'm about to lose."

"A bet?"

"Oh, there's always a bet going when there's a new couple to focus on," Maya explained. "You should've heard the number of bets people made when Nick and I first got back in touch. There were like a hundred of them."

"More like ten, and I won five of them. That was a glorious month. I got to go to the spa for a massage with my winnings and everything," Lindsey said.

"Yes, she had her mustache waxed," Maya offered, then giggled like a maniac when Lindsey tried to elbow her in the ribs.

"We're just saying that everybody in town has decided to place bets on you two right now," Lindsey offered. "I thought you already knew." Her gaze landed on Ava. "You've lived here your entire life. How did you miss it?"

"No one's mentioned it," Ava replied.

"I don't care who is betting on what," Griffin said. He was over all of it. "If people are bored and want to place bets, more power to them. For the record, we were down south to pack up my old place last weekend. I'm putting it on the market so that I can finance renovations here."

"Because you're moving here permanently?" Maya asked.

Griffin hesitated, then shrugged. He knew what he wanted to answer, but he also didn't want to lead Ava on. "I don't know. In theory, I would like that. I just don't know if I can survive in a place that doesn't have midnight grocery shopping or a liquor store that sells more than two kinds of vodka. I also don't know if I can survive the winter. We'll see."

Maya studied his features. He found the moment stressful, yet the way she smiled at him told him she was happy with what she found there. He wanted to ask why, but

Lindsey's presence had him keeping his mouth shut. The sooner the two of them left, the better. He wanted to go back to spending time with Ava alone.

"Here's the information." Maya handed over a flier. "We're going to be there. You guys can meet January and Jake while you're up there too. I think you'll like them."

"Thank you. We've met and they're great." Griffin took the flier, looked at it briefly, then folded it to put it in his pocket. "Anything else?"

"Just one thing," Lindsey replied. "If you two could declare your love and devotion by Christmas, I would greatly appreciate it. I have that window in the pool, and I could really use one of those Himalayan salt massages. They're expensive, though."

Griffin made a face. "I'll do my best."

Lindsey gave a surprisingly sweet smile. "That's all I ask."

22

TWENTY-TWO

va borrowed a dress from Maya, and when she showed up at the farm, she felt unbelievably nervous. She carefully navigated the rutted driveway in heels, taking longer to make it to the door than she'd anticipated. It opened the second she reached it.

Griffin stood there in a beautiful black suit—something that probably cost more than her entire wardrobe combined—and his dark hair was slicked back from his face, making him even more attractive than ever, which should've been impossible.

"Wow," she said.

"You took the word right out of my mouth." Griffin looked her up and down then shook his head as his gaze returned to her face.

"Is something wrong?" Ava gripped her hands together in front of her, her nerves jangling. "Should I go home and change?"

"No. Absolutely not. You look amazing."

"Then why are you staring at me like that?"

He blinked rapidly. "Because you look amazing."

"Oh." Ava didn't know how to respond. "Well, thanks."

He smirked. "You're not used to people complimenting you, are you?"

Ava shrugged. "I don't date much."

"Yeah, I wasn't talking about dates." He slowly lifted his hand and brushed a stray hair away from her face. She'd gone all out and pulled her hair back, something she almost never did. "I'm starting to get the feeling that nobody has ever paid you your due."

"What do you mean?"

"Just that you deserve to be worshipped by everybody you come into contact with. I don't think anybody has ever taken the time to do it correctly."

"Oh." Ava's cheeks heated. "That might be the nicest thing anybody has ever said to me."

"And that's the problem." He leaned in to give her a soft kiss.

Ava caught his face before he could pull away and ran her thumb over his lips to remove the gloss that had transferred there. "Are you nervous?" she whispered.

"Actually, I'm not." Griffin flashed one of his heart-stopping smiles. She was getting far too reliant on them. They were like a drug to her. "Are *you* nervous?"

"A little. I can't walk in heels very well."

Griffin glanced down. He looked caught between worry and laughter. "Well, how about you keep a firm hold on my arm all night, and I'll make sure you don't fall? That will be the trade-off."

"That sounds convenient for both of us."

"It does." Griffin held out his arm, and she slid hers through it. "Come on. Let's go to a holiday party."

"I hope they have good food," Ava said as he led her to

his SUV. "I think I'm going to want to load up so that I have plenty of energy for later."

Griffin frowned. "What's later?"

"When we come back home. Or I mean, to your place."

"Ah." A grin spread across his handsome features. "I think we're both going to need to bulk up for that."

***HOME.* THE WORD WAS** all Griffin could think of as he secured Ava in the passenger seat and navigated toward the resort.

With each passing day, he was starting to think more and more that he was home. That thought both exhilarated and terrified him. He liked the idea of making the farm his permanent home. He felt a comfort there that he hadn't felt anywhere else. Still, one problem remained. Griffin simply didn't know if he could be happy in the country over the long haul. He needed to figure that out ... and fast.

Though he'd been to the resort as a child, he'd never driven there, so Ava had to direct him. When they coasted the final hill to the summit lodge of Sylvan Slopes Ski Resort & Lodge, he gasped when he got a gander at all the beautiful Christmas lights.

"Wow," he said as he found a parking spot.

"That's the second time you've said that tonight," Ava teased him. "Should I be offended?"

"Why would you be offended?"

"Because the first time you said it, you were talking about me."

He shook his head. "No. You're still the most beautiful thing I've seen tonight. The lights are pretty fabulous, though."

"They are."

Griffin collected Ava on the other side of the vehicle, making sure to keep a firm grip on her arm as he led her to the sidewalk. It hadn't snowed yet, but she really did seem uncertain in her heels. Truth be told, he liked being able to touch her whenever he wanted. Her shaky steps seemed as good a reason as any other.

When they walked through the huge glass doors at the front of the resort, Griffin was struck by the beauty of it all. To his right was a large check-in desk for the guests. To his left, a huge lobby spread out, all organized around a wood-burning fireplace that crackled cheerfully and beckoned for them to pick a couch to curl up on.

"Maybe I should take up skiing," Griffin mused as he absently helped her remove her wrap. When he turned back to her, his heart skipped a beat because the cold outside coupled with the warmth inside had her glowing. "Or we could just order hot chocolate and snuggle on one of those couches and pretend we went skiing."

Ava snorted. "That sounds like an interesting plan."

"I thought you would like it."

"I can teach you to ski if you want."

"Is that a fact?" Griffin arched an eyebrow. "I didn't know you could ski."

"I don't recall you asking."

He cocked his head, considering. "Fair enough. How long have you been skiing?"

"Since I was a kid. That's one of the few things to do up here in the winter. My friend Jake Jeffries's father owns the resort, and he set up a program where kids from low-income families could borrow skis and have free lift tickets whenever they wanted. I had to learn from the other kids who had taken lessons, but it wasn't that hard."

She didn't talk about her past often, though she let

bits and pieces slide. One thing that had become glaringly apparent was that she hadn't grown up with a lot of money. People like Lindsey and Maya didn't care, but he had to think there were others in the area who weren't so open minded when it came to something like that. "I would love for you to teach me how to ski." The words were out of his mouth before he could think better of it. "I don't want to get hurt, though, so we should take it slow."

Ava locked eyes with his. "Yeah, getting hurt would suck."

Her words were loaded with double meaning, and when Griffin reached out to fix her hair again—there wasn't anything wrong with it, but he liked touching her—he was prepared to lay his heart bare. He didn't get the chance, though.

"Oh my god! Ava, you look amazing," someone said in a high-pitched voice, and when Griffin turned, a willowy brunette was scurrying toward Ava. The woman was clad in a powder-blue dress and sparkled as if she belonged on top of the tree.

"You do too," Ava replied. She swiveled smoothly and offered the woman a hug. "That dress is out of this world."

"Jake had it made for me," the woman replied, her eyes briefly drifting to Griffin before they focused on Ava again. "He thinks blue is my best color, for some reason."

"Oh, don't go getting weird," a man chided her as he moved up behind her. He was dressed in a charcoal-gray suit, but he had a blue pocket square offsetting the muted color. It matched the woman's dress perfectly. "I like you in every color."

Ava beamed at the couple as the man slid his arm around the woman's waist. If the coordinated outfits hadn't been a dead giveaway that they were a couple, the way he looked at her would have. He was completely besotted.

"You guys look perfect together." A flash of wistfulness came to Ava's face, then she straightened. "Griffin Holden, this is Jake Jeffries and January Jackson. We all went to high school together."

Griffin had to absorb the names for several seconds. "That's a lot of *J*'s," he said finally as he extended his hand toward Jake.

Rather than find the statement odd, Jake laughed. "We sat next to each other in every class growing up because of those names."

"Ah." Griffin nodded. "You fell in love in high school."

"Oh no." January shook her head. "We hated each other in high school. We did horrible things to each other."

"It's true. In seventh grade, we went on a field trip, and she purposely spilled water on my crotch and told everybody I'd wet myself. I spent the entire second half of the year explaining that I didn't wet myself because cider made me giddy."

Griffin froze, unsure how he was supposed to respond, then he burst out laughing. "I see."

"You really don't." Jake's smile made Griffin understand that he was over whatever teenage tortures he and January had doled out. "We were horrible to each other."

"Yet you're together now," Griffin pointed out.

"Yup." Jake tightened his grip on January. "Now and forever. We just had some things to work out when we were younger."

"All his fault," January said as she jerked a thumb at him.

"Yes, I was the one who spread the rumor about myself crying during sex at the senior prom."

"Oh, I forgot about that one," Ava said. "I think the worst part of that story was that you told everybody he dressed up like a clown before he did the crying and could only find release if he honked breasts. I was afraid to go near him for a full year."

Jake glared at January. "I didn't know about the clown part."

Sheepishly, she replied, "It all worked out in the end."

Jake wagged a warning finger in her face. "You're going to pay for that later."

"Oh, I'm shaking in my heels." January shot him a petulant look before focusing on Ava. "You look lovely. I wasn't certain you would come, but I made sure to ask Maya and Lindsey to extend an invitation. I don't have your number right now, and you didn't respond to the message I sent you on your blog."

"Oh crap!" Her hand flew to her mouth. "I haven't checked the messages on my blog in ... well ... weeks. I can't believe I forgot. What if something important is in there?"

"I'm sure someone would've tracked you down if there was," January replied. Her eyes drifted to Griffin. "It sounds like maybe you got distracted."

"Griffin and I have been catching cats in his barn," Ava admitted. "We're trying to get them all vaccinated and fixed. We also got all the kittens out so that they can be properly socialized and find homes. So if you guys are looking, there are some adorable fluff balls at the rescue right now."

January turned pleading eyes toward Jake.

"Oh, you want a cat?" Jake's nose wrinkled. "I thought we agreed no pets and no kids for at least two years."

"We said no kids right away," January countered. "We didn't say anything about a cat."

"I don't know." Jake looked distinctly uncomfortable. "I'm not sure I'm ready to be responsible for another living creature. I can barely take care of myself."

"We can do it together," January insisted. "Please? We can even get two so they can keep each other company. I've always wanted a cat. My mother would never let me."

The second January mentioned her mother, it was like a switch was flipped behind Jake's eyes.

"We can get two kittens," Jake said automatically. "You have to help me figure out how to take care of them, though. I'm going to need help."

"I'll make a list." January happily tugged Jake toward what looked to be a restaurant. "You guys should follow us. The food and drinks are this way."

"We'll be right there," Ava promised as she watched them go.

Griffin, however, watched her instead of them. "Are you close with January?"

"Yeah. We had a lot in common as kids."

"Like what?" Though Griffin wanted a drink, he wanted to learn Ava's secrets even more. He felt as if he was on the precipice of learning something important, so he forced himself to be calm as he waited.

"Oh, it's nothing." Ava gave a dismissive wave. "It's just … we both didn't have a lot of money growing up, and it was embarrassing sometimes. I don't want to dwell on that tonight, though. Can we just focus on having fun? I just want to eat good food, drink amazing cocktails, and forget about all the serious stuff for a few hours. Can we do that?"

Griffin nodded. "We can do that." Though he wanted more information about her past, he didn't have to ruin the magic of the moment to get it. He had time. "What sort of cocktail do you want?"

"Something yummy."

"I think that can be arranged."

GRIFFIN DRANK SO MUCH THAT HE TOLD AVA HE DIDN'T feel comfortable driving home. Apparently, January and Jake had thought ahead, though, and set aside a block of rooms just in case. January was more than happy to show Ava and Griffin to their room shortly before midnight.

"It was smart of you to do this," Griffin said as she ushered them inside. "It never occurred to me that you don't have working rideshare up here."

"We do, but it's hit-or-miss." January smiled. "It's fine, though. We have the open rooms, and we want people to have a good time."

"Awesome." Griffin shot her a thumbs-up before heading toward the bathroom.

"Thanks for doing this," Ava said. "I don't think he expected to have as much fun as he did."

"Yes, well, I'm willing to bet that Luke's famous snowball martinis didn't help." January made a face. "I told him to cut the alcohol in those things. Obviously, he didn't listen."

"They're deceptively delicious," Ava replied. On impulse, she reached over and squeezed January's hand. "You seem happy."

January beamed back. "I am. I've never been this happy."

"I'm glad. I always knew you were going to find happiness with Jake."

January snorted. "People keep saying that, but I don't believe them."

"The chemistry was always there," Ava insisted.

"What about you?" January asked pointedly. "Are you going to find happiness with Griffin? You guys seemed awfully lovey-dovey tonight."

The question caught Ava off guard. "I don't know. He's not sure he can stay up here long term. He's a city boy at heart."

"And you're always going to be a country girl. If it matters, I didn't see a guy waffling on where he's going to end up tonight. He seemed pretty happy."

"But what if it doesn't last?" Ava's smile momentarily slipped as her heart squeezed.

"I think he's going to surprise you, Ava. It might not be the city he's looking for but something else. He just needs to realize that he's already found that something else."

Ava sighed. "Thanks again for the room. I'm going to fill him full of water and ibuprofen then dump him into bed. Your party was amazing, by the way. So much better than the stuffy ones they used to have up here."

"I wish I could take credit for that. That's all Jake. He's the fun one in our relationship."

"I happen to think you're fun together."

"Maybe. Perhaps you and Griffin can be fun together too."

Ava glanced at the closed bathroom door. "Maybe. I'm afraid, though. With each passing day, I feel more than I thought possible when it started. What if I'm the only one?"

"You're not. Anybody who looks at that man when he's in a room with you can see that."

"It's already too late," Ava admitted. "I'm head over heels for him."

"Just be brave." January squeezed her hand. "It's going to work out. Have faith."

Ava wished she could, but if her past had taught her anything, it was that nothing good ever happened to her over the long haul. "Thanks again for the room. We'll see you in the morning."

23
TWENTY-THREE

"What do you think?" Ava stood at the end of Griffin's bed and modeled her "smart" pantsuit. She'd showered, done her hair to perfection, and had even put on makeup. She wasn't expecting applause or anything, but a wolf whistle wouldn't have hurt her ego.

Instead, Griffin's brow furrowed as he looked her up and down. "You're overdressed for a day in bed."

The holiday party was two weeks in their rearview mirror, and ever since, they'd been joined at the hip—and well, other places. They were fully comfortable with each other.

"We can't spend the day in bed."

"Why not? It's supposed to rain all day. The weather forecaster even said it might turn to snow after dark. You know what that means." He waggled his eyebrows.

"What does it mean?" she asked blankly.

"It means we can add whipped-cream-flavored vodka to our hot chocolate and cuddle in front of the fire all day.

As cute as you look in your little suit—and you do look cute —I happen to think the fireplace thing sounds better."

"It does sound lovely. But we can't do it."

"Why not?" Griffin whined. "I had plans. Why do you think I bought that stuff to throw into the Crock-pot? I've got it all taken care of. We don't even have to leave for food."

Ava had been the one to introduce him to Crock-pot cooking. So many people used Instant Pots lately, but she was a traditionalist. In the past two weeks, they'd made chili and chicken together in Chuck's ancient Crock-pot, and both meals had turned out delicious. While glad that Griffin had embraced the concept of Crock-pot cooking, it wasn't on the agenda for the day.

"We have to leave for the Career Day thing at the school," she reminded him. "I thought we could stop at the coffee shop for some caffeine and doughnuts before then."

Griffin's scowl deepened. "Career Day? What are you even talking about?"

Ava planted her hands on her hips and stared him down. "Don't even. I was here when Nick asked you to participate. You agreed. So did I. That means we're going because I keep my word."

"Oh jeez." Griffin threw up his hands and fell back against the pillows. "I forgot all about that." He grabbed the blanket and tugged it over his head, hiding his naked torso from Ava's avaricious stare. "I don't want to do it."

"Nobody *wants* to do Career Day," Ava replied. "Heck, even the kids don't want to do it. We agreed, though."

"Tell me again why I agreed."

"I believe, if my memory of the conversation is accurate, you agreed because you were put on the spot."

"So that means the agreement shouldn't be binding."

Ava didn't change her stance, only narrowed her eyes. When the silence extended for far too long, Griffin poked his head from under the covers and met her steely-eyed glare.

"You're not giving me a choice on this, are you?"

"Nope." Ava vehemently shook her head. "You're going. We'll stop to get caffeine and doughnuts beforehand so that we're both sugared up and ready. Then after, we're going to hit the grocery store for food. We can do the hot chocolate and whipped-cream-flavored vodka when we get back."

"What about my roast? I wanted to make pot roast."

"Well, since I'm already ready, I can go downstairs and start the pot roast."

"The whole point was for us to do it together."

Ava's expression softened. "The important part is the gravy. We can't do that until later. I'll start the main stuff, and we'll make the gravy together later."

Griffin looked resigned. "Fine. I'm not going to be pleasant, though."

"Just dress up in one of those nice suits you brought back from Detroit," Ava suggested. "I'm betting you clean up really nice for more than just parties, and if you wear one, I'll have something to look forward to stripping off you later."

Griffin didn't consider the order long. "Okay. I expect some vigorous undressing later. There'd better be music ... and a little dance ... and a feather boa."

Ava snorted. "Where am I going to get a feather boa?"

"I have no idea, but that's on you. I want one, and you're going to get it."

She could only think of one person who might have a

feather boa. "Just get in the shower. We need to leave in twenty minutes."

Griffin moved fast when he finally got out of the bed, catching Ava around her waist and kissing her with a loud smack before she could squirm away. "I look forward to your undressing me in exactly three hours. That's all the time I can stand to be away from you and this bed."

"I'm going to be there with you," she reminded him.

"Yeah, but you can't undress me in front of the kids. That will send a bad message."

"Good point."

"Just wait for the point I'm going to drive home in three hours. That's going to be even better."

"Ah, something to look forward to."

GRIFFIN LET AVA PICK OUT HIS SUIT BECAUSE he didn't care what he wore, and she seemed amused by the process. He even allowed her to tie his tie, which ended up slightly crooked, but she was so excited that he couldn't be the bearer of bad news.

He held her hand as they walked into Maya's café, and he even did his best to ignore the taunting from Maya and Lindsey when they strolled up to the pastry case together.

"Well, look who is finally out and proud," Lindsey drawled.

"That could be taken the wrong way," Griffin noted as he studied the display case. Maya was a gifted baker, and he'd been sampling her offerings since he got to town. "Ooh. I want whatever that is." He pointed.

"That would be a cheese Danish," Maya replied. "It's Nick's favorite too."

"That's what I want."

"Let's go back to talking about the way my words could be taken," Lindsey pressed. "What wrong way are we talking?"

"Yeah, I'm not getting into that, because you'll trap me." Griffin flashed her the sort of smile he knew would irritate her. "I'm not falling for that on Career Day. I have enough to worry about."

"Wait," Ava said. "Are you afraid of the kids or something?"

"I'm not *afraid* of them," Griffin countered, avoiding eye contact so he could focus on making sure his arm cuffs were even. "I just don't know what I'm going to say to them."

"I think Nick wants you to talk about architecture," Maya replied. "I'm going to be talking about opening my own business. He told me just to cover the basics and not let them rattle me."

"Except I'm not really an architect any longer, am I?" Griffin recognized his voice had taken on an edge, but there was very little he could do about it.

"Griffin..." Ava frowned with uncertainty as she studied him.

Rather than explode, which was something Griffin was worried would happen, he closed his eyes. "I'm sorry. I'm just a little nervous."

"Because your last building fell like a Kardashian on a pub crawl?" Lindsey asked.

Griffin shrugged. "I know it wasn't that long ago, but I feel removed from that situation now. My reputation has been forever tarnished by what happened. I'm no longer going to be the guy who designed the Taft Building near the river. That's what I was known for before this, in case you're wondering. I'm always going to be the guy who killed two people with his incompetence."

Griffin shoved his hands into his pockets and went back to staring at the pastry case. He knew Maya, Lindsey, and Ava were exchanging worried looks without having to raise his chin.

"It's going to be okay," Ava promised him as she wrapped her hands around his wrist. "They're not going to be interested in that stuff. They just want to hear how you design buildings."

"Except I don't do that any longer," Griffin reminded her.

"I kind of think you do," Ava pressed. "You've been drawing up plans for the farm. I saw them the other day. You have plans for eventually expanding the main house, and I saw what you want to do down the line. I saw that barn house you want to build. It's amazing."

Taken aback, Griffin asked, "You saw that?"

"It was on the kitchen table. You can't expect me not to look when the Oreos are sitting next to it."

Griffin huffed a laugh. "I guess I'll remember that for next time." For some reason, her praise grounded him in a way he didn't know he needed. "You really liked it?"

"Yeah. The only thing that barn was missing was a little balcony off the upstairs window so that you can watch the stars."

"That's an interesting idea."

"I'm full of them."

He smiled softly. "You kind of are."

"Aw," Lindsey said when they leaned in to kiss, causing both of them to pull back. "You guys are just the sweetest. You're so cute that you make Nick and Maya look cold and disinterested. Kind of makes me want to puke."

Ava glared at Lindsey. Then she said, "I need a feather boa. Any idea on where I could find one?"

Lindsey nodded. "I have one in my car. You can have it."

Griffin's jaw dropped. "You have a boa in your car?"

"Three, actually. You can have the purple or the pink. The blue one is Bear's favorite, so you can't have that one. Not that you would want it or anything. He sweats a lot when we're ... well, you know."

"Yeah, we're done with this conversation." Griffin shook his head. "And here I thought the kids were going to be terrifying. Who knew it would be Lindsey who would terrify me before we even got started?"

Ava shot her hand in the air, and so did Maya, making them giggle.

Griffin caught Ava's chin and gave her another kiss to settle himself. She was his ray of sunshine on a cloudy day. "I just want to get this over with. Then we're totally doing the whipped-cream-flavored vodka thing."

"Kinky," Lindsey drawled. "Now I know what you want the boa for."

"Let's just get our coffee and doughnuts," Griffin said to Ava. "I need to get away from her and fast."

"On it." Ava stepped forward. "We'll be out of here in three minutes. Time me."

AVA WAS ONE OF THOSE PEOPLE WHO DIDN'T apologize for being different. When she took center stage in the classroom and explained what she did for a living, she tuned out the snorts and eye rolls. Instead, she laid everything out, including how she managed to secure advertising for her blog. When she was finished, not only had she wowed all the kids, but she had the few adults present smiling as well.

"There are different ways to make a living," Nick said as

he took over the conversation from Ava, who had already graced the kids with two bows and a little dance. "Ava is an example of someone who created her own gig. We've talked about the gig economy, right? How things are different from when your parents—and especially my parents— were younger. You guys are going to have to roll with the punches more than ever."

A pretty brunette with a button nose and a skirt so short that it likely flouted the school's dress code raised her hand. "My mother says that Ms. Mason makes her money off the misery of others. Supposedly, she hides in bushes and eavesdrops, then prints what she hears on the internet so she can shame people."

Ava kept her composure, but her insides had begun to squirm. It took everything she had not to smack the girl in her stupid button nose.

Lindsey, who'd told Ava she had decided to come along because she was bored and simply didn't want to be left behind, stirred in the back left corner of the room. "Savannah, tell your mother that everybody in town would've known about her and the Roto-Rooter guy regardless because nobody has that many toilet problems."

Wide-eyed, the girl said, "You take that back."

"No." Lindsey made a face. "Just for the record, kid, nobody needs their pipes snaked twice a week." She paused. "Wait. That might've come out wrong."

"You're done regardless," Nick warned Lindsey, jabbing a finger in her direction. "Do not turn this into a weird situation."

"What? I was just telling the truth."

"You're done." Nick turned to Griffin, a pleading look in his eyes. "You're the last one of the afternoon. Kids, please welcome Griffin Holden. He's an architect, which is not the sort of job we hear much about in these parts. Please give him a warm welcome."

The classroom broke out into polite applause, but Griffin didn't step to the lectern to speak. Instead, he remained rooted to his spot.

Concerned, Ava edged closer to him. "You're up," she whispered.

When he raised his eyes from the floor, where they'd been fixated for the past five minutes, Ava saw the panic there. He was as pale as a ghost and balling his hands into fists at his sides.

"I can't," he whispered. "I just can't do this. I don't want to."

Ava had fallen victim to the same problem more than once herself. He was about to careen over a mental cliff into panic-attack territory. She should've listened when he put up a fight that morning. He'd been saying more than she realized when he unleashed his anxiety in Maya's shop.

She couldn't let him lose himself in public on her watch. She knew how painful that was.

When Ava moved back toward the lectern, she had a bright smile on her face. Sure, she recognized it looked a little deranged, but she launched into the tale of the Holden farm renovation.

She told the kids how there was a plan in place to turn the house into a bed-and-breakfast. Then she made them laugh with tall tales of catching cats in the barn. That led to a discussion about the local cat rescue and what good work they did. By the time the bell rang, Ava had control over the situation ... and Griffin had retreated into himself in the corner of the room.

"You did well," Nick said to Ava when all the kids were

gone. He looked relieved. "Way to go." He shot her a thumbs-up then darted a worried look toward Griffin.

"You need a cape when you do stuff like that," Lindsey noted. Her expression was hard to read as she looked Nick up and down. "I didn't cause him to go off the rails, did I?"

"You certainly didn't help by making him uncomfortable earlier," Maya hissed.

Ava tuned them out and approached Griffin with her palms turned out. She didn't know how she was going to tackle the situation until the words were already coming out of her mouth. "Are you ready for pot roast and hot chocolate?"

Griffin jerked up his chin, seemingly surprised that she wasn't giving him a hard time. "I'm sorry. I don't know what happened there. I was okay until I wasn't. It just ... came out of nowhere."

"It's fine," Ava assured him. She refused to let him see her worry. "I swooped in and saved the day. The kids love me. Even Savannah, and I outed her mother's affair with the Roto-Rooter guy."

"Everybody knew about that affair," Lindsey insisted. "We were taking bets."

Ava extended her hand to Griffin. "Come on." She needed him to take it so that she could get him out of the high school and back to the farm. He would be okay once he was there.

Griffin stared at her hand for what felt like a really long time, then linked his fingers with hers. "I don't think I can ever be an architect again." He seemed resigned and almost relieved. Ava saw a little something else hidden in the depths of his eyes, too—despair.

"You're not alone," Ava promised as she brushed his hair back from his face. "We'll figure it out together." She already had a few ideas on that, although she couldn't say them out loud. "Let's go home and get naked in front of the fire." She realized what she'd said when it was too late to take it back. "Your home, I mean."

Either Griffin didn't pick up on her slip, or he didn't care. Instead, he gripped her hand tightly and let her lead him to the exit. "Yeah, let's go home. I think I want to be done with this day."

"Definitely. It's hot-chocolate-and-vodka time."

He managed a wan smile. "That sounds like a plan to me."

24
TWENTY-FOUR

Ava decided to go to the city without telling Griffin. She wasn't certain when she'd made the decision but seeing the way he'd fallen apart over a simple Career Day discussion had spurred her to action.

So on a day when he was working in the attic with Bear's team, Ava drove south. She'd researched the building incident on the internet and knew the name of Griffin's former company—Holden Architectural. They had an office in Royal Oak, so Ava pointed herself there.

She didn't have an appointment—she'd thought about making one but opted against it—and she was nervous when she walked through the front door. The lobby wasn't what she was expecting. It had sleek lines and gray hues, with no splashes of color. When she spent time with Griffin, all she saw was color.

"Hello." Ava rubbed her hands over her pants as she approached the receptionist's desk. "I'm hoping to talk to Gerald Holden."

The secretary blinked rapidly, looked Ava's outfit of

simple jeans and a T-shirt up and down, and made a face. "He's a very busy man."

"This is regarding his son."

"His son no longer works for the firm."

"I'm well aware. I know his son and have something I need to talk to Mr. Holden about." Ava wasn't used to being shut down. She had one of those personalities that meant she always got her way.

"Maybe you should just tell me what that something is, then you can go back to … wherever it is you came from."

Ava might have been out of her element, but she was in no mood to be ignored. "I've driven all the way from Bellaire this morning, and I don't have time for crap because I have to drive back again this afternoon. I need fifteen minutes of Mr. Holden's time, and I'm not leaving until I get it."

"I could force you to leave."

"You could, but the last thing this firm needs is negative media attention, and I wouldn't go quietly, so there would be reporters all over your front walkway within an hour. Is that what you want?"

The secretary considered it, then inclined her head toward the lobby sitting area. "Give me a few minutes."

"Lovely." Disgruntled, Ava moved to sit in one of the chairs.

After Ava had spent a few minutes staring at an abstract painting that featured eight different shades of gray, the secretary called out to her.

"The first door on the left on the second floor," she announced.

Ava managed a flat smile. "Thank you." She forced herself to walk with more attitude than she felt, and when she arrived at Gerald's office, she'd almost convinced herself she was in charge of how the conversation would go. She was a big proponent of "fake it till you make it." Then she saw the imposing man sitting behind the desk, and all her bravado fled.

"My secretary said you want to talk about Griffin?"

Ava's mouth went dry. "Yes."

"Well, then have a seat." Gerald looked as if he was in a hurry. "Close the door too. Nobody needs to hear my family's private business."

Ava did as instructed, then stepped lightly to one of the chairs across from his desk. They were unbelievably rigid and uncomfortable.

"I knew your father," she blurted.

Gerald studied her. "Is that so?"

Ava nodded. "He was famous in Bellaire. He used to have the best Halloween parties."

"Halloween is a waste of time. Adults dressing up like morons? No, thank you."

Ava barely managed to hold it together. "Well, I didn't come here to argue about Halloween." She took a breath. "Although you know what? Halloween is awesome. Who doesn't like a night when you get to dress up as something exotic, drink themed cocktails, and eat as much candy as you can carry?"

"I would be that person," Gerald replied.

"Well, that tracks." Ava was even more annoyed than she'd anticipated. "I'm not here to talk about your father."

"That's good. My father squandered all of his potential, and it still makes me angry. He had a great eye for design, and he never used it. Instead, he insisted on wasting his life on that stupid farm. There's not much to talk about."

Ava worried she was about to Hulk out and balled her hands into fists on her lap, reminding herself she was there for a specific reason—Griffin, not Chuck. Chuck had recognized what his son was a long time ago and made his peace with it. Also, Chuck was gone. Griffin was the one who was suffering.

"We need to talk about your son," Ava said. Just thinking about Griffin's tortured face at the Career Day event made her have to center herself. "I think you need to do what's right for him for a change."

Gerald's expression didn't change, yet a gleam came to his eye. "And what's that?"

"You need to take responsibility for the Peck Building falling."

Gerald was clearly the sort of man who liked to keep his cool, but his jaw dropped. "Excuse me?"

"I know it was you. You're the one who hired the construction crew who did shoddy work. You forced your son to take responsibility because you didn't want to deal with the blowback. He's suffering, though."

Gerald ran his tongue over his teeth, seemingly debating how he wanted to respond. Ava knew it wouldn't be pretty, but when he did open his mouth, his words had an extra layer of vitriol. "How is this any of your business?"

"Because I care about your son."

"I guess I know what he's been doing up north," Gerald muttered. "I knew when he said he was focusing on the farm that he had to be making it up. It's so typical of him to be distracted by something so mundane."

Ava refused to rise to the bait. "You need to take responsibility so that this doesn't crush Griffin," she insisted. "He knows it wasn't his fault, yet everybody believes it was. That's not fair. People died."

"Life isn't fair," Gerald replied evenly.

Ava wanted to smack him. "That's true. But you're

stacking the deck against him to protect yourself. What sort of parent does that?" Her mind flashed to her parents. She understood having a selfish parent better than most. Gerald might've had more money than her parents, but at his core, he was no different.

"I think I'll refrain from conversing about my parenting ability with a country girl like you." Gerald looked bored. "There's no way you could possibly understand the intricacies of this situation. You have no frame of reference."

Though she could tell she was being dismissed, Ava remained in her chair.

"I don't care if you look down on me," she said in a low voice. "You don't have to like me. I don't have to like you. None of that is important. What is important is Griffin."

"And I'm guessing you're going to tell me about my son, because you somehow know him better than me after a few weeks."

"I know that he's a good man, and he's mired in guilt and uncertainty right now," Ava replied. "He wants to honor his grandfather's memory because that's all he has to focus on. You're taking away what he's good at to protect yourself, and that's not what a parent does."

Ava stood. Her legs were shaky, but she was determined to finish. "Your son is a good man with a heart of gold. He tries so hard to do the right thing. That's kind of amazing because the standard you've set is the opposite. Do you want him to give up his gift?"

"O-Of course not," Gerald sputtered. "This will all die down by summer, and he'll be welcomed back to the firm."

"He won't come back to the firm as long as this is hanging over his head. He'll hide away up north for the rest of his life if you don't do something to set the record straight. You've ruined this place for him as it is."

Gerald narrowed his eyes. "And what is that supposed to mean?"

"It means that he's selling his house and leaving this place. He's already making plans."

"But … that's preposterous." Gerald shook his head. "He doesn't belong up there."

"I don't actually believe that, but he deserves choices," Ava replied evenly. "I want him to have options. I don't want him staying up north because he has nowhere else to go. I want him to want to stay."

"I could face criminal charges. I'm not saying your accusations are correct, but if they were, I would be in trouble. Griffin doesn't have to worry about that."

"Is that your argument for throwing him under the bus?" Ava demanded. "God, you're a freaking terrible parent."

"I am a man who does his best," Gerald shot back. "What do you want from me?"

"I want you to do what's best for your son for a change. He deserves to be able to steer his own ship. You're not giving him that option, and it's not fair."

"As I said, life isn't fair."

"You're still the parent. For once in your life, do what's right for him. How hard is that?"

"You might be surprised."

Ava stared him down for several beats, then shook her head. "I was stupid to come here. I hoped that you would do the right thing for him. What an idiot you must think me for believing that."

Gerald narrowed his eyes. "My son will have a great future. He was destined for it."

"Your son needs to be able to decide what he wants," Ava shot back. "He can't do that when you've taken away all but one of his choices. Why can't you see that?"

"Because... Because..."

"Because you refuse to see yourself as what you truly are."

"And what's that?"

"You're the villain in your son's story. Who wants to acknowledge that?"

"I think it's time for you to go."

"Yeah, I was just thinking the same thing."

DEJECTED, AVA DROVE HOME. The day felt wasted. In hindsight, she knew it had been a risk to drive four hours each way just to spend fifteen minutes with the devil. She was exhausted, yet she found herself in the Holden barn just as the dinner hour was rolling around.

The black cat sat in the middle of the barn, watching her as she opened the trap and plopped down on the ground.

"I need a win today," she said plaintively. "I need you to get in this cage." She pointed.

The cat lashed his tail and didn't move.

"Come on," she pleaded. "Can't you do the right thing for once in your life? I swear we'll bring you back once we get you checked out."

The cat merely stared at her, his luminous eyes betraying nothing.

Ava opened her mouth—she didn't know if she was going to cry or scream—but footsteps behind her made her swivel.

Griffin appeared in the opening, dressed in jeans and a T-shirt. He was covered in what looked like dust and had some cobwebs in his hair. But the look in his eyes made her still.

"I was starting to wonder if I was going to see you at all today," he admitted as he started for her. "I was getting depressed until I looked out the window and saw your car."

"I had some stuff to do," Ava replied dully.

"I know. Driving to Royal Oak and back in the same day is quite the feat."

Ava's body went rigid. Not for a moment had she thought he would find out about her trip. When Gerald had dismissed her so callously, she'd believed that was the end of it, but obviously not.

"Who told you?" she asked.

"Who do you think?"

His face was neutral, giving no clue to his feelings.

"Are you going to yell?"

"I'm not sure." He sat next to her on the floor. When he crossed his legs, he didn't accidentally touch her like he normally would. That lack of contact left her bereft.

"You probably think I'm a busybody," she said.

"You're definitely a busybody."

"I didn't mean to insert myself in this. I just couldn't help myself." Tears threatened to stop Ava's voice.

To her surprise, Griffin reached over and held her hand. "Baby, I knew you were a busybody the day I met you. Nothing has changed there except maybe your motivations."

Ava didn't know how to respond. "Meaning what?"

"Meaning that I understand why you did what you did today." He seemed to be choosing his words carefully. "What happened at Career Day was embarrassing."

"No." Ava vehemently shook her head. "That wasn't your fault. Nobody is judging you for that."

"I'm judging me for that."

"I didn't mean to stick my nose in business I had no right to, but … well … I couldn't help myself."

"I'm sure."

She was silent for a moment then exhaled a shaky sigh. "Your dad is a putz."

"He is. And he would never deny that."

"He basically told me I was an idiot."

"My father would not understand your appeal."

"Because I don't wear pencil skirts and I'm a rainbow instead of a slate-gray color wheel?"

Griffin opened his mouth, then shut it, cocking his head. "That is a very interesting take on my father."

"Is it wrong?"

"No."

"Well, then it was a totally wasted trip." Ava had to work hard not to cry. Tears would only make the conversation worse. "I get that I overstepped my bounds. If you want to break up with me, I wouldn't blame you."

"You *did* overstep your bounds."

"Yeah." She couldn't meet his eyes.

"But I've never had anyone in my life who cared enough to do what you did."

She froze as he flipped her hand over and traced the lines in her palm.

"I was angry when I first heard," he continued. "I couldn't believe you'd gone down there. Then the more that I listened to him, the more I realized it was the nicest thing anybody had ever done for me. You weren't down there because you wanted me to go back to the company. You were down there because you wanted to make sure I had all the options in front of me."

"Pretty much." Ava's lower lip trembled as she finally

found the courage to meet his gaze. "I don't want you to stay here because you have no other options. I want you to want to stay here."

"I know." Gently, he brushed her hair out of her face. "My father is sending in a new incident report regarding the building failure. He's taking responsibility."

"Seriously?"

"Seriously." He bobbed his head. "My name will be cleared. He's already forwarded the new report to me, and there's no doubt I'll be exonerated."

Ava let out a breath. "That's good, right? Your reputation will be restored."

"Yes. I don't like people thinking I'm responsible for killing people."

"Does that mean you'll be going back there?" Ava hated asking the question, but she had no choice.

"No." He cracked a smile. "It means I'm continuing what I already started. I want this farm refurbished." He hesitated but only for a moment. "I don't know what's going to happen, but I'm not leaving. I want to continue working on what we've been doing."

He leaned closer. "I want to keep spending time with you."

She let out a shaky breath. "That's good. I like that idea."

He chuckled. "What you did today—while coming from a place of loyalty—might not have been your best move."

"Yeah."

He leaned in and pressed a soft kiss to her lips. "I appreciate it, though."

"You do?" Ava was so relieved that she wanted to throw herself at him, but she refrained.

"Yes, but we still need to talk about boundaries."

"That's fair."

He stood, extending his hand. Ava took it and allowed him to pull her to her feet. Before he could pull her tight for a hug, however, his gaze fell on the trap, and his eyes widened.

Confused, Ava turned and found the black cat had gone into the trap and was patiently waiting for the door to close. "No way."

Griffin chuckled. "I guess you got more than one win today."

"Fancy that."

"You're still a busybody."

"Yeah, and I probably always will be."

"I think I can work with that."

"How do you feel about discussing my busybody tendencies over pizza? I can pick it up after I drop off the cat at the vet."

Griffin grinned. "I think that's the best offer I've had all day."

25
TWENTY-FIVE

A thin blanket of snow covered the ground when Ava woke on Thanksgiving morning. Though it looked cold outside, it was warm in the bed she was sharing with Griffin.

He breathed deeply, his face peaceful in sleep, and she took the opportunity to study him in the warming light and marvel at how pretty he was. His thick hair had grown several inches since she'd met him. Coupled with his morning stubble, it gave him a rough-and-tumble look she found appealing. When he'd first arrived on the scene, he might've been dressed down in simple jeans and a shirt, but he still had that city air about him. That had disappeared, and it wasn't just because he'd taken to wearing flannels because he'd come to appreciate how important layers were when working in the barn.

He'd turned the muscles he'd earned in a gym down south into the sort used for everyday work on a farm, and the worry lines she'd seen dogging him at the start had slowly melted away. He looked like a content man, and that gave her hope. She just didn't know if she should embrace it.

"Why are you thinking so hard this early in the morning?" Griffin asked without opening his eyes. He reached for her, wrapping his arms around her waist as he tugged so that she was pressed against him.

"How did you even know I was awake?" She giggled.

"You have a certain energy, Ava." His eyes were still shut, as if he was trying to savor those last few moments of rest before greeting the day. "When you're awake, you're always thinking. You're coiled and ready to pounce on whatever new task you want to tackle. When you're asleep, it's the only time you relax. You're unguarded and quiet."

"Are you saying you prefer it when I'm quiet?"

"God yes." He smiled, but she refused to let him off the hook.

"I can be quiet when I'm awake."

"All evidence points to the contrary."

"I can. Have you ever considered there's such a thing as too much quiet, though?"

"No. Shh." He stroked the back of her head and rested his cheek against her forehead. "It's quiet time."

She frowned. "I can be quiet."

"Shh," he practically crooned.

"I can be," she muttered more to herself than him. "I'm totally a quiet and relaxed individual." As if to prove it, she zipped her lips.

That only lasted for thirty seconds before she lost her patience. "So, we're having the big Thanksgiving Day dinner today at Maya's café. I offered to bring something, but she said she had it handled. You don't think that was a dig on my cooking abilities, do you?"

Griffin opened one eye. "You can't be quiet, can you?"

"I can, but I don't choose to be now. It's Thanksgiving, and we agreed to go to dinner together. That's kind of a big deal."

He opened his other eye and grinned. "Are you nervous about coming out as a couple?"

"No." Ava averted her eyes, but she and Griffin were pressed so tightly together that the only place to look was at his neck. "We already came out as a couple. Everybody knows."

"Everybody?"

"Well, everybody I care about."

"I don't care who knows. I like you. I like this. And I don't want anything to change. If others don't like it, they can suck it."

The words warmed Ava all over while also making her uneasy. "What if someone asks questions about how we met?"

"I'm going to tell them I found you hiding in the bushes because you couldn't contain your hormones and were warm for my form. After my initial shock, I decided to give you a chance because I figured your blood sugar was low that day. I've since found that if I keep you fed, it cuts down on the weird stuff."

Ava's jaw dropped. "You cannot tell them that!"

He laughed at her outrage. "It's my story. I'm going to tell it however I want."

"Well, then I'm going to tell them how you walked around naked in an attempt to entice me."

"That didn't happen. If you want to tell that story, though, more power to you. It makes it sound like I'm such a glorious sight when naked that you couldn't keep your hands off me."

Ava growled deep in her throat. That was true.

His smile only grew broader when she finally met his gaze again. "It's going to be okay. It isn't as if the others didn't know where this was going. I'm looking forward to a fun meal with friends."

"Do you like Thanksgiving?"

"I like the food. I've always found Thanksgiving to be a weird holiday, but I don't hate it or anything."

"What's your favorite holiday?"

"Until now, it's been New Year's Day because of all the football. I'm pretty sure it's going to be Halloween going forward, though."

"Why?"

"Because you love Halloween."

Ava went so gooey that she thought she might sink into the mattress. "I ... um..."

He laughed. "You're finally speechless. Look at that."

"Oh, whatever." Ava gave him a shove but didn't pull away. "We have exactly one hour before we should get up and greet the day. I promised to help deliver dinners to the area seniors for the Meals on Wheels program. It's going to take a few hours."

Griffin's eyes widened. "I didn't know you did that."

She shrugged. "I try to help when I can. It's not always just about me."

"Well, I want to help too." He kissed the tip of her nose, then rolled her so that she was under him and had no choice but to look into his eyes. "If we have an hour, though, we'd better not waste it."

Everything inside Ava sighed with contentment. "Definitely not."

. . .

GRIFFIN COULDN'T REMEMBER EVER ATTENDING the sort of raucous Thanksgiving dinner like the one Maya and Lindsey were hosting at the café. Even when he was a kid, Thanksgiving dinners had been a formal affair. His father often invited business associates over for a catered dinner to wine and dine them, and Griffin was expected to dress appropriately. Even then, he was told to only speak when spoken to.

Thanksgiving in Bellaire was something entirely different.

"What is that heavenly smell?" he asked as he moved into the kitchen with Ava and watched her go to work helping Lindsey and Maya put sides together.

"That's me, honey," Lindsey drawled. "That's my natural musk."

"Ew." Maya wrinkled her top lip. "Don't say 'natural musk' that way. It makes me want to gag."

"How are the cats?" Ava asked Maya as she grabbed an apron.

"They're wonderful." Maya's expression turned dreamy. "We're having so much fun with them. Nick and I are using them as a test run to decide when we want kids. When we feel they're not too much work, we're going to start talking about adding a little one to the mix."

"Aw." Ava beamed at her. "That sounds cute. How many kids do you want?"

"Five," Lindsey replied for her. "She wants five because she wants to keep up with me."

Maya looked horrified at the thought. "We're thinking one. But we might add a second if the first one is really good. We're going to play it by ear. We're just not sure we can handle more than one with two full-time jobs."

"You have parents in the area, though," Lindsey pointed

out. "In fact, you have four grandparents who will be more than eager to help. You should take advantage of that."

"We'll see. What about you two?" Her gaze moved between Ava and Griffin. "How many kids are you going to have?"

Ava practically choked. Her face grew so red that Griffin worried she might pass out. He, however, refused to let the question get under his skin. A few weeks ago, he might've freaked out. Nothing seemed as scary as it had then. For some reason, the biggest thing Ava had brought to his life was a sense of calm. The future wasn't some black void any longer. It had form, and that form looked a lot like Ava.

"We haven't talked about kids yet," Griffin replied. "The second we do, though, you'll be the first to know."

Maya chuckled. "Sorry. I couldn't help myself. You guys are just so cute together."

"We *are* cute together," Griffin readily agreed as he slipped behind Ava and looped an arm around her. "What can this cute couple do to help?"

Lindsey looked shocked. "You want to help us with the food?"

"Of course." Griffin bobbed his head. "Why wouldn't I want to help?"

"Because you have a penis. The penis brigade is in the other room. The men are watching the children while we handle the food. You should join them."

"But I want to help," Griffin insisted.

"If you stay in here, we can't grill Ava about the sex," Lindsey shot back. "Now, as much as I like bossing men around in the kitchen—and pretty much anywhere else I can get away with it—I would much rather hear whether you're a grower or a shower."

It took Griffin a moment to grasp what she was saying.

"You're trying to scare me away with that talk. It's not going to work."

"Fine." Lindsey barely blinked before turning her attention to Ava. "Does he know where the clitoris is? Because—and I'm going to be honest here—the haircut he showed up with suggests he didn't. This new haircut gives me hope, but I'm not entirely convinced."

That was enough to push Griffin straight through the swinging kitchen doors and into the café. "I'll see you in a little bit." He blew a kiss toward Ava, then tried not to take it personally when they burst into laughter.

"Did they chase you out?" Nick was holding one of Bear's children—a boy who looked to be about five or so—and continuously flipped the kid up and down to keep him laughing.

"Pretty much," Griffin replied. "I tried to offer to help, but Lindsey brought up the clitoris, and I figured it was best to get out of there."

"That's my motto when Lindsey mentions her clitoris," Bear deadpanned. He had a kid tucked under his arm and was standing at the counter so that his daughter—who couldn't have been more than six—could apply makeup to him.

"What's a 'itoris?" the boy Bear was holding asked.

"It's a mystical creature that only pokes its head out when the moon is full and the legs are shaved," Bear replied. "Its superpower is complaining, and it likes to hide when you're feeling lazy."

The boy looked as if he was contemplating Bear's answer with a great deal of concentration. "It sounds like a turtle," he said finally.

"It's exactly like a turtle." Bear put the boy on the

ground. "Go play with your brothers. Try not to destroy anything."

"Can I tell them about the turtle?"

"Absolutely." Bear went back to focusing on his daughter. "Am I pretty yet?"

The little girl, who looked exactly like her mother, wrinkled her tiny brow. "Almost there."

"That's what her mother says when I'm looking for the clitoris," Bear mused.

Griffin had to choke down his laughter, and when the bell over the front door rang, he jerked up his head to see who else was joining them. He didn't recognize the older woman. She had gray hair that had likely been red at one time poking out from under a hat, she was dressed in a coat that looked as if it had been turned inside out, and her pants had only one leg cuffed. She was a mess.

"Can we help you?" Griffin asked.

"I'm looking for my daughter."

He didn't know what to make of the woman. The way Nick responded, however, had him curious.

"Hello, Mrs. Mason," Nick said calmly. He gave the kid he was entertaining a light push toward the back of the café and his brothers. "It's been a long time."

"Has it?" The woman's expression was blank. "I'm not even sure I know who you are, so I guess it has." She held out her hands, shrugged, then laughed like a loon. "Seriously, I know my daughter is here," she said when her smile disappeared. "I need to speak to her."

Nick kept darting worried looks toward Griffin. *Does he not know who she is either? Wait, that's not right. He said her name.*

"Mrs. Mason, why don't you take a seat, huh?" Bear said as he pulled away from his daughter and faced the woman.

He had a face full of makeup but didn't seem to care. "We can get you some coffee."

"I don't need coffee," the woman spat back. "I need my daughter. Get her."

Is this Lindsey's mother? It was the only thing that made sense to Griffin, yet the woman didn't look like Lindsey. Something was familiar about her, but he couldn't place it. She was very clearly soused, though. He could smell the bourbon from across the room, and it made his stomach twist.

"I don't think that's a good idea," Nick said, catching Griffin off guard.

Why would he keep this woman from Lindsey?

"You've clearly been over at the tavern, and I don't think Ava should have her holiday ruined because you can't drink in moderation."

All the air whooshed out of Griffin's lungs. "Ava?" He'd heard the last name but it hadn't registered.

Nick jerked his eyes to him. "Oh, right. You don't know Mrs. Mason." His tone was measured, but a great deal of dislike radiated from him. "Let me solve that problem. This is Darla Mason. She's Ava's mother."

"Oh, I don't know if I want to take responsibility for Ava today," Darla slurred as she rested her hand on the counter to keep her balance. "In fact, I almost never want to take credit for her these days because she's not good for much. When she was younger and more likely to listen, I would take credit for her fifty percent of the time. Now it's more like ten percent. Is she here, though? I need some money. I'm out, and they won't extend my tab at the tavern."

Nick's lips twisted. He'd obviously dealt with Darla more than once, and he didn't like her. Griffin finally realized why Ava had so carefully avoided almost all conversation regarding her parents. If Darla was the only representation she had, there was no reason to claim her.

"Should I get Ava?" Griffin asked in a low voice, conflicted. He didn't want to ruin the holiday for Ava—she'd been so excited about spending time with him and her friends—but if their roles were reversed, he would want to be the one to handle the situation.

"I would rather not, but I don't see that we have a choice," Bear replied. He looked weary and annoyed at the same time. "She's not going to leave, and I'm not giving her any money."

"Well, Ava won't give her money," Griffin said with a laugh.

Nick and Bear shot each other dubious looks.

"Right?" Griffin pressed. He was growing more and more uncomfortable with the conversation.

"Sometimes it's hard to say no to a parent," Nick replied softly. "I know exactly how she feels on this one. *Exactly.* But she's going to have to deal with it."

Griffin stared at Darla a moment longer, then nodded stiffly. "I'll get Ava."

Resigned, Bear dragged a hand through his hair. "Yeah, I think that would be best."

26

TWENTY-SIX

Ava was having a good time in the kitchen when a worried Griffin appeared in the doorway, his face pale.

"Have you decided on a childless life after spending time with Lindsey's brood?" Ava teased him.

Griffin shook his head. "They're fine. Um ... there's someone here to see you, though."

Ava furrowed her brow. "Me? Who's here to see me?"

"Nick says it's your mother."

She sighed and rolled her eyes. "Of course she's here." She moved to the sink to wash her hands.

"I can get rid of her for you," Lindsey offered. "I've dealt with Darla before."

"It's not your job," Ava replied.

"It's not *your* job either," Maya said softly. "I think you can be done if you want to be."

When Ava glanced at Griffin, he looked confused. She'd been purposely vague about her childhood, not trying to keep the truth from him, but she hated talking about her parents because it made her irrationally angry—and ridiculously sad.

"I'll get rid of her." Ava dropped the towel onto the counter. "Did she say what she wants?" she asked Griffin.

"She said she needs money because she's out, and they won't extend her tab at the bar."

"Well, that sounds about right." Ava dragged a hand through her hair, gathering her strength, then moved woodenly toward the swinging door. "Welcome to the shitshow," she muttered.

Griffin's hand shot out, and he wrapped his fingers around her wrist before she could disappear through the door. He looked as if he wanted to say something, but no words came out.

"This is what she does," Ava said. "It's normal. I've got it. You can stay in here with Lindsey and Maya. It will be better than listening to whatever nonsense she's decided to spew today."

Griffin flicked his eyes to Maya and Lindsey, and Ava couldn't decide whether he was seeking permission to stay or asking for clues as to what he should do. Ultimately, he straightened his shoulders and smiled.

"My father essentially framed me for murder," he reminded her in a low voice. "How bad can your mother possibly be?"

"You might be surprised." Ava managed a wan smile.

When she walked into the dining room, her spine was rigid, and she scanned the space, looking for the one person she'd been hoping not to see that day. "Hello, Mom," she said tightly.

She could smell Darla when she was still ten feet away and internally cursed the woman. "Nice to see you went out of your way to get cleaned up for us."

Darla either didn't catch on to her daughter's sarcasm or didn't care. "I need some money," she announced.

"So you can drink some more?" Ava didn't get too close —the last thing she wanted to do was give her mother a physical target.

"Oh, don't take that tone with me," Darla sneered. "I don't need your attitude today of all days."

"And what's today?" Ava asked. "Why is today any different from any other day, as far as the whiskey is concerned?"

"It's Thanksgiving." Darla sniffed and conjured up fake tears. "You know Thanksgiving was your father's favorite holiday."

Ava was immune to her mother's machinations on the subject of her father. At least, she wanted to be. "Last time I checked, any holiday when Dad could have a drink was his favorite. He wasn't all that particular about it."

Darla shot Ava a death glare. "Your father was a good man. Don't you dare talk that way about him."

"I don't particularly remember him being good at anything but drinking, putting holes in the drywall with his fist, and coming after me with a belt, but if you say so." Ava reached into her pocket, where she always kept money in case of an emergency, and peeled a twenty off. "I can't spare more than this."

Darla grabbed it as if she was afraid Ava would snatch it back and made a face. "This is it? I can barely get three drinks for this."

"That's all I can spare," Ava replied firmly. "You should go now."

"Like I want to stay here with this group." Darla sent Bear's makeup-covered face a grimace. "You should come with me, Ava. I guarantee we're having more fun over there than you are here."

"I'm good," Ava replied. She ushered her mother toward the door. "You should leave now."

Darla lowered her voice, but she was a rampant drunk and had no volume control. "Did you do what I said and seduce that guy so you can steal his farm? It looks like that plan is coming to fruition, huh?" She tried to wink but blinked both eyes.

Ava froze with her hands on the door. "I can't believe you just said that." She risked a glance at Griffin and found him watching the scene with his hands in his pockets. He didn't look angry or even shocked. His face was unreadable.

"I've never understood your attachment to that farm, but there's only one way to get it," Darla said. "I told you that when I saw you right after he arrived. It looks like you're making progress. Keep it up." Darla tapped the side of her nose and grinned. "I think that advice deserves another twenty."

The frustration Ava had been trying to keep in check bubbled up, and she shoved her mother through the open door.

Darla stumbled over the uneven concrete and went down in a heap. "What's your freaking damage, Ava? Are you trying to kill me? I wouldn't be surprised. You've always hated me. Well, just know there's no life insurance. Even if there was, I wouldn't leave it to you."

"Oh, don't worry, Mom." Ava could contain her anger no longer. "I don't expect anything from you. I learned it was a mistake to rely on you at all long ago."

"Hey! I taught you to be self-sufficient." Darla extended a warning finger. "I'm the reason you're as good as you are at getting what you want. When you finally get your hands on that farm, it will be because of me and what I told you to do."

Ava wanted to pull her hair out to feel anything other than the rampant disappointment rolling through her. She knew better than to let her mother get to her, yet it always happened. Darla was a master at crushing Ava's spirit, and Ava was convinced she only showed up when she did because she wanted to remind her that there was no escaping her past.

"I don't want you coming around anymore," Ava blurted, taking herself by surprise as much as her mother. "I just ... don't want to see you again."

Darla blinked rapidly, then started laughing. She still made no attempt to get up from the ground. "Are you kidding me? I'm the only family you have. I'm your only support system."

"That's not true." Lindsey appeared in the doorway. Bear had a firm grip on her arm and appeared to be trying to drag her back inside. "Stop it, Bear!" She shook herself free and shot him a warning look.

"Don't insert yourself into this situation, Lindsey. It's none of your business."

"When has that ever stopped me before?" She stomped over to Darla and hunkered down so that they were at eye level. "You're a bad person, Darla. I used to think it was the drugs and drink that did this to you, but at your core, you're rotten. They just make it worse."

"Like I care what you think," Darla sputtered.

"That's fine," Lindsey replied evenly. "But you need to care about what's best for your daughter. You've never done that. Not when we were back in school. Certainly not when she was a kid and didn't even have money for lunch half the time. Did you know my mother and Maya's mother used to take turns packing extra stuff in our lunches so that we could give food to Ava without embarrassing her? Why is it that our mothers cared more about her than you do?"

Ava blinked back tears. She hadn't known the extra food was packed for her, but she'd recognized that Lindsey and Maya were always open to sharing with her. They were the reasons she didn't go through the day wondering if she would even get a single meal.

"You suck," Lindsey continued. "That's all there is to it. You well and truly suck, and it's not fair that you keep doing this to your kid. Why can't you just stop?"

"Because she belongs to me," Darla spat, her eyes filled with anger. "She's the one who is going to take care of me in my old age. That's what she's supposed to do."

"Yeah, that's not how it works." Lindsey shook her head. "You're her mother. You're supposed to take care of yourself. She didn't ask to belong to you, and I'm fairly certain when they were doling out kids to parents, someone made a mistake and saddled her with you. I'm fixing that mistake."

Lindsey grabbed Ava's arm and dragged her back toward the restaurant. "Now she belongs to us," she called back. "You have no claim to her. We don't want to see you around again, and if we do, we're going to start tipping off the cops about the stuff we see you shoving into your pockets when you meet your *friends* on dark street corners. That gives them probable cause to search you, just FYI."

Darla's eyes narrowed into dangerous slits. "You're going to want to be very careful about the threats you toss around."

"I'm not afraid of you," Lindsey replied. "Just stay away from your daughter. She doesn't need you. She never did." With that, Lindsey shoved Ava through the café door. She then made a big show of locking the door and pulling down the shades.

"That's better, huh?" Lindsey flashed a bright smile, but it didn't elicit one in return from a numb Ava.

"Where's Griffin?" Ava asked quietly. All she really wanted was him. He'd become adept at soothing her, and he didn't even realize it. In the moment, when her mother was likely still collecting herself on the sidewalk, all Ava wanted was to have his arms around her.

One look at Maya's face told her that wasn't in the cards.

"He took off," Maya replied. She looked as if she wanted to burst into tears. "He said he wasn't hungry and thanked us for inviting him. Then he left through the back door."

"He asked if we could give you a ride back to your place," Nick added.

Ava's heart sank, but she couldn't speak.

"It was the stuff about the farm I think," Bear said. "In his head ... um... He might be having some doubts about why you're with him. You've never hidden the fact that you want that farm."

Even in her weakened state, Ava couldn't deny that.

"But I want *him* now," she whispered. "I want him, not the farm."

"I know." Bear looked pained. "I tried to tell him that. He needs some time to decompress, though. You need to give him tonight to come to grips with this. Your mother is toxic. But in his heart, he knows the true you."

Does he? Ava wasn't so sure. "I think I'm going to take off too." She started toward the kitchen to grab her coat and purse. "I just ... need some time to think."

"Don't go," Maya said. "You should stay with us."

"Don't go to the farm," Lindsey ordered in a low voice. "That will just make things worse. Give him some time."

"I'm not going to the farm," Ava assured her. "I just need some time to myself. I don't want to ruin your Thanksgiving."

"You won't ruin it," Maya insisted. "Just ... don't go off by yourself."

"I've always been by myself," Ava replied dully. "Maybe that's how it's supposed to be." With that, she trudged into the kitchen. She was barely cognizant that Lindsey and Maya had followed her. She didn't look over her shoulder to acknowledge either of them when she left.

GRIFFIN DIDN'T KNOW WHAT TO THINK. PART of him understood that Darla was a sad woman who didn't care what she said. She had no impulse control and was more interested in bleeding her daughter dry than anything else. But he couldn't shake the idea that maybe she was right.

Was all this a con? Did Ava start bonding with me in an attempt to get me to care for her so I would hand over the farm? Is she capable of that type of duplicity?

Deep down, he didn't want to believe she was. But her attachment to the farm was palpable. He'd never understood why. He'd loved his grandfather, but a farm was just a farm.

Right?

Griffin changed out of his clothes and pulled on a pair of jogging pants and a T-shirt. There was leftover pizza in the refrigerator, but he didn't have an appetite. All he could picture was Ava's resigned face as she stood in front of her mother. The way she'd balled her hands into fists at her sides and seemingly braced herself for an onslaught of ugly words—and possibly slaps—was seared into his brain. He had no doubt Ava's mother had been more than just verbally abusive to her when she was growing up. So many things were starting to make sense.

But that didn't mean Griffin knew what he was supposed to do. He wanted to be with Ava—so much that he was already aching—but he couldn't allow himself to be used. If he fell any harder for her, there would be no picking up the pieces if she shattered him later.

Because he needed a distraction, Griffin moved toward the trunk of journals Bear and Nick had helped him carry downstairs that first day. He sank to the floor, leaned against the wall, and opened the one on top of the pile. It was dated from almost twenty years ago, and Griffin couldn't help smiling at his grandfather's familiar writing.

Ada showed up with bruises again today.

The first line caused Griffin's blood to run cold. Grandma showed up with bruises? How is that possible? She died more than twenty years ago.

He kept reading.

She was crying. I knew she was running from that mother of hers. She's a terrible woman. I took her to the loft and told her that she could always hide there if need be. I don't want to spell it out for her in case it leads to trouble, but I won't be able to live with myself if something happens to that child. I want her to think of the barn as a refuge.

Griffin blinked rapidly then looked at the name again. His grandfather had clearly written Ada. *What if he meant Ava, though?* The timing would've been right. Ava had said she considered the barn a refuge.

I talked to the Social Services people, but they say I'm too old to serve as a foster parent to Ada. I've asked around, but nobody else can take her. But she can't stay where she is. Her mother

*might kill her when she loses her mind in one of her states. I
don't know what to do.*

Griffin felt sick to his stomach as he squeezed his eyes
shut. He'd known that Ava's childhood hadn't been good
but hadn't wanted to see the truth that was right in front of
him. Her childhood hadn't just been rough. No, it had been
torture. She was lucky to be alive.

The last line on the journal page jumped out at him,
and not just because his grandfather had actually spelled
Ava's name correctly for the first time.

I have to save Ava.

"You're not the only one, Grandpa," Griffin said with a
raspy voice as he let the tears fall. "I'll do what you
couldn't. I swear it."

27
TWENTY-SEVEN

Griffin stayed up all night reading the journals, though he didn't realize he was going to until he finished them. Some didn't mention Ava. They were love letters to his grandmother, a woman Griffin wished he'd known better. The journal entries made it clear that both of his grandparents were disappointed in his father.

He couldn't blame them. He was disappointed in the man too. The only good thing he'd done in decades, as far as Griffin could tell, was finally take responsibility for the mess he'd made.

But the entries about Ava drew him in. His grandfather had first met Ava when she was hiding in his barn. She'd broken in when her parents had been fighting, and she just wanted some peace and quiet. Because he was a good man who saw a child in distress, Chuck went out of his way to give her a safe space to hide. He seemed to realize that there was little he could do for Ava other than listen to her. Her parents weren't physically abusing her, at least as far as she was willing to admit. But that didn't mean Ava wasn't a neglected little girl.

Chuck paid attention to Ava. He helped her with homework. They talked about her dreams, and Chuck was well aware that Ava wanted to take the farm and turn it into a bed-and-breakfast. His grandfather had mixed feelings on the subject—he was a guy who valued his privacy—but the one thing he seemed to understand was that Ava needed something to make her feel safe, and that was the farm.

Griffin was exhausted when he finished. He also needed to think. An idea had begun to form as he read the journals, but he needed rest to make sure it was a good idea. With that in mind, he tumbled into bed. One way or another, he was going to fix things with Ava that day. He just needed a little sleep first.

HOLLOW-EYED AND TIRED, AVA made her way into Maya's café for coffee. She felt numb, somehow disconnected from her world, and she was confused about how it had happened. One minute, she'd been happy—happier than she could ever remember being—and more importantly, she'd felt as if she belonged. But in a split second, her mother had ruined all that. Ava was hardly surprised. If there was one thing Darla was good at, it was making Ava feel as if she had no control.

"How are you?" Maya asked when she caught sight of Ava.

Immediately, Ava plastered a fake smile onto her face. "I'm fine. You don't have to worry about me."

Understandably dubious, Maya asked, "Did you talk to Griffin?"

"No. He's done with me."

"You don't know that."

"He thinks I want to steal his farm from him." Ava leaned against the pastry case and briefly shut her eyes. "And the truth is when I first heard he'd paid the taxes on the farm, that's exactly what I wanted to do. I wanted to find a way to chase him out of town so that I could get my hands on it."

Maya didn't respond, seeming to wait for her to continue.

"I wanted him to go away. I had this dream for how my life was going to turn out, and it involved that farm. I didn't really care what happened to him."

"And how do you feel now?" Maya asked as she opened the pastry case and grabbed a cheese Danish without prodding.

"Empty," Ava replied. "I feel empty."

Maya nodded. "You love him."

Stunned, Ava whipped up her head. "I don't love him."

Maya cocked an eyebrow but otherwise remained silent.

"I don't," Ava growled. "We barely know each other."

"You've been spending time together for almost two months now. You don't think that's enough time to fall in love with someone?"

"No." Even as she said it, doubt filled her. She would've laughed at the suggestion a month ago or even a week ago. But the pit inside her felt as if it would never get filled. She missed his laugh, the warmth of his body, and the way he listened to her even when she was prattling on about nonsense. *If that isn't love, what is it?* "I don't know," she amended.

Maya's eyes filled with pity as she handed Ava the Danish. "I only have one question for you."

"Yes, my mother is always like this," Ava replied automatically.

"It's not about your mother. We're all well aware of who—and what—your mother is. It's not your fault she was so limited. She's a narcissist. Some people shouldn't be parents, and your mother is one of them. But I'm glad she only cared about her own interests and not what was best for anybody else when she had you, because otherwise, you wouldn't be here ... and I happen to like you."

Ava swiped at a tear as it slid down her cheek but didn't respond.

"I know how you saw things going on the farm before you met Griffin," Maya prodded. "How did you see them yesterday, though?"

"What do you mean?" Ava sniffled. She hated crying in public, but she couldn't seem to stop.

"If I'd asked you how you pictured your future yesterday, before anything went down with your mother, what would you have said? Were you alone on that farm when you pictured it?"

Ava's lower lip began to tremble. "No."

"I didn't think so. Were you standing next to Griffin, maybe with a belligerent cat or two at your feet?"

Tears had begun cascading down Ava's cheeks. "Yeah."

"Then I think you need to tell him."

"What am I supposed to say?" Ava asked angrily. "I did want him gone at the start."

"I'm pretty sure Griffin knows that. I'm positive, in fact, that he was aware of that the day he caught you spying, and you called him a pervert."

"He told you about that?"

"He told Nick and Bear. He said that even when you were being obnoxious, he couldn't help marveling over how pretty you were, and before he found out who you were, he thought you were saucy and delightful. I believe those were his exact words."

"How do we make this work, though?" Ava asked. "He's always going to wonder about me."

"I'm not sure that's true." Maya handed Ava the latte she'd been brewing and motioned her toward a booth. "Sit."

Ava did as instructed, though she didn't like following orders. But she was at a loss and knew she needed help.

"The first thing you're going to do is eat that Danish and drink that coffee," Maya instructed her. "You're going to get all those tears out, too, because you don't want your face to be red and puffy when you go and talk to him. You need to look your best. That's going to require a shower and a different outfit."

Ava glanced down at her jogging pants and T-shirt. "I'm never going to be some fashion plate like he might meet in the city. If that's what he's looking for, he's looking in the wrong place."

"Ava, you have a pair of panties stuck to the ass of those jogging pants," Maya replied. "I'm sure that's because of static cling in the dryer, or maybe I'm just hopeful that it wasn't a deliberate choice. Either way, you need a different outfit."

Ava didn't disagree. "I'm afraid," she whispered.

"I know you are. I was afraid when it was me too. You have to open yourself up to the process, though, because if you do, you might get everything you've ever wanted."

"What if I don't?"

"I think you're going to. If you don't, though, at least you'll know. You won't be living in doubt."

"I guess," Ava replied, still unconvinced. "I really miss him."

"I'm willing to bet he misses you too."

GRIFFIN SLEPT FOR FOUR HOURS. Though it wasn't enough, it was all he was going to get. He had things he wanted to do—the weather forecaster was predicting measurable snow, and he wanted to be ready for it—and waiting wasn't an option.

He showered, dressed in jeans, a T-shirt, and a flannel shirt, then he googled Darla's name. He found her address almost immediately. It was so close that he could walk there, so that was exactly what he decided to do.

He picked a path through the woods, trying to imagine young Ava doing the same in the opposite direction when she was afraid, and each step filled him with peace instead of rage. He was about to give her the one thing she'd always longed for—safety. That started with her mother.

Griffin rapped loudly on the door of the run-down house. Griffin couldn't believe the state of it. He hoped it hadn't been falling down around Ava when she was a child, but he was a realist. The house, with its sagging porch and boarded-up windows on the east side, had been losing its fight for survival for some time.

It took Darla a full two minutes to answer the door, and when she did, her eyes were bloodshot, and she had a cigarette hanging from her lips. Her hair stuck out in eight different directions and didn't look as if it had been washed in days. Darla was in the same outfit she'd worn the night before, but the shirt was inside out. Griffin had a few theories about how that might've happened at the bar, but he didn't care enough to ask.

"What do you want?" Darla demanded. Her gaze was unfocused. "If you're a bill collector, I'm fresh out. I paid your bill last week. It's not my fault you didn't get it."

Griffin made a face. "How do you know what bill I'm here to collect on?"

"I paid all of them last week."

He had watched Darla demand money from Ava for drinks the previous evening and knew that was a lie. But he was beyond caring. "I'm not here to collect money for bills."

"No?" Darla puffed on her cigarette and gave him a long once-over. "What are you here for? If it's something romantic, I just need five minutes to get cleaned up."

Griffin tamped down the bile that threatened to spew forth. "I'm definitely not here for that."

"Then what do you want?" Darla looked to be at the end of her rope. "I'm nursing a hangover here, and nobody has time for you." She narrowed her eyes. "You look familiar. Are you the mailman?"

Griffin called on his limited patience and held it together. "I'm the man who is going to tell your daughter he loves her today."

Realization dawned on Darla's face. "You're the Holden boy."

"My name is Griffin, not that it matters." Darla needed to know where she stood and what would and wouldn't be allowed where Ava was concerned. He wouldn't allow his woman—*his heart*—to be hurt by that monster again.

"Well, Griffin," Darla drawled. She suddenly had pockets of energy she hadn't had seconds before. "What can I do for you?"

"You can stay away from Ava."

Darla snorted. "Um, she's my daughter. A mother doesn't stay away from her daughter."

It took everything Griffin had not to shake the woman and scream, "You were never a mother to her!" in her face. Histrionics wouldn't help anybody. He needed to be firm because he wasn't doing it just for Ava. No, he was doing it for both of them and the life he wanted to share with her.

"I don't want to take much of your time," Griffin said. "I'm sure you're a busy woman."

"I am." Darla smirked.

"I just want you to know that what happened last night isn't going to happen again."

Puzzled, she asked, "And what happened last night?"

"You embarrassed your daughter in front of her friends. You crushed her, although I'm guessing that's a weekly occurrence with you. But it honestly doesn't matter how often it happened in the past. What matters is that it's done happening."

"What are you trying to say?"

Griffin steeled himself as he prepared to drop the bomb on her. "You're not allowed to see your daughter unless you get it together."

"Excuse me?" Darla's eyes practically bugged out of her head. "Who are you to say what I can and can't do when it comes to my daughter?"

"I'm the man who loves her," Griffin replied simply. "I'm the man who wants better for her. You have never been the parent she needs. You neglected her. I've heard the stories about how you took off for months at a time when she was a kid."

"She stayed with her grandparents when she was a kid," Darla fired back. "It's not as if we left her alone."

"What about after she was fourteen?"

"She was old enough to take care of herself then."

Griffin could do nothing but shake his head. The woman didn't understand the damage she'd done to Ava. She was a narcissist—much like his father—and only cared how things affected her. "I don't have time for nonsense." He planted his hands on his hips. "This is how it's going to go down."

He laid it out for her, holding nothing back, and explained how he was going to be with Ava, and how they were going to build a bed-and-breakfast together. He even explained how they were going to catch feral cats together, although he almost lost Darla's interest with that tangent, so he swiftly returned to the main issue.

"I'm going to take care of her," Griffin insisted. "I'm going to love her so much that she's going to forget that you didn't. I'm going to make her feel safe. I'm going to make her happy. We're going to build a life together."

Darla blandly pulled another cigarette from the pack. "Do you want an award for that or something?"

"No, I want you to understand you're not going to be part of that life. You're an alcoholic. I'm guessing you're a drug addict, too, although that hasn't been explicitly spelled out for me."

"I have trauma!" Darla barked.

"We all have trauma. Your daughter has trauma. The problem is you've never cared about her trauma. You only care about yours. You never once thought about pulling yourself together so you could be a better mother to her, did you?"

Clearly affronted, Darla replied, "Ava's always been a self-starter. She likes to be the one I go to."

"No, she doesn't. She just doesn't think she has any other options. But she does. I'm going to put Ava first. I'm going to make sure she eats her dinner and gets her rest and laughs at least ten times a day. You're not going to be part of that."

"You don't get to dictate whether I see my daughter," Darla snapped.

If Ava wanted to see her mother, he couldn't stop her. But deep down, he finally understood what Ava truly needed. She just wanted someone to care enough to put her first, and that was what he intended to do.

"If you cross onto my property, I'll have you arrested," Griffin said blandly. "I'm going to ask Ava to block your contact name on her phone. It's time for you to be the adult and start fixing some of your problems."

"You don't get a say in it!" Darla screeched.

"I do," Griffin replied. "I want to make things better for Ava, so I get a say. She has a dream she wants to see fulfilled, and somehow—although I'm not sure when this happened—her dream became my dream."

He smiled when he realized how true the words were.

"So I'm going to take care of her—actually, we're going to take care of each other—and you're not invited to the party. If you want to go to rehab and make yourself a better person, we can talk when you've been sober for six months. Otherwise, you're not allowed in our lives."

Griffin turned his back on her and started down the rickety stairs. He paused when he was at the bottom of them. "And it's going to be a beautiful life. Just FYI. You'll be missing a lot."

With that, he headed toward the woods that led to his farm. *No, our farm.*

Despite Darla's sputtering behind him, he didn't look over his shoulder. She was in the past. It was time to look forward to the future.

28
TWENTY-EIGHT

The snow fell hard as Ava sipped her coffee and looked out the window of Maya's café. She always liked how pretty it looked, and it meant winter was beginning in earnest.

She'd thought she would be watching the snow from the Holden farm, maybe in front of the fire with Griffin at her side. But that wouldn't be possible. She'd lost him, and it was all her fault.

"Do you want a Danish?" Maya asked as she stopped by Ava's table, looking concerned.

Of course, this is my second visit of the day. Why shouldn't she be concerned? Ava mused.

Sitting around, mainlining caffeine all day was out of character for her. Normally, she would be out doing something. But it felt as if she had nothing to do. She was aimless, and she hated it.

"I'm fine." Ava flashed a fake smile. She was far from fine but didn't want to dwell on it. If she did, people would ask questions, and the last thing she wanted to talk about was her mother.

And Griffin—she wanted to forget he'd ever been part of her life. It hurt too much when she thought about him. She had a Griffin-sized hole in her heart, and she couldn't help but wonder if it would ever be filled.

Before him, she'd been so focused on the farm that romance wasn't even on her radar. He'd snuck under her defenses and made her feel safe.

Why does it have to hurt so much?

"You don't look fine. In fact, you look downright miserable." She sat in the booth across from Ava without an invitation. "Have you called him?"

Ava wanted to snap at Maya to go away, but she didn't. Maya was a lovely woman, and it wasn't her fault that Ava had screwed things up. Maya cared, and she shouldn't be punished for it. "What would I even say to him? My mother wasn't technically wrong. I wanted the farm when I first started going out there."

"Maybe, but you weren't with Griffin simply because of that."

Ava rubbed her cheek. "Wasn't I? What if I was and deluded myself into believing otherwise?"

"That's not what happened."

Maya sounded so sure of herself that all Ava could do was cock an eyebrow.

"You fell in love with him. Don't deny it."

Ava swallowed around the lump in her throat. "Griffin's gone. He wants nothing to do with me. What I did or didn't want doesn't matter."

"You don't know that."

"I do. I *do* know that. He hates me."

"That's just your anxiety talking. I know a little bit about thinking you've screwed something up."

Ava snorted. "No offense, but everybody knew you and

Nick were going to end up together. Even when you guys were fighting it, everybody else knew. There was a pool and everything."

"I know."

"So it's different for me."

"How so? There's a pool for you, too, you know."

Ava froze with her coffee cup halfway to her mouth. "What?" She'd known people had been gossiping and even betting on when she would hook up with Griffin. *Has it gone further than that?*

"There's a pool for you and Griffin too," Maya repeated. "It started the week he arrived here as something of a joke. You were obsessed, and he was hot. Then Nick and Bear saw the two of you together and spread a bit of gossip—don't be mad, because we all spread gossip around here—and things picked up in earnest."

Ava had no idea what to say. "But ... no." She shook her head. "Nobody seriously thought we were going to be together for more than a fling. If they were betting on us, it was just a joke."

Maya held Ava's gaze. "You're wrong. Everybody knows you and Griffin are meant to be together. The only person who doesn't is you."

"I'm pretty sure he doesn't know either," Ava shot back. "That's why he never wants to see me again."

Before Maya could respond, Ava's phone lit up. They both looked down at the table. Griffin had sent a text.

I need your help at the farm. Please come.

Maya raised her eyebrows. "Are you absolutely sure about that?"

Ava's heart rate picked up a notch. "He probably just needs help with the cats." As soon as she said it, she embraced the belief. "There are a few stubborn ones out there."

Maya looked as if she wanted to argue but just smiled. "I guess you need to go out there to find out."

AVA TRIED TO KEEP HER ANXIETY IN CHECK as she walked from her car to the barn. The door was open, despite the snow. Maybe Griffin had caught one of the cats and needed her help because he didn't know where the rescue was located.

Yes, that's probably what it is.

Even though Ava was determined to keep her hopes in check, she couldn't help but hold her breath as she stepped through the open door … and walked into a ridiculous romantic fantasy.

Griffin stood in the middle of the barn, surrounded by flickering tea lights, and he held a single rose in his hand. He looked as nervous as she suddenly felt.

"W-What…?"

"Hey." Griffin shifted from one foot to the other. "Hi. How are you?"

Ava didn't know whether to laugh or cry. "Good."

"Good?"

"Good-ish."

Griffin didn't respond.

"Horrible," she amended as she struggled to hold back tears. "I feel sick to my stomach, and I'm so sorry about my mother. She's a terrible person and always has been."

"She *is* a terrible person. I think she might be a sociopath. She seems unable to accept the fact that she's not the center of the universe."

Ava frowned. "When did you talk to her?"

"This morning. We had a long chat, in fact. I told her she wasn't allowed to terrorize you any longer. I'm not sure it matters, because it's not as if she's suddenly going to respect me, but we'll take that as it comes."

"We will? I don't understand."

"I know. I'm doing this all wrong. I knew I would." Griffin moved closer to her and brushed the snow from her hat before handing over the rose. "I had grand plans," he explained. "I was going to be smooth and do that whole grand gesture thing. But I'm a mess when it comes to this stuff."

For some reason, that made Ava smile. The situation wasn't funny, yet he was being himself. He wasn't putting on a show for her. He was trying.

But to do what?

"Griffin—"

He shook his head. "I need to do this. You have to let me do this."

Because she didn't know what "this" was, Ava merely nodded.

"Look around," he said quietly. "What don't you see?"

Ava searched the barn because it seemed to be important to him. At first, she didn't see anything out of the ordinary. After a few seconds, however, something became glaringly apparent. "There aren't any cats in here."

"There aren't." Griffin looked relieved that she'd figured it out. "I've been working for hours to catch them. It wasn't easy. That Maine Coon was the last one. I was so frustrated that I sat down next to the cage and cried. I also might have been missing you, so that didn't help with the tears. Do you know what he did?"

Ava shook her head. She didn't know, but she was invested in the story.

"When I started crying, he gave me this disdainful look. Like a 'You're so pathetic that I can't even deal with you' look. Then he walked into the cage."

Ava had no idea what to make of that, so she only said, "Huh."

"Yeah." Griffin gave a watery laugh. "The cat felt sorry for how pathetic I was."

"Is he...?" Ava was horrified by the mere thought that the cat might already be gone.

"I got a call about an hour ago," Griffin replied. "All the final cats have a little something wrong with them. They all need medication, and the black cat, who I'm calling Toby, is going into kidney failure. That's why they'll all be living in the house with us this winter, and we'll make decisions on the other cats once they've been medicated for a bit."

Ava had no idea what to say. "Us?" she prodded.

"Us." His eyes gleamed. "We'll keep the original framework for the barn, but all the walls have to be replaced, and we're going to need to run plumbing out here, if we plan to actually turn it into a house. It's not going to be fast, but I do think it's going to be worth it." His eyes never moved from her face. "In fact, I know it will."

Dumbstruck, Ava stared at him. Then she replied, "You want to turn this barn into a house. That's what you're saying."

"It's more like I want to build a house for us that looks like this barn. It needs a lot of work, and it's going to be cheaper to keep the shape but start all over."

"Huh. What about the house?"

"We'll live there over the winter. I'm going to need your help deciding what to do with each room. I believe B and Bs have theme rooms, if I'm not mistaken, and I've never been very good at picking out themes."

"You want to turn the house into a B and B and the barn into a house for us."

"Am I not getting my message across clearly?" Griffin asked. "I'm nervous and probably not making any sense." He sucked in a breath. "Let me start over."

He seemed calmer when he walked to the ladder. "The second floor will be a huge master suite. It's going to have a bathroom where your spot in the loft used to be, and we'll have one of those huge tubs with jets so that we can look out on the farm—and still have privacy—no matter the season."

Ava's heart had leaped into her throat, and she felt the need to sit down. Since there were no chairs, she remained on her feet through sheer force of will.

"We're going to have to stay in the main farmhouse for at least a year. I figure it's going to take us eight months to do everything up right anyway, so I was thinking we'd aim for the fall—you know, the run-up to your favorite season —to host the grand opening."

"You want me to help you with this?"

"Oh, Ava, I want you to do this with me," Griffin said earnestly as he stepped in front of her. "It's not just that I'm out of my element and have no idea what I'm doing. It's also that when you told me about your dream for this place, I could see it. Somehow, over the last few months, it's become my dream too. There's nobody I would do this with but you."

Ava could have sworn her heart had doubled in size, but she didn't immediately run to him and throw her arms around his neck. "How do you know this will work?"

"I don't *know* it's going to work," he replied. "I just know I don't want to be without you."

"You say that now, but what happens if you hate winter and decide you need to move back to the city?"

"That's not going to happen."

"How can you be sure?"

"Because you're not in the city."

It was what Ava needed to hear, and it left her breathless. But that didn't mean she was ready to lower all her walls and throw herself at him so that they could celebrate. She was still afraid. "But ... you could have anything you want. Your father admitting the building falling was his fault and not yours opens doors for you. You could go back to your old life."

"You know what's funny about my old life?" Griffin asked.

Ava shook her head.

"I wasn't all that happy before the building fell. I thought I was. Well, actually, I think it's fair to say that I was content. I didn't realize I was missing anything, because I'd begun to gloss over the details of my life. There was no happily ever after for me down there because I couldn't see beyond work. Since I met you, all I've seen is potential for a happily ever after."

"You mean when you caught me spying on you?"

"That was the day I got the first glimpse." Griffin gave a lazy smile. "There's little I love more than a mouthy woman."

"Then you must love me to pieces," Ava muttered.

"I do."

Ava's heart shattered at the words, and she had to suck in a breath to steady herself. "What?"

"I love you, Ava." Griffin moved even closer to her. "I'm not sure when it happened—although there's a distinct chance it was when you made me eat leek-and-morel macaroni and cheese then marched me through a haunted maze—but it has happened. I love you with my whole heart.”

“Even though I only got into this mess because I was trying to figure out a way to steal the farm from you?”

“Yes. I knew what you were trying to do when you first volunteered to help with the cats. I’m not a dumbass.”

Ava opened her mouth to argue the point, but Griffin silenced her with a shake of his head.

“You can let some of them go,” he said sternly, causing Ava to smile.

“I wasn’t really angry with you when I left Maya’s café yesterday afternoon. I was just ... surprised. Then I found myself getting angry with myself, not you. Your parents are terrible people, Ava.”

“They are.”

“But I’m not your parents. I’m not going to leave you for long stretches of time ... or ever. I want to be with you. I told your mother I’m going to love you the way you deserve, the way she never did, and I meant it. I want to build my life with you. But I need you to meet me halfway. I can’t do it all by myself.”

Ava was rocked to her very core. “You told my mother that?”

“Yeah. I also told her there would be rules when we were building our life together, and until she gets her shit together, she’s not invited to visit. I want us to live in a happy bubble. Your mother is not a happy person.”

“Wow.” Ava lifted her fingers to his cheek. His skin should’ve been cold because of the weather, but it was warm, and it made her want to rub her cheek against his.

So she did. She stepped forward, their chests coming together, and pressed her cheek to his. “I love you too.” She couldn't see his face, but she could feel his heart pounding against hers.

"I know."

"I'm still going to be a lot of work."

"I know that too. And I want to be the one putting in the work."

Ava briefly closed her eyes, and when she opened them again, somehow, he'd moved his mouth so that it was directly above hers. But he didn't close the final inch. Instead, he waited.

"I can't wait to do this with you," she said finally. "It's more than I ever hoped for."

"That's exactly what I wanted to hear." Griffin cupped the back of her head and pressed his lips to hers, the world swirling around them.

Things wouldn't always be easy for them. They would disagree and snipe at each other whenever the opportunity arose. But some loves were meant to last a lifetime, and they were destined for that sort of love.

"You're going to set the barn on fire if you're not careful," Ava said as she pulled away and swiped at her teary eyes. She still hated feeling vulnerable in front of people, but she was getting used to it. "That's a lot of candles."

Griffin narrowed his eyes. "Way to ruin the romance, Ava. Also, those aren't candles. They're battery-powered tea lights."

"Oh. I guess that means we can get naked in here, up in the loft, and we won't be endangering the barn. It will be a sort of spiritual cleansing. We can watch the snow fall."

"I think that sounds like the best idea I've ever heard."

Ava took his hand and led him toward the ladder. "I can't believe you caught the rest of the cats."

"That's how much I love you. I wanted the cats to be the grand gesture."

She paused halfway up the ladder. "You did well."

"We're going to do great together."

She felt the words to her very core. "We really are."

EPILOGUE
TEN MONTHS LATER

“What do you think?”

Griffin nervously fluttered his hands and looked out at the farm, which was decked out in all its Halloween glory. He thought it looked pretty good but needed confirmation, which was why he'd brought Nick and Bear out to survey his handiwork.

“That's a lot of pumpkins,” Bear noted as he took in the driveway that led to the old farmhouse, which was the new B and B. It would be opening for the first time in three days, and it looked bright and shiny compared to the way it had looked a year ago.

Griffin made a face as he took in the pumpkins. They weren't real. He'd considered carving thirty pumpkins for the weekend—he had something special planned and wanted to be authentic—but it seemed like a waste of money. Instead, he'd bought decorative pumpkins when he saw Ava looking at them online. She'd ruled them out because she thought they were too expensive for their first year. Griffin had felt otherwise.

They were an investment in their future. If she wanted

the pumpkins, he wanted the pumpkins.

"They're for ambiance," Griffin explained. "When Ava gets here, I want her to see them when driving up. Everything is going to be lit up."

"Okay." Bear scratched this cheek. "I'm still confused."

"Of course you are," Griffin grumbled. "What has you confused?" He'd only known Bear and Nick for a year, but their friendship had grown so strong that it was almost as if they'd been friends since grade school. Sometimes, Bear even said, "You remember" to Griffin when referring to a story he couldn't possibly remember. It had become part of their schtick.

But that didn't mean Griffin didn't find Bear annoying on a regular basis.

"It's September," Bear said. "Why is all your Halloween stuff out in September?"

"Because Halloween is Ava's favorite holiday, numb nuts," Nick replied. "He wants to make the proposal magical for Ava. This is how he's going to do it." He shot Griffin a thumbs-up. "I think it's great."

Griffin gave a nod of thanks.

"I get that Ava loves Halloween," Bear continued. "She's always loved Halloween. That's hardly a surprise. What I don't get is why you're having Halloween in September."

Griffin scowled at him. "Because I'm going to propose and want it to be memorable," he snapped. "Our first date was at a corn maze. I'm trying to remind her of that ... without having an actual corn maze." He cast his gaze toward the empty field. "We can't deal with a cornfield on top of everything else, although I'm considering renting the plot to a local farmer so that he can tend and harvest it, and we can turn it into a maze after. That's for next year, though."

"The kids will love a corn maze," Nick said. "I get not wanting to deal with an actual crop field, though. That seems like a good trade-off."

"Right?" Griffin was nervous about that too, although he had a few months to figure out the logistics. "Anyway, it looks good, doesn't it?"

Griffin had filled the yard in front of the B and B with inflatables, arches, and fake pumpkins. Fake ghosts filled the side yard, a cauldron doubled as a fog machine, and eerie noises played from a speaker in the second-floor window of what used to be the barn. It still looked like a barn from the outside, but inside, it was a beautiful house that Griffin shared with Ava. It had only been livable for two months, but they'd immediately moved in and made it their home. The rest of the stuff could wait until the following spring. Then they would finish the finer details. Their home was perfect for the moment, and that was all that mattered.

Home was a word Griffin hadn't been sure he would ever be able to use after the Peck Building fell. But Ava had changed everything, and he would be forever grateful.

"Tell me it looks good," Griffin barked. His anxiety was spiking, and Bear's refusal to get on board with his plan was starting to chafe.

"It looks great," Bear assured him. "I'm just not sure why you're doing Halloween in September. If you want all this stuff out when you propose to Ava, why not just wait until next month to do it?"

Griffin sighed. "Because next month, we're completely booked—I'm talking the whole month—and there's going to be no time to celebrate. I want to celebrate."

"Ah." Bear nodded knowingly. "You want a weekend full of sex. Why didn't you just say that?"

"You make me so tired," Griffin lamented.

"Let me see the ring," Nick prodded.

Though Griffin had no doubt he was trying to redirect the conversation to something innocuous, he was more than happy to show off the ring. He'd spent weeks picking it out, researching the different cut and clarity aspects for engagement rings.

He pulled the velvet box out of his pocket and dropped it into Nick's hand, then chewed on his bottom lip as Nick opened the box and looked inside.

"Nice," Nick said with a grin. "*Very* nice. Two carats?"

Griffin nodded.

"Princess cut?"

"No, it's a cushion cut. The edges are more rounded and softer. When I looked at the stones next to one another, the cushion cut just felt more like Ava." Anxiety spiked through him again. "You don't think I made the wrong choice on the ring, do you?"

"I think you made the perfect choice," Nick assured him.

"Calm down, Esmerelda," Bear drawled as he took the box from Nick. "The ring is awesome. It's so awesome, in fact, that my wife is going to ask why I didn't get her a ring like this, even though we were barely out of high school when I knocked her up and we got married."

"You know what's interesting about that story?" Nick prodded.

"No, and I don't care to hear what you think is interesting about it."

Nick ignored him. "What's interesting is that she's birthed five of your big-headed babies and still has a tiny engagement ring. Maybe a good husband—say, one who owns his own construction business and brings in a decent amount of money—should consider updating his wife's engagement ring to reflect the anguish she absolutely had to go through to birth those aforementioned big-headed babies."

"Ugh." Bear handed the ring box back to Griffin. "You're going to suggest this to Maya, aren't you? She'll tell Lindsey, and I'm going to have no choice but to drop twenty grand on a ring that shouldn't be necessary because my love is more important than any diamond."

Nobody spoke for several seconds.

"That's not going to work if I use it as an excuse for why I'm not buying her an engagement ring, is it?"

"Nope," Nick and Griffin replied in unison.

"I didn't think so. This is such crap."

Nick patted Griffin on the shoulder as a surly Bear started stomping toward his truck. "You're going to do great. The decorations are nice, but they're not important. In the moment, when you're holding that ring and looking at her, you're going to realize what's important."

"And what's that?"

"You'll see."

AVA TURNED IN TO the driveway that led to the Holden farm. Technically, it was her home, but she still thought of it as the Holden farm. She was hoping to get over that. Though it was probably just a habit, she couldn't help but consider that she was finally living a dream she'd practically given up on, and it didn't quite seem real yet. She was hoping she would get over that too.

The radio blasted eighties songs as she rocketed down the driveway. Griffin had insisted on getting it smoothed because he didn't want its ruts to damage any vehicles. But

Ava sort of missed the little dip that made her feel as if she was going airborne.

She was halfway down the driveway when she noticed the pumpkins, and her stomach clenched.

"He bought them," she said, shaking her head. She'd first spied the pumpkins in her favorite Halloween catalog but had immediately discarded the notion of buying them —at least until next year—because they were expensive. Obviously, Griffin had been paying more attention than she'd realized.

"Wow." Getting out of the car, she grinned at the pumpkins, then her attention moved to the lawn in front of the B and B. Since they lived in the barn, Ava rarely parked over there. The glare of the setting sun nearly made her miss the lights, but her heart did a happy roll because she recognized exactly how everything would pop when darkness fell.

"I can't believe you did this," she called out to Griffin, who was standing underneath a hilarious archway. It reminded her of something that would be used as a prop in a high school movie featuring a dance—well, other than the skeletons and pumpkins hanging from every black branch. "It's amazing."

"Yeah?" Griffin didn't move to intercept her, which was odd. Normally, she would already be in his arms.

"It's a little early, but it's amazing. Our first guests are going to love it."

"Yeah."

Ava's nose wrinkled when Griffin remained rooted to his spot. "You're kind of quiet tonight." She put her purse on the top of her car and glanced around again. Something felt off. "Has something bad happened?"

Griffin shook his head. "No." He took an exaggerated

step forward. "Why would you think that?"

"Because you're acting weird."

"I'm not acting weird."

"You're glued to that spot under the arch like a big freak," Ava countered. "What's going on? You're going to make me melt down."

"Don't melt down."

"Then tell me what's going on." Ava wrung her hands. "Is it Darla?" She rarely mentioned her mother since she'd been cut out of their life. Griffin's declaration to Darla had done nothing to change her attitude, so they'd simply moved on. They were both happier for it. But that didn't mean Ava wasn't braced to hear bad news about her.

"No, baby, this has nothing to do with your mother." Griffin looked pained as he took another step forward.

Then Ava noticed he was holding something. In the waxing light, it was hard for her to make out. "What's that?"

Griffin straightened and tightened his fist around the box. "What's what?"

"That box in your hand." Ava pointed, her breath catching in her chest. "Is that...?"

"This is not how I saw this going," Griffin groused under his breath. "Not even a little."

"How you saw what going?" The fear Ava had been feeling moments before gave way to excitement. "Are you going to propose?"

"Not now." Griffin made a face. "It was supposed to be a surprise. Like ... a grand gesture. I even put light-up collars on the barn cats." He gestured toward the new barn, which wasn't as big as the old barn but was still chock-full of personality. Sure enough, in the grass in front of the barn, several lights could be seen moving to and fro.

"You put light-up collars on the barn cats," Ava repeated, dumbfounded.

"I was hoping they would rush in to see you like they usually do, but they're cats. They don't do what they're supposed to."

"No." Ava licked her lips, her eyes moving back to the box. "Can I see what's in there?"

"I don't know. My whole plan is shot now. It was supposed to be a Halloween wonderland, something to remind you of our first date, and now it's all messed up."

For reasons she couldn't identify, that made Ava grin. "Nothing is messed up. In fact, this is perfectly us."

"Yeah?" Griffin arched an eyebrow. "Well, in that case, maybe I should just suck it up and realize nothing is perfect."

"Not even me?" Ava teased, her cheeks heating.

"Not even you," he confirmed, shifting from one foot to the other. "You're as close as humanly possible, but you've got a few quirks I could do without."

"Like what?"

"Like refusing to put the new toilet paper roll on the holder and instead leaving it on the floor for the cat to shred."

Ava smirked. Toby was still alive. He was on special food and had lost a lot of weight, but he was still around, and he slept in the chair in the bedroom every night so that he could look through the window at the same view he'd had from the barn loft when he was wild and free. "I'm just trying to be a good cat mom."

"Uh-huh." Griffin rubbed his free hand over his pants. "You know I love you, right?"

Ava nodded. "I love you too."

"This was supposed to be a grand gesture, a big speech,

then we were going to dance to 'The Monster Mash' before going inside to watch a horror movie to get you in the mood."

Ava laughed. That sounded like something he would plan. "I don't need that."

"I know." Griffin rolled his neck. "But that doesn't mean I didn't want you to have it."

"I'm okay just knowing you love me," Ava admitted. "You're the only one I can say that about and mean it." Her eyes burned, and she had to blink back tears. "Can I see what's in that box?" She didn't care that she sounded impatient.

"Just a second." Griffin kept moving until he was directly in front of her. "I'm not the only one who has ever loved you. There are plenty of people in this town who do. But I'm the one who loves you best. I want to wear that title for the rest of my life."

He dropped down to one knee, causing Ava's heart to seize, and opened the box. She almost fell over when she saw the size of the diamond.

"I love you, Ava Mason. I want to keep living this wonderful life with you. I want to keep working this wonderful job with you. Eventually, I even want a kid or two with you, although it might only be one, if our kid ends up with your attitude, which is a distinct possibility."

Ava gave a watery laugh as she dropped down next to him. "I think that sounds like a pretty good life."

Griffin nodded as he slipped the ring onto her finger. She hadn't said yes, but there was no way she would say no. They'd been working toward it for a year and would continue working on it for the rest of their lives.

"I love you," he whispered. "So, so much."

Ava sniffled so hard that it sounded as if she were running a snot factory. "I love you too."

"Don't cry." Griffin used his thumb to wipe away a tear. "This is a happy day."

"Maybe these are happy tears."

"Maybe." He leaned in and gave her a soft, lingering kiss. "I set up an outdoor inflatable screen on the other side of the house, and I have the original *Halloween* cued up. "Do you want to move the celebration over there?"

Ava nodded wordlessly. He'd thought of everything.

"There's champagne, popcorn, and Reese's Peanut Butter Cups," he added.

Okay, he really *had* thought of everything. "That sounds like the perfect night."

"Oh, Ava, it's not about one night. We're about to get our perfect life."

And finally, Ava knew what real peace was. He'd made her feel safe, and she was home. They were about to embark on forever, but it was the safety she treasured most.

"You're going to get really lucky tonight," she said as she glanced at the ring, which fit perfectly on her finger.

"I got lucky the day I caught you spying in the bushes. Everything else is gravy, baby."

"I'm going to remind you of that when I eat so much junk food tonight that I wake up with a sugar hangover tomorrow."

"Somehow, I think that sounds like the best thing I've heard all day."

That made two of them.

"So, a movie and some vigorous snuggling?" Ava held out her hand to him.

He took it and tugged her up to stand. "Forever," he said, dropping a kiss on her forehead. "Forever and always."